A
Dawn &
Rosie
Adventure

Paper
Daffodils

# TITANIA
# TEMPEST

First edition

ISBN 978-1-77933-204-2

## CHAPTER ONE

Is it possible for loneliness to become a personality trait? Rosie Bishop pondered this as she stared out the grimy kitchen window, idly fiddling with the spoon in her half-empty teacup. After so many years, it certainly felt like it could. It seemed to be the only emotion that kept her company anymore – that, and a seeping bitterness that coloured every waking moment.

With a sigh for her thoughts, she abandoned her cold tea and moved closer to the window, wrapping her arms around herself in a vain attempt at comfort. Beyond the glass, the claustrophobic winter sky spoke volumes, and she couldn't shake the feeling that the world had a gaping hole in it. A shiver passed over her, and she dropped her gaze, only to have it arrested by a flash of yellow. She frowned, and stared; there along the dull verge, daffodils danced in defiance of the moody day. Bright and incorrigible, they kept up a cheerful waving in the stiff breeze outside, and Rosie tilted her head, reminded of something she couldn't quite put her finger on. Vaguely, she associated them with... something. Their liveliness transfixed her for a long moment, taking her back to memories she almost recalled, but at last, she shook her head, for the sentiment refused to bloom into true recollection. Her face puckered into a scowl. She didn't care, anyway; she didn't care about anything, anymore. The colours of life had long since faded into monotonous shades of grey, and the bright flowers were merely a callous reminder of that fact.

With a huff, she turned her back on the view and her aimless feet bore her down the hall, her footsteps echoed by the slow ticking of an antique clock as it kept incessant track of nothing-much. Callous, the timepiece reminded her that she had nothing much to do today – or any day – and she shuffled away to the other side of the house in a bid to escape its judgement.

She meandered through room after lifeless room, until she found herself standing in front of the bay windows in the parlour. There, unbidden, her gaze found another bunch of cheerful daffodils, and she paused again. Despite her melancholy, she marvelled at their audacity. Spring was a mere suggestion, winter still holding fast in the snap of brittle air, and yet, the undaunted daffodils unfurled their crowns. In tiny echo of their gallantry, the corners of her lips twitched into the ghost of a smile, and a strange warmth tugged at her. Indeed, they *did* remind her of someone, but she couldn't quite pin down—

"Mum?" A call echoed through the house, dousing her musings.

The front door slammed, admitting a clatter of footsteps – more than one person, by the sounds of things – and Rosie's tentative smile vanished.

"In here!" she snapped.

Beneath furrowing brows, her eyes lingered on the daffodils, but then she turned and stalked into the hall. Her daughter Mary appeared a heartbeat later, laden with shopping bags, and two boisterous children bounded in behind her.

"Mum, it's freezing in here! Why haven't you got the heating on? You know, at your age—"

"I don't recall inviting you," Rosie interrupted. She was only sixty-two, for God's Sake.

Mary rolled her eyes. "It's Tuesday, Mum – you told me to pop past on Tuesday."

Rosie faltered for a brief moment. *Was it really Tuesday already? Felt like a second since last Tuesday – and a lifetime.* Composing herself, she growled, "I know. I just didn't… realise the time."

"Odd, seeing as you sit and stare at the clock all day," Mary said, before wisely changing the subject. "Here – let me put these down – I brought you a few groceries. Boys, say hello to Grandma."

"Hi, Grandma!" came the shrill chorus.

Rosie almost smiled, but then reminded herself she wasn't in the mood. "Wipe your feet!" she barked as they skipped past her, and they exchanged impish grins as they whizzed around again to obey.

"*So-rr-y*, Grandma!" Tommy wiggled his eyebrows at her.

Nate snorted into his sleeve at the insincerity of his brother's apology, and Rosie gave a resigned sigh as they scampered off. But it was all she could do to control the quirk of her lips – despite her persistent woe, their antics always managed to brighten her day.

"What have you got in there, then?" she snapped at Mary as she followed her into the kitchen to supervise the unpacking.

"All the usual, plus a few chocolates," said Mary mildly. "And… I've got a surprise for you."

She held out an envelope, and Rosie eyed it suspiciously before accepting it with long fingers. "What is it?"

Mary raised an eyebrow and waited for her to open it. Scowling, Rosie did so and pulled out a sleek brochure and a folded piece of paper neatly typed with provisional details.

"It's a Retreat," Mary prompted. "A week in the countryside."

Rosie looked up from what she was reading. "For *seniors*?"

Mary allowed herself a long-suffering blink. "As in, over fifty-five. Come on, Mum, you've been holed up in this house for months, and you need to get out. It's nothing fancy, just a nice relax in the Lake District – a little wine-tasting, walks in the woods, perhaps even a spot of fishing—"

"*Fishing*?!"

"Look, just think about it, will you?" Mary's gaze softened, and she came to cup her mother's hands beneath her own. "I'm worried about you, Mum. I know the divorce hasn't been easy for you, but it's been over a year, and you've hardly set foot outside of this house. You've not checked in at the office, you seldom go shopping… Even I'll admit that Dad was a bastard, but honestly, you need to stop wallowing. You're a free woman, and it's time you took your life back."

Rosie spluttered, a veritable cascade of indignant protests burning on her tongue. But over Mary's shoulder, the daffodils beyond the window caught her eye again, and she swallowed her bitter retort. After a moment, she huffed, "Fine. I'll think about it."

Mary's tired face creased into a smile – the first one Rosie had seen cross her lips for a very long time, she realised. Something stirred deep within her numb heart, just for a second, and, gently, she squeezed Mary's hands around the envelope.

"I'll think about it," she repeated, more softly. "I promise."

Blinking rapidly, Mary gave a brisk nod and turned away before a tear could escape her. She inhaled deeply to compose herself and then yelled into the abyss of the house.

"Boys! C'mon! Let's go – we've a lot of errands to run!"

Rosie's face fell. "You won't… stay for a cuppa?"

Mary's eyebrows shot up in surprise. "I didn't expect" – she cleared her throat – "I'd love to, Mum, but I've got to get Tommy to practice, and Nate's got a play date."

"*Mu-um*!" Nate complained, overhearing as he tumbled back into the kitchen. "It's not a play date. Me and my mates are just hanging out."

"That's what I meant," Mary said, ruffling his shaggy mane of blond hair.

He yelled and pushed her off, setting to furiously straightening it out again, and Rosie watched with soft affection. They were growing so fast – Nate was nearly nine already, Tommy ten. Real little lads, now.

"Yes, yes," Rosie said, hiding the spark of disappointment behind a casually dismissive wave. "Of course. Next time, then. Thanks for bringing the shopping."

Mary managed half a smile as she ushered the boys out, and her gaze fell to the papers still clutched in Rosie's hand. "The Retreat's in April, but I have to confirm by the end of this week."

"I'll think about it," Rosie repeated once more, firmly setting the envelope and its contents down on the countertop.

Her daughter met her eye, noticed the stubborn glint, and sighed.

"Well," she said, "let me know." She pressed a kiss to Rosie's wan cheek. "Bye, Mum."

"Bye Grandma!" the boys shouted as they raced to the car.

Rosie leaned against the door frame, watching them wrestling along the way, both of them utterly undaunted by the icy drizzle. Mary glanced back as she made the driver's side and offered a small wave as she ducked into the car. Rosie returned it, feeling strangely that more than just the winter was beginning to thaw. The car pulled away, turned out of the cul-de-sac, and disappeared from view, leaving her alone once more. With a sigh, she made to turn away, but from the verge, the daffodils caught her attention with a cheerful wave. She watched them dance in the damp breeze for a long moment, feeling again the tugging of vague, impalpable memories, and something sparked within her.

Maybe she would go on that trip, after all.

# CHAPTER TWO

Two months later, Rosie found herself tailing Mary across the carpark of a quaint hotel, leaning into a biting wind and sincerely regretting her decision to come. As the breeze snarled her hair into knots, she pushed her hat more firmly down atop her head and growled at Mary, "I can't believe I let you talk me into this!"

"It's only the Lake District, Mum," Mary said with a smile, and her blue eyes – Rosie's eyes – held a hint of mischief. "It's not another country."

She tugged her mother's small suitcase up the front steps of Greenside Inn before Rosie could protest further, and at the top, turned to admire the view. In the distance, the sun was beginning to set, painting the fresh, damp sky in pretty pastels.

Mary paused with a small, contented sigh. "Gosh, would you look at this place, Mum? It's gorgeous!"

Rosie stalked up to stand next to her and narrowed her eyes as she looked out. "There's a bloody coach coming, Mary," she said, scowling at a vehicle heading up the drive. "Full of *old* people."

"Bet none of them are as obnoxious as you," Mary quipped, ducking into the reception.

Rosie spluttered and stormed after her, but found her already talking with the manager – a weaselly young man who introduced himself as Pip – and had to content herself with a dreadful glower. When Mary had finished showing him the booking confirmation, the pimply youth turned to Rosie with an insipid smile.

"Welcome to Greenside Inn, Mrs Smith."

"It's Bishop," Rosie snapped. "*Miss.*"

"Very well, Miss Bishop." His smile widened, just a touch, and she fought the urge to wipe it off his face. He signalled a red-headed young woman from nearby. "If you'll follow Liz, here, she'll show you to your room."

Rosie glared daggers at her daughter, but Liz had already caught up her suitcase and was pulling away.

"Off you go!" Mary prompted.

"We're going to have words about this when I get back!"

Mary smirked. "I've no doubt. But in the meantime, you're here, so you might as well attempt to enjoy yourself."

Fuming, Rosie vacillated on the spot, Liz drawing away with her personal belongings on one side, and her daughter turning for the door on the other. But Mary gave a jaunty wave and disappeared outside, and then there was nothing left for Rosie to do but follow her small, lonely suitcase down the hall towards the lift.

"You're on the third floor, Miss Bishop," Liz said brightly, pinging the button to summon the contraption.

Rosie swallowed as she followed her in; she'd rather have taken the stairs. But the ascent was smooth and uneventful, and the silver doors soon slid open to reveal a cosy passageway lined with large windows, that offered a commanding view of the Inn's attendant lake. Liz continued the entire length of the hall, stopping at the very last room to slide a key card into the slot. She pushed the door open and stood back for Rosie to precede her, and then followed to deposit the suitcase.

"Your itinerary is on the fridge," Liz said, "but the activities are optional. You are quite welcome to simply relax and take in the scenery. Your booking's for the whole package, though, so you can take advantage of any of the activities on offer." She tipped Rosie a jaunty smile and turned for the door. "Enjoy your stay, Miss Bishop. I'm sure your roommate will be along shortly."

"My... what?" Rosie dropped the TV remote she'd been inspecting and spun around, but Liz was gone. The door clicked softly closed and Rosie found herself alone, and furious. This was not what she'd agreed to! The odd group activity she could put up with, because, if she were honest, she loved being out in the country, but a *roommate*? That wasn't part of the deal! She pursed her lips to a thin white line. No, she wouldn't have it; she'd march back downstairs, catch that weaselly manager Pip by the scruff of his neck, and demand a solitary room. Three thunderous steps took her to the exit and she snatched at the handle – but the door swung inward before she could touch it. It bounced off her toes, making her yelp, and she skittered backwards with a hiss. An extended second passed before a woman's confused face popped around the door to see what the obstruction was, and Rosie steeled for a skirmish.

But an odd feeling of déjà vu accosted her, and she wavered. Equally perplexed, the other woman's hazel eyes widened beneath a thick fringe of silver hair. She took Rosie's measure, and then her eyebrows lifted high.

"Good God... Rosie?"

Recognition clanged through Rosie like a brass bell, and her jaw dropped. She stepped out of the way to let the door swing wide.

"Dawn?!"

Amazed, Dawn Clermont shook her head, tossed her suitcase aside and swept to engulf Rosie in a hug. "What in the bloody hell are you doing here?!"

Rosie laughed – oh, the first time she'd laughed in so long! – and returned her fierce squeeze. "What am I doing here? I'd never take *you* for a 'seniors retreat' kind of girl!"

Dawn pulled back with a grin. "I'm not, usually, but I won a free holiday at bingo night so—"

"*Bingo?*" Rosie interrupted with a splutter. "Not bingo, Dawn!"

"Honestly!" Dawn laughed. "I started playing a couple of years ago, not long after Jack died. I joined a few other clubs too; a book club, a gardening club – a gin-making club…"

She smiled around the cheeky anecdote she'd tacked onto the end, but Rosie's face had greyed.

"Jack's… dead?"

Dawn's amusement faltered under the unexpected clarification. She squeezed her eyes shut and nodded unevenly, and Rosie gently wrapped her up into another hug.

"Oh, Dawn… I had no idea… I'm so sorry."

Against her shoulder, Dawn sighed, "It's all right, Rose. It's been four years, but I still… miss him, you know?"

They stood for a long moment, until, at last, Dawn drew back to dab at a small tear. Rosie squeezed her hand in solidarity, and then ventured: "Tea?"

Dawn nodded. "Please. Milk—"

"Two sugars." Rosie finished, smiling gently. "I know."

Dawn managed a watery smile in return and settled onto the couch as Rosie busied herself at the small kitchenette. When she shortly held out a cup, Dawn reached gratefully for it and sipped deep, drawing fortitude from the sweet warmth.

"Thank you," she murmured.

Rosie plopped down beside her and patted her arm. "Not much a good cuppa can't solve."

Wiping at her nose with a sleeve, Dawn gave a derisive huff. "Ridiculous, really – haven't seen you in twenty years, and the first thing I do is burst into tears."

"Mmm." Rosie raised a judgemental eyebrow at her. "I know I've aged a little bit, but I must say I didn't quite expect *that* reaction."

Dawn snorted, almost spilling her tea. "God, I've missed you, Rose."

Rosie sighed and leaned comfortably against her shoulder. "I've missed you too."

"Really, how did it get to twenty bloody years…?"

"That's life, I suppose. Spending too much time on trivial things, and not enough moments on those that matter."

Dawn huffed in amusement. "And when did you become such a melancholic sage?"

"Round about the time Richard left me."

"What!" Dawn cried, actually spilling her tea. "Shit." She wiped the liquid from her lap half-heartedly as she stared at Rosie. "Richard *left* you?"

Rosie tilted her head with a wan smile. "Bloody did. Just over a year ago, now. Found himself a younger model."

Dawn made a rude noise and thumped her half-empty cup down on the coffee table. "Poor bloody woman," she exclaimed. "Well, to hell with Richard. I never liked the bastard anyway."

"You introduced us," Rosie reminded her mildly.

"Oh. Yes…. Shit, sorry."

Their eyes met for a silent moment, and then they collapsed into laughter – real, raw, gut-wrenching laughter that persisted until tears flowed and neither could breathe.

At last, when Dawn had recovered enough to speak, she took Rosie's hand and gave it a gentle squeeze. "He didn't bloody deserve you, Rose. I hope you know that."

Rosie's smile softened. "It's not all bad, I suppose. I did get Mary out of it – and my beautiful boys."

"Boys?" Dawn frowned. "What boys?"

Rosie laughed. "Tommy and Nate – Mary's sons."

Dawn sat perfectly still for a moment, processing – and then unleashed a crow of amusement. "You're a *granny*?"

"You're not so young yourself," Rosie shot back.

"Yes, but Rose… you have *grandchildren*."

"So do you, technically," Rosie replied, raising an eyebrow in challenge. "Mary is your god-daughter, after all."

"That's hardly the same thing."

"It counts."

Dawn harrumphed, affronted. "It does not!"

Rosie smothered her amusement with her fingers pressed over her mouth, and Dawn glared at her, fighting a losing battle with her own quirking lips. Somehow, everything was funny. Their crumbling lives, their chance meeting, the state of their tedious affairs – all of it. So damned depressing all one could do was laugh it off. And they did, dissolving back into giggles, clutching at their ribs, holding on to that amusement as if it were a last, desperate lifeline.

"Stop it!" Dawn gasped. "Stop it, Rose – you're going to make tears run down my bloody legs!"

Rosie couldn't respond for the mirth tumbling from her lips, and it redoubled under Dawn's ludicrous comment. Helpless, she shook her head, trying to catch a breath as her eyes streamed, and Dawn clutched at her arm, clinging to it for dear life as they rode the wave of mild insanity.

But finally, they calmed and sat staring at each other with school-girl grins, vibrant and alive upon the small moment of shared hilarity.

"Thanks," Rosie panted as she wiped at her eyes. "I really, really needed that."

"Me too," Dawn agreed. "But now I'm stuffing exhausted. What do you say we pop a bottle of Bolly and rehydrate?"

"I hardly think champagne counts for rehydration," Rosie snorted, but they rang for room service anyway.

"*Order two*," Dawn mouthed, hanging over Rosie as she tried to keep her composure on the phone.

"What? I'm sorry what did you – how many, what – glasses? Oh. Two." Rosie batted Dawn violently away with her free hand. "And two bottles. What? Am I... what? Am I sure I want the glasses...? Of course I'm bloody sure."

Dawn snatched the phone. "Yes, thank you – two bottles, two glasses. Bucket of ice."

She hung up before Rosie could claw the handset back, and Rosie glared daggers at her.

"Ah, there's the intimidating individual I remember," Dawn said with an air of sagacity. "You don't scare me, though, you know."

Rosie deflated. "I know, damn you."

Shortly after, Liz knocked on the door and held out a tray with two bottles, a silver ice bucket, and two champagne flutes.

"Sent the glasses, I see," Dawn quipped, relieving her of the whole lot.

Liz gave a puzzled frown. "I – what?"

"Never mind," Rosie said, gaily shutting the door in her face.

By the time she'd turned around, her friend was already pouring. Stone-faced, Dawn thrust a brimming flute into her hand and then necked her share straight out of the bottle.

Rosie sent her gaze heavenward. "Should have just got one bloody glass, after all."

Dawn grinned wickedly and smacked her lips. "Cheers, Rose! Here's to seeing you again – un-bloody-believably! – and, to getting into far more trouble than we can handle."

Rosie cracked a smile. "Just like old times."

"Just like old times," Dawn agreed, holding the bottle out.

Glass clinked, and laughter echoed.

# CHAPTER THREE

Rosie woke to sunlight streaming through a chink in the curtains. With a groan, she clutched at her head and, cautiously, sat up to survey the carnage with bleary eyes. How had that cushion ended up perched on top of the TV? She squinted at the debris around it. Empty champagne bottles – far more than two – littered the scene; her upturned suitcase had spilt its contents across the floor – she vaguely remembered attempting to find a gaudy shawl (a gift from the boys) to show Dawn – and half the furniture had moved. Had they been dancing? Yes. Yes, they had. Badly, if she recalled.

Her lips twitched; it had been fun, though. Even her throbbing headache this morning was completely worth it. With a yawn, she reached up to rub slumber from her eyes but found her arm caught up in a swath of fabric and realised she was still wearing the bloody shawl. Laughter caught soft between her lips, and she turned to wake Dawn to share the ludicrousness once more.

But the other bed was empty.

She started in unpleasant surprise, staring at neatly made corners and pristine covers. It did not appear slept in – which was impossible because surely, she'd seen Dawn collapse onto it last night with an empty champagne bottle still clutched in her fist? Freeing her arm from the shawl, she tucked the orange-bobbled fabric around herself and slipped from her own bed. With shuffling steps, she crossed warily to the couch. That was empty, too.

Perplexed, she searched the bathroom, opened the door to squint into the hall, and even peered into the fridge. But there was no sign of Dawn. Stifling a shiver, Rosie clutched the shawl tighter. Had she imagined the whole thing? Finally tipped over the edge of misery into the dark void of true psychosis…? Perhaps drowned her sorrows beneath a plethora of champagne and hallucinated happier times?

Surely not…

Her lip trembled, and she worried it with her teeth.

Surely—

The corner of a suitcase caught her eye, tucked mostly under the other bed. Oh, thank God – Dawn *had* been here. *Was* here… somewhere. The relief of the realisation dropped Rosie onto the side of the couch, and tears welled; caught in the downswing of adrenalin, she buried her face in her hands and sobbed. Her own reaction surprised her, the sheer magnitude of fright and despair that sunk claws into her heart at Dawn's sudden absence; the fear, the feeling of loss, was more potent than anything she'd experienced before, and she shook with it.

It took her some time to gather herself again, but at last, she pushed heavily to her feet. Her trembling hands resettled the shawl, and the window drew her, pale sunlight streaming through a crack in the heavy curtains. She decided she could use some air. Drawing back the curtains, she pushed the window wide, shut her eyes, and leaned her head out into the crisp morning. Against the helpful ebullience of cold air, she drew a deep, calming breath.

A quiet murmuring caught her attention, then, and her eyes flashed open. She cast about, and her heart fluttered on a wave of reprieve when she spied the source, for down below – talking to the bloody daffodils – was Dawn. All on her own in the misty gardens, she cradled a steaming cup of tea in one hand and gesticulated animatedly with the other, clearly quite caught up in whatever she was discussing with the flowers. As Rosie's pounding heart settled, a broad smile eased over her lips. It was just like Dawn to be out communing with nature in such a ridiculously literal fashion. One thing was for sure, she'd never quite grown up – and approaching mid-sixties had made sod all difference to that fact.

Warmed by contentment at the surety her dear friend was still nearby, Rosie made herself a cup of tea, too, popped on her wellies, and went down to join her. As she stepped out through the side doors of the Inn, a wash of cool, damp air engulfed her, driving a delicious shiver down her spine, and she took an indulgent sip of hot tea before she proceeded down the steps. At the bottom, she discovered the grass was wet, but she'd worn her wellies for just that possibility and clumped happily onward with dry feet.

On her left, the grounds rolled away to the edge of a silvery lake, while to the right a magnificent oak forest stood tall, providing safe harbour for two skittish roe deer that bounded away as they caught sight of her. Somewhere in the distance, a fox barked, hailing the morning, and blue tits scolded from glossy-leafed holly bushes at the tree line. Rosie let her gaze rove, drinking in the beautiful scenery as she meandered across the lawns to where Dawn was perched on a small bench beside a riotous spring flowerbed.

As she drew near, Rosie composed herself and snipped, "Talking to the fairies again, are we?"

"More interesting company than you so far this morning," Dawn shot back.

Rosie plastered a dreadful scowl across her face. "You nearly gave me a heart attack with your disappearing act."

Dawn scoffed and straightened her beanie. "I hardly did it on purpose."

"You even made the bed!"

"I always make the bed."

Rosie's glower darkened. "I was really worried, Dawn."

Dawn widened her eyes innocently. "Damn. Should have hidden in the cupboard to watch your reaction."

"It's not funny."

Dawn cocked her head, lips twitching. "It's a *little* bit funny. That shawl really suits you, by the way."

Rosie's eyes narrowed and she pulled the gaudy thing tighter against her chest. But she couldn't maintain the façade for long in the face of Dawn's impish smile; it was a little bit funny – now that she'd gotten over her initial fright. And besides, there was too much of last night's good spirits still circulating in her veins. She plopped down on the bench next to Dawn, noticed her teacup was empty, and poured half of her own into it for her.

"What are you doing out here so early, anyway?"

"'Talking to the fairies,' obviously."

"Scintillating." Rosie leaned back on the bench and looked across the sprawling vista. "God, what a shit view."

"Bloody dreadful, isn't it?" Dawn sighed happily. She sipped her borrowed tea and made a face. "You cow, couldn't you at least have added *one* sugar?"

"Consider it repayment for this morning. Drink up."

They sat comfortably together, watching the birds and the clouds passing by until, at last, Dawn's stomach rumbled.

"I've finished my cuppa, anyway," Rosie said with a smile. She got up to stretch. "Let's go in for breakfast. I've heard that they serve the best scones in all of England at this Inn."

"Scones are for tea, not breakfast," Dawn muttered, meandering next to her across the dewy grass. "But... I do *love* scones... so I'll allow it. They'd just better put the bloody jam on first, though – none of this ridiculous strawberry-dollop-plopped-on-top nonsense."

They reached the steps, but Dawn paused before she ascended, distracted by a single daffodil that had established itself beside the entrance. She touched one fingertip to its valiant, full-blooming crown, whispering encouragement, and Rosie pushed past with a roll of her eyes. But she jerked to a halt again upon a wave of realisation.

Dawn. *That's who the daffodils had reminded her of.*

She turned back, and Dawn looked up with an unsuspecting smile.

"Daffodils are my favourite," she explained when she noticed Rosie's perplexed face. "They're such bright, brave little things."

"I remember," Rosie replied, frowning. After a heartbeat, she added, "Strange… they're the reason I came on this trip in the first place."

Dawn straightened with a cheeky pout. "Aww, missing me, were you?"

Rosie scoffed, dousing the moment. "Haven't spared you a thought in twenty years."

"Course you haven't. Come on, I'm starving. And we've got a big day planned."

As the words sank in, Rosie scowled. "Do we?"

"Yup," Dawn chirped. She bounded up the steps. "I've signed us up for everything."

# CHAPTER FOUR

An hour and a half later, Rosie sat tight on the couch with her arms folded. "I've told you; I don't want to go."

"C'mon!" Dawn admonished, rushing about the room. "We're going to miss the bus!" She grabbed the guidebook off the small kitchen table and threw two bottles of water – and Rosie's purse – into a tiny backpack.

"Hey!" Rosie exclaimed as she noticed. "That's mine!"

She flew over to rescue it, but when she was close enough, Dawn looped an arm through hers and propelled her out the door. It clicked locked behind them before Rosie could break free, and then Dawn held up the key card.

"Stay in the hall, then," she challenged, flaunting it.

Rosie blew irritably through her nose, arms akimbo as she watched Dawn escape down the passage. As she made the lift, Rosie suddenly realised she was serious, and stormed after her. "Give me the bloody card!" she shouted as Dawn hammered the buttons. "Damn you, Dawn, you bloody—!" The lift pinged closed, Dawn gifting her a cheeky wink just as it did so, and Rosie slammed a fist against the doors. "Dammit!"

She hissed a stream of curses under her breath as she turned for the stairs, taking them two at a time with little regard for her knees. She swirled around the bannister post at the bottom and found her *friend* holding the front door open, ready to bolt.

"The lobby's nice, too," Dawn suggested.

She scarpered, and renewed oaths poured from Rosie's lips as she dashed after her. "I'll kill her!" she muttered as she scooted across the car park in hot pursuit. "I'll bloody kill her…!"

Dawn ducked onto the full coach, speeding all the way to the very back seats, and Rosie surged aboard. She paused with her fingers clawed into the seat-tops on either side of the aisle, nostrils flaring as she glared at her trapped prey, and Dawn shrunk lower into her seat, watching apprehensively as she stalked towards her.

But when Rosie had closed three-quarters of the distance between them, Dawn shouted, "For the love of God, man, DRIVE!"

The coach suddenly lurched forward, toppling Rosie into the seat beside Dawn, and she spluttered her indignation. Dawn gave her a cheeky grin as she righted herself. "I knew you'd be difficult about this, so I made friends with the bus driver." She lowered her voice conspiratorially. "Popped him twenty quid."

Rosie gritted her teeth as the coach pitched around the corner of the drive. "You are stuffing impossible."

Dawn beamed. "Thank you."

"I think there *may* be a reason I haven't spoken to you in twenty bloody years."

"I'll make up for it," Dawn promised with a wink, and Rosie rolled her eyes so hard they hurt.

They fell to silence, and Dawn flipped through the guidebook while Rosie stared stubbornly out the window with her arms folded. But as the drive stretched, Rosie began to fidget.

Dawn carefully ignored her.

At last, Rosie huffed. "Where *are* we going, exactly?"

Dawn slowly licked her thumb and turned the page. "It's a surprise."

"I don't like your surprises."

Rosie stared her down until, at last, Dawn gave an exasperated sigh and held out the book. Rosie craned to look at the spot where her finger rested, and then her flummoxed gaze flashed up again.

"A *tree-top* adventure? Are you mad? We're sixty, not sixteen!"

Dawn gave a one-shouldered shrug. "It sounds like fun. And it says it's appropriate for all ages."

Rosie eyeballed her. "Dawn. You are *deathly afraid of heights*."

"I know," Dawn said defensively, "but… I promised myself that this year I would try the things that scare me. And I really want to try." She averted her gaze, then, and admitted, "I'm not very brave, though… which is why I wanted you to come. I… really want to do this, Rose."

Caught between irritation and understanding, Rosie stared. "You could have just said."

Dawn made a face. "And missed out on your mad dash to the bus?"

Rosie's eyes glittered. "Safer bet would have been to just tell me. Who's to say I won't leave you up a tree somewhere, now?"

Dawn paled. "You wouldn't…"

"Wouldn't I?" Rosie pasted her most aloof, untouchable expression across her face and turned to gaze serenely out of the window once more.

Dawn studied her for a long moment, trying to judge just how serious she was, but her mask was as impossible to read as ever.

"Oh, look," Rosie breezed after a moment, "here we are. How lovely."

The coach turned onto a gravelled drive and Dawn plastered herself to the window, staring white-faced at a spider's web of ropes and netting stretched between a magnificent collection of oaks and conifers. They debussed, and she wavered as she turned her gaze up, up, to the underside of a wooden platform far above them. Turning slightly green, she extended a hand vaguely back towards the vehicle and made to turn around. "Maybe I'll just… wait here…"

"Nope!" Rosie clipped. She caught Dawn's outstretched arm and dragged her onward. "This was your bright idea."

Dawn leaned back against her tugging, but Rosie was persistent, and they soon found themselves kitted out and strapped into safety harnesses. Dawn clutched white-knuckled at the helmet fastened firmly onto her head, wondering what the hell the point of it was when a fall could break every other bone in her body.

"Ready?" Rosie goaded, gesturing flamboyantly for her to precede up a stout ladder affixed to a grand old oak tree.

Dawn tried to say no, but all that escaped her was a small squeak. They were the last buddy-pair of their group to ascend, and she swallowed as she reached for the rungs.

"Move it," Rosie snarked, "or we'll miss the bloody bus *back*. And then I'll be really miffed!"

Taking a deep breath, Dawn began to climb. It took her far longer than any of the others, and though she stop-started all the way up, Rosie patiently blocked her way back down. At last, they reached the top and paused to catch their breath. Ahead, an innocuous wood-and-cable bridge stretched, offering passage to the next tree, and Dawn clutched at the safety ropes, teetering on the brink of a meltdown.

"You can do this," Rosie murmured, placing a calming hand on her back.

Dawn leaned back against her touch for a moment, and then nodded and squared her shoulders. Tentatively, she placed one foot onto the bridge – and found it far firmer than she had expected. She shuffled forward, gasping against her terror.

Rosie moved with her, one hand keeping contact against her shoulder blade. "Breathe. You're all right. I'm right here."

Inch by inch, they progressed, over the first bridge, across the next, and the next. Rosie shadowed Dawn's every step, whispering encouragement, until finally they made it to the last platform before the descent. But there, a zip-line loomed, and Dawn backed against the tree trunk, grey-faced and shaking.

"I can't, Rose," she gasped, a tear escaping to roll down her cheek. "I can't…"

Rosie turned a savage expression on the attendant waiting to attach Dawn's harness.

"Can we go tandem?"

The youngster shrank back and nodded mutely.

"Good. Strap us in. Come here, Dawn – come here, come *here*."

Pointing to the spot in front of her, she bullied Dawn into position. Under her baleful supervision, the attendant hurriedly affixed clips and straps and then scuttled back out of the way. Rosie manoeuvred Dawn to the brink, but Dawn baulked and pushed back against her with a fearful cry. Rosie let her pause. "Put your arms out," she suggested softly against Dawn's ear. "It'll be just like flying."

"F-falling, you mean," Dawn said with a small sob.

Rosie hugged her from behind, lacing her hands together over Dawn's sternum. "You've conquered it, Dawn. We're almost there. You can do this. Trust me. I'm right here – I won't let go."

With a despairing shake of her head, Dawn slowly raised her trembling arms out to the sides, and then Rosie pushed off from the platform. The air whizzed past, tearing a tiny gasp from Dawn's lips instead of the scream she found herself too terrified to voice. Rosie held tight; chin tucked against the top of Dawn's shoulder. Over and over, she murmured against the wind: *I've got you. You're okay, I've got you.*

The descent seemed to stretch forever, but at last, the zip angled upward, slowing their headlong rush, and then they were safe on a gigantic mat. There, a bevy of attendants sprang to release them from the harnesses, and Rosie caught the nearest one by the collar.

"Fetch a Coke!" she demanded. "Now!"

The attendant yelped and scurried to obey, and soon Rosie had manhandled Dawn onto the closest bench and thrust the sugary beverage into her hands.

"You look like shit," she said with a scowl.

"Th-thanks," Dawn managed to respond.

"Drink." Rosie sat down beside her, rubbing her back with a gentle concern that belied her acerbic tone. "Bloody mad, you are. Putting yourself through that."

Dawn took a shaky sip of her coke and then turned a green smile on her friend. "Hated every minute of it, to be honest."

Rosie softened. "But... you did it."

Dawn's smile broadened, gentle and pleased. "I did, didn't I? Thanks, for coming with me."

Rosie wrapped an arm around her shoulders and gave her a squeeze before eyeing the half-drunk Coke. "Finish that, mind. I have to pay for it."

"A-actually, Miss," ventured a hovering attendant, "you can have that complimentary."

Rosie's glare reignited. "Who bloody asked you? Bugger off – go, go!" She waved them away, bristling protectively in front of Dawn as the attendants retreated between surreptitious glances. "Nothing to see here, you little shits!" she called loudly after them.

Beside her, Dawn sniggered, and then the vice-grip of her fear abated, dropping her into a full fit of giggles in the backwash of adrenalin. Rosie rounded on her.

"And what the bloody hell are you laughing at?"

"Your... people skills," Dawn gasped between laughter. "Absolutely... fabulous."

Rosie's lips quirked, and she pulled Dawn to her feet.

"I assume you can walk?" she asked acidly.

Dawn rolled her eyes. "I didn't break anything."

"I know. You're welcome."

Arm in arm, they meandered back towards the coach, and then Rosie helped Dawn clamber aboard despite her shaky legs.

When they had dropped into their seats, Dawn reached for the guidebook, and Rosie cleared her throat in warning.

Dawn gave a sheepish grin. "Back to the hotel for lunch, and then… on to the next activity."

"Do I dare ask?"

"It'll be fun."

Rosie gave a dark sigh. "Oh, how enthused I am."

# CHAPTER FIVE

After lunch and a too-short rest, Rosie found herself loaded into the coach again, an extra coat tucked firmly onto her lap. It was a warm, bright afternoon, and she didn't feel she needed it, but Dawn had insisted they each bring one. It couldn't hurt, she supposed – the Lake District was notorious for showers, after all.

As the coach rumbled down narrow lanes, she leaned over to peer into Dawn's guidebook. "Where are we going this time?"

"Windermere," Dawn replied, showing her a picture of England's largest lake.

Despite herself, Rosie was impressed. "That's lovely, actually."

"Isn't it?" Dawn smiled. "We're going kayaking."

"We're bloody *what*?"

"Kay-yak-king," Dawn repeated. "You know, little boaty-floaty adventure, out in the nature…"

Rosie fixed her with a withering glare. "If I'd known you were going to drag me into all these ridiculous things, I'd have thrown you out of my room the minute you arrived."

"Our room," Dawn corrected jovially. "I've been kayaking once before, it's wonderful fun."

Rosie folded her arms around her coat and fell to muttering. Dawn paid her no mind, continuing to pour over her guidebook.

After a long moment, she commented, "There's lots of butterflies, this time of year."

Appropriately baited, Rosie stopped swearing under her breath.

"Peacocks and tortoiseshells in April, it says," Dawn continued conversationally, as if she were completely unaware of Rosie's piqued interest.

Rosie vacillated and then snatched the book to see for herself. She poured over pictures of the pretty little things painting the landscape, feeding on heather, sunning themselves in meagre rays on the lake shore. Her eyes widened as they scanned the page. "Did you know that there are *forty-one* species of butterfly in the Lake District?"

Dawn's mouth twisted with amusement. "*Really?*"

She didn't give a flying fig about butterflies if she were honest, but she knew Rosie loved them, and contented herself with half-listening to her commentary as she turned her gaze out the window. Beyond, the world of the Lake Poets rolled by. A blaze of yellow stretched to secretive, bluebell-filled woods, and she sighed as she remembered the last lines of one of her favourite poems by Wordsworth. Quietly, she murmured, "*And then my heart with pleasure fills, and dances with the daffodils…*"

Rosie looked up. "What?"

"Nothing." Dawn smiled at her irritable expression, that same face that hid so much light, love, and warmth.

Rosie snapped the book shut. "Are we there yet? I feel like we've been driving forever."

"It's been fifteen whole minutes. But yes, we're nearly there."

Shortly after, the coach scrunched to a halt on the shores of Lake Windermere.

"Leave that," Dawn snapped when Rosie got up with her extra coat.

"But I thought you said—"

"For *after*, silly. You can't take it on the kayak."

Rosie dumped the coat, muttering something incredibly rude under her breath as they stepped off the coach. But she fell to abrupt silence as she looked up from the step – wide-eyed, they both stared, taken aback by their first proper view of the magnificent body of water in its entirety.

"It's huge!" Rosie whispered, reverent. "Look, Dawn!"

"I've got eyes," Dawn murmured back, equally awed.

Rosie swallowed. "Are you sure you want to head out in a tiny boat onto *that*?"

Dawn squared her shoulders and nodded. "I climbed a tree. I can do anything."

"*Technically*," Rosie muttered, following her across the car park towards a small building that had canoes propped up against its walls, "you climbed a *ladder*."

Dawn signed the indemnity and retrieved a pair of life jackets from a friendly guide named Ben, who then led them to a two-person kayak bobbing beside the wharf.

"Know what you're doing, ladies?" he asked in an easy-going tone.

"Yes of course," Dawn said, lowering herself into the boat. "I have plenty of kayaking experience."

"Once!" Rosie snapped. She caught Ben's eye as she passed him. "She's been kayaking once."

Ben leaned against a bollard and gave a relaxed smile. "Once is plenty. You'll be all right – it's a calm day today, no wind for waves. Maybe don't go too far, though. It can be quite tiring paddling all the way back."

"We're not geriatrics," Dawn snapped as she settled into the rear of the kayak. "Get in, Rose, before Mitch Buchannon here decides we need armbands."

Ben laughed, graced them with a jaunty salute, and went on his way.

"Could have at least helped me get on the bloody thing," Rosie muttered, clinging to the pilings for balance as she reached for the bobbing craft with one foot.

Dawn pulled the boat closer to the dock and offered a hand. With a scowl, Rosie stretched for it and shakily managed to sit down. Once she had settled, she felt a bit more secure, but then Dawn pushed a paddle at her. Rosie greased her with a glare over her shoulder. "Doesn't this thing have a motor?"

"Your ignorance astounds me."

Rosie harrumphed and turned her gaze forward as they floated away from the dock. "Why do you get to sit at the back? I don't like you sitting behind me."

"I'm sitting at the back so I can steer. And do this."

Dawn slapped the paddle blade against the water, dousing Rosie with a well-aimed splash. Rosie yelped and turned to berate her, but the craft tilted dangerously as her weight shifted. She dropped her paddle and grabbed at the sides as it rocked, and Dawn laughed, snatching up the wayward oar before it could float away.

"Should have left you up the bloody tree!" Rosie howled.

"Yes, too bad about your heart of gold," Dawn replied. She handed back Rosie's paddle. "Here, you're going to need this."

"I don't even know how to use it."

"Easy, dip and pull."

"Oh!" Rosie shook her head violently as Dawn demonstrated. "No – I don't have the balance, Dawn, you do it – you do it. I couldn't possibly – I'll just… sit here and try not to fall out."

Dawn rolled her eyes and set to, choosing a course not too far off the bank so they could admire the floating butterflies at the water's edge. At length, Rosie relaxed, captivated by their gorgeous surroundings as they drifted along, and Dawn propelled them a fair distance before turning to explore a quiet bay.

"Stop, Dawn!" Rosie gushed suddenly. "Stop, stop – there's something in the water! There, near the shore!"

Dawn dipped the oar to bring them to a halt and peered in the direction Rosie was excitedly pointing.

"It's an otter!" Rosie exclaimed, craning to see better. "Oh, Dawn, look!"

It wasn't just one – three pups gambolled around their mother and then dashed up to wrestle on the muddy bank. The two women watched in perfect silence, delighted by their chirps and squeals, and Rosie reached back a hand to clasp Dawn's as they shared the heart-warming moment. They sat watching for ages – the otter family seeming in no hurry to get anywhere – and the day began slowly to fade around them. But at last, Mum chirped at her pups, scolded the one that nipped her tail, and led them off for an evening's fishing.

Dawn roused from the reverie first. "Shit, Rose, it's quite bloody late. You're going to have to help me row, or we won't make it back to the dock before dark."

Rosie glanced up at the sky with some trepidation and realised she was right. Gamely, she lifted her paddle. "Pull and dip, right?"

Dawn groaned. "Dip and pull!"

Rosie's first few strokes were shallow and ineffective, but after a couple of corrections from Dawn, she was paddling with sure rhythm. Dawn synced time, and they glided out of the bay at a reasonable speed. They stuck close to the bank as they had on the way out, and Rosie pointed out a red stag with a single unshed horn that she wished they could stop and observe. But daylight was running, and they pressed on.

When they finally docked in deep twilight, concerned Greenside Inn staff were hovering. As they halted alongside the jetty, Ben came forward with an impish grin to offer a hand to Rosie. "Dunno what all the fuss is about," he said with a shrug. "I told them two tough old birds like you'd be fine."

Rosie caught his outstretched fingers in a vice grip, making him wince. "If you use that word old – if you use that word *one more time…*" Buoyed by ire, she shoved his hand aside and stood up of her own accord in the small craft.

Dawn yelped. "NO, Rose! Wait – stop!"

Too late. The kayak pitched dangerously, throwing Rosie off-balance. Dawn lunged for her as she teetered backwards, but the shifting centre of gravity was too much – the whole boat flipped sideways and dumped both of them in the water. They came up spluttering, gasping against the cold and weighted down by heavy clothes. Dawn, a swimmer in her youth, grabbed hold of the back of Rosie's life jacket as she floundered, and pulled her towards the side. Ben dived in to help; the water wasn't especially deep near the dock, and a few strokes of his powerful arms pulled them into the range of standing. There, Dawn caught an arm around Rosie's waist to steer her to safety, and Ben surged out and sprinted to his office for blankets. He returned shortly, looking chaste, and Rosie glared at him with chattering teeth as he draped a blanket over her shoulders. Sheepishly, he offered one to Dawn, too, and she gave him a small nod of thanks as she wrapped it around herself.

Pip, accompanying that day's tour, hovered over them. "My goodness, ladies! I'm so sorry about all this! Are you hurt?" When they shook their heads, he rounded on Ben, sputtering as he puffed up his gangly frame and raised an accusatory finger. "I will have your company shut down for this! This is, this is… reckless endangerment! These are my *clients*, Sir! You will be hearing from our lawyer, you will—"

"All right," Rosie interrupted around her chattering teeth. "That's enough. It's hardly his fault the boat tipped over."

Ben, who had bowed his head beneath the tongue-lashing, looked up with an expression so intensely relieved it was strange to see it on the face of a grown man.

"Yes," Dawn agreed. "He can hardly accept responsibility for two crazy *old* ladies messing about on a lake."

"Oh!" Rosie howled, throwing her head back. "That word!

What did I say about that word!"

"I'm really sorry, Miss," Ben mumbled.

Rosie fixed him with a diabolical expression. "For dropping me in the drink? Or for calling me *old*?"

Ben swallowed. "Um…"

Dawn gave an exasperated huff. "She's having you on – ignore her." She turned to peacock-Pip. "Are we going to stand here all night, dripping wet, or are you going to take us home?"

Pip deflated. "Oh, uh, yes, of course, yes." He gathered himself and caught his simpering smile between his teeth once more. "Let's get you to the coach, shall we? Get you nice and warm, shall we?" He offered his arm, but they ignored it, hanging on to each other instead.

"Oh, spare us the condescension, would you," Rosie huffed. Pip clamped his mouth shut and Ben grinned. Rosie narrowed her eyes at the boatman as they passed, making his smile falter, but Dawn offered him a wink. "Cheers, Ben. Thanks for the rescue."

"Oh, yes," Rosie snarked. "Our hero!"

"She's grateful, really," Dawn assured him. "We'll recommend you anytime – it was a lovely afternoon."

Ben blushed. "Thanks, Miss. You take care now, be sure to get warm as soon as you can."

Rosie deigned to gift him half a smile, and then they made their way back to the coach. Inside, Dawn caught up one of the extra coats waiting on the back seat and wrapped it around Rosie in an attempt to placate her violent shivering.

"Not exactly what I had in mind for that," Rosie said wryly.

"Bet you're glad I made you bring it, though," Dawn replied.

She added her own coat over it as an extra layer, and Rosie frowned beneath her gentle hands.

"Aren't you cold?"

Dawn gave an impish smile and pulled her damp blanket closed again. "Freezing – but you're trembling like a leaf. I'll be gutted if I made you go kayaking and then you catch hypothermia."

Rosie raised an arm to hold the coats open. "Get in here."

Dawn tucked in next to her, and Rosie adjusted the coats around both of them. The body heat helped, but the drive home still felt exceptionally long, and Rosie's cold had set in deep by the time they arrived.

"Come on," Dawn said, helping Rosie up when the coach had finally stopped. "I could do with a whiskey."

Rosie, too cold to respond, merely nodded and let Dawn guide her off. They made their way slowly to their room, Rosie having chased Pip's concern away with a single chattering snarl, and Dawn immediately drew a steaming bath when they walked in. As soon as it had run, she unpeeled the damp coats and blanket from Rosie's trembling shoulders and pushed her gently towards the bathroom.

"Y-you sh-should—" Rosie tried to say, but Dawn cut her off.

"Shut up. Get in there and get warm. I'll throw on something dry for the time being and put the kettle on. There's whiskey in the minibar – we'll have an Irish."

"Th-there's n-no cream."

Dawn rolled her eyes. "Hurry up, now, before you freeze to death."

When Rosie had emerged and donned several layers of clothing, Dawn thrust a laced coffee into her hands and went to shower. She was quick about it, being more concerned about Rosie than she let on, and soon reappeared dressed in nightclothes and a thick robe.

Catching sight of the slightly bluish tinge of Rosie's lips, and the still-persistent shiver plaguing her, she frowned. "How are you feeling?"

Rosie cradled her hot coffee like a lifeline. "I'm so c-cold… It's in my b-bloody b-bones…"

"Come on," Dawn said, "let's get you under some blankets. I swear to God – if you freeze, I'll never forgive you."

She stripped the beds for every cover they had and settled Rosie beneath them on the couch. Tucking in beside her, she pulled Rosie's trembling form against her and arranged the blankets over both of them, and Rosie sighed at the cocoon of body heat.

"What a bloody day," Dawn said sheepishly, attempting to rub some warmth back into Rosie's arms.

"M-mm," Rosie agreed. "T-tomorrow, *I'm* ch-choosing the activities."

Dawn laughed. Encompassing her icy form as best she could, she held Rosie tight until the first hint of warmth seeped back through her. The hot whiskey coffee helped, too, and Rosie tucked her head against Dawn's shoulder as she finally began to warm up. With better comfort came fatigue, and Rosie found she couldn't hold her eyes open a moment longer; cuddled against Dawn's side, she yawned and drifted off to sleep.

## CHAPTER SIX

When Rosie woke, it was still dark. She tried to stir but found herself buried beneath a veritable mountain of blankets. *Had Dawn used everything in the bloody room?* Something heavy was caught around her waist, too, and she struggled against a momentary surge of panic at feeling trapped. But Dawn shifted beside her at the movement, and she relaxed as she realised it was only Dawn's arm, tucked firmly around her. In the half-dark, she made out her friend's face and realised that they lay lengthways on the couch, her head pillowed against Dawn's chest. The revelation came softly, of how safe and warm she felt cradled in the arms of her dear friend, and she sank into it with a sigh. Closing her eyes, she listened to the steady beat of Dawn's heart, drew comfort from the rise and fall of her chest, and wondered how she'd lived without her for so bloody long.

But Dawn's arm tightened suddenly, and a small, miserable murmur slipped from her lips. She gave a violent twitch, and Rosie pushed herself half-upright to stare down with concern.

"Dawn?" she whispered.

Dawn's eyes squeezed tighter, her mouth contracting to a

grimace and her hands fisting against the nightmare that plagued her. Rosie supported herself on one elbow and reached to cup her cheek. "Dawn…"

Another whimper tore from Dawn's lips, the distress of it cutting claws into Rosie's heart, but then her eyes flashed open.

"Rose!" she cried, groping through the dark.

Rosie caught her flailing hand and shushed her softly. "I'm here – I'm here."

Dawn rolled up to catch her in a crushing hug, gasping against a primal fear. "Oh, thank God – you were in the water, you went under. You – you didn't come up…"

"Except I did, you damned fool," Rosie murmured, squeezing her fingers. "Would you relax? You can't get rid of me *that* easily."

Dawn flopped back down with a shudder. "True… you're a bitch to do in." But her lip trembled, undermining her snarky attempt, and she dropped her gaze. "You must be more careful, Rose, please. I can't… lose you, too."

"I'm not going anywhere," Rosie promised. After a second, she added, "Want some coffee?"

"It's the middle of the bloody night."

"Yes, but I'm awake now."

Dawn groaned. "And I suppose that means I have to be awake, too?"

"Your intuition amazes me, sometimes."

Rosie rolled over and slipped off the couch, flipping on one of the wall lamps and nicking a blanket to wrap around her shoulders before padding to the kitchenette. As the kettle boiled, she rinsed their cups from earlier and added the trappings for a decent coffee.

"Another whiskey?" she called over her shoulder.

"Do you even have to ask me that?"

Rosie smirked and added a generous dash to their cups. She returned with a mug in each hand, and Dawn sat upright to take a hearty sip of hers.

"Ahh, absolutely bloody perfect. Thanks."

Rosie dropped onto the couch beside her. "So," she said with a wink, "what misadventures do you have in store for me tomorrow?"

"Oh-ho, no…!" Dawn grimaced, shaking her head. "I'm done making the plans."

"Aww, I get to pick?"

Dawn blew through her nose as if the admission were painful. "Yes."

"Excellent. I vote a sit-in with a good book in the morning, and then a lazy walk around the grounds in the afternoon."

"Wow." Dawn blinked sardonically. "Be still my beating heart."

"Books are their own kind of adventure," Rosie stated.

"Don't get me wrong, I do love a good book."

"Good. I brought a few – you can read one of mine. In fact, I've one I think will drastically appeal to you."

"Oh? What's it called?"

"*Bonkers.*"

"Better not be some kind of dodgy serial-killer romance with a title like *that*."

Rosie snorted. "Hardly. It's an autobiography, by a famous comedian."

"Oh. Well, I do like comedians."

"I know. You've spent your whole life trying to be funny. This book actually *is*."

Dawn sat back, affronted. "*You* think I'm funny."

"Sometimes," Rosie allowed, taking a sip of her coffee. She choked, almost spilling it. "Christ, that's strong!"

Dawn sniggered. "You bloody poured it!"

Rosie cleared her throat, took another swig, and pulled her legs up onto the couch. Dawn caught an arm around her shoulders, fussing with the blankets, and Rosie settled in against her side. "This is nice," Rosie sighed, cradling her coffee.

"Isn't it?" Dawn agreed.

"Better than you trying to drown me."

"Or you threatening to leave me up a tree."

"You've no leg to stand on, there, you pillock. That was *your* idea."

They fell to companionable silence for a time, watching fluid moonlight filtering through a crack in the curtains. At length, Dawn shifted, pulling her arm down from Rosie's shoulder to cup her coffee with both hands. She took a sip and then stared into it, and a melancholic sigh escaped her.

"D'you think…" she trailed off, and then met Rosie's eye. "D'you think we're too old for these sorts of shenanigans…?"

Rosie contemplated her for a moment, weighing up the question. Somehow, it didn't seem like the time for a flippant response. Slowly, she replied, "Day before yesterday, I'd have said yes. But then you came along, out of the blue, and reminded me what it feels like to be alive. Something about you makes me… brave."

Dawn studied her. "You make me brave, too. I'd never have dreamed of crossing stick bridges strung between trees if you hadn't been there."

"I'm proud of you for that," Rosie said softly. "I know how scared you are of heights."

Dawn gave a small, sad chuckle. "I can't believe I did that, actually." She took a breath, and her face clouded. "Oh, Rose… When did life get so glum? I don't want to be old and lonely."

"Me neither, but we're only in our sixties," Rosie said, patting her arm. "And we have each other. Besides, after today, I don't see there's much stopping us doing all the things we want to do. We might just do them a little slower, that's all."

A small smile shone through Dawn's melancholy. "*You* might do them a little slower – bugger-all wrong with *me*." She winked, drained her cup, and cradled the empty vessel on her lap. "I think a calm day tomorrow is a good idea, though. I must admit, I'm a tiny bit exhausted."

Rosie's eyes crinkled. "Me too. We'll take it easy, and then the day after you can sign us up for another wild adventure."

"Excellent. I have so" – Dawn yawned wide and prolonged – "many plans."

"Come on, you – let's call it a night."

Dawn reclined, her heavy eyes closing. "I think I'll just... sleep here. Can't be arsed" – yawn – "to move all the blankets back."

Rosie rescued the cup before it slipped from her limp fingers and set it beside her own on the coffee table. She got up and turned off the wall lamp, waited for her vision to adjust to the pale moonlight from the window, and then turned back to retrieve a blanket so she could sleep in comfort in her own damned bed. But Dawn had them all tucked up tight around her, under her, and pulled up to her chin, and was almost asleep.

"Can I have one of those please?" Rosie said, looming over her with her hands on her hips.

"Mmm," Dawn muttered without opening her eyes. She snuggled down deeper, fisting at the blankets. "So... comfy..."

Rosie stalked closer to tug fruitfully at the corner of one, but Dawn had done a fine job of wrapping them to immovability. "At least let me get in, then," she huffed. "It's bloody freezing standing out here."

Dawn slurred something unintelligible but flopped out a sleepy arm to admit her. Muttering under her breath, Rosie clambered over and squeezed into the tiny space Dawn had opened for her. Peevish, she fidgeted with the blankets and cushions, trying to force them to some kind of comfortableness, and Dawn tucked her arm in again, trapping Rosie against her side.

Rosie squirmed. "You're squashing me!"

Dawn gave her half an inch, and she settled with an exasperated sniff, pushing her hair irritably out of her face as she laid her head at an awkward angle against Dawn's shoulder. She huffed and fidgeted a little more, but finally managed to get comfortable, and, at last, as she warmed up, her ire dimmed. Exhaustion began to tug heavily at her, too. Dawn's arm tightened around her, and she relaxed. She yawned, spared a smile for sleepy

Dawn, and then leaned up to pop a kiss on her cheek – but Dawn responded subconsciously to the movement. She turned her head as Rosie shifted so that she accidentally met her mouth instead. The unexpected shock of the connection – so soft and intimate – widened Rosie's eyes, and she froze with her soul pressed suddenly against Dawn's lips. And Dawn kissed her – really kissed her – for a long, heartbeat moment, but then, mumbling, let her head loll back to the side and sighed into a deeper slumber. Rosie jerked back and hung by a thread, one hand hovering over her trembling mouth in disbelief.

"What the bloody hell was *that*…?" she whispered. Her heart lurched, erratic, and her hand dropped to press against her chest instead. Hardly daring to breathe, she outlined Dawn's peaceful face with anxious eyes before settling on her mouth, full and shadowed in the indistinct light. Subconsciously, Rosie bit at her bottom lip, worrying it with her teeth. That had… struck a chord.

Which was weird.

"You're over-tired," she muttered, tearing her gaze away and crushing the odd feeling beneath a savage frown. "Go to sleep, for God's sake."

With a heavy sigh, she reclined and buried her head in the blankets.

# CHAPTER SEVEN

Rosie groaned, lifting a hand to shield her face against streaming sunlight as Dawn tugged open the curtains.

"Wake up, sleepy head," came Dawn's singsong voice. "It's after nine and I'm making tea. It's a beautiful day."

Dawn returned to perch beside her and Rosie's eyes suddenly flashed open, fully awake – accusatory. She stiffened. "You... kissed me."

Dawn tilted her head with a bemused smile. "What?"

"You kissed me!" Rosie repeated, scrambling upright on the couch to glare at her reproachfully.

"That's an odd thing to say first thing in the morning," Dawn said, perplexed by the sudden accusation.

"You did!" Rosie's hand flew to her lips, feeling the odd, slow tingle that still echoed. "You kissed me!"

"I did not."

"You did, last night!"

"Now, Rose – I think I'd remember if—"

"You did, Dawn, you bloody did!" Rosie shouted, leaping free of the blankets.

"All right," Dawn said, holding up her hands.

Rosie's eyes flashed side to side with disquiet, her hands fisting and unfisting at her sides.

"Christ," Dawn said, watching her, "that must have been one hell of a dream."

Rosie spun away in a fit of irritation, stalked back again. "I didn't bloody dream it! God, I can't believe you don't remember – honestly, I know you were half asleep, but—" Her face suddenly fell, and she considered the possibility that it might be better left alone, anyway. "It doesn't matter – forget it – it doesn't matter." She dropped heavily onto the couch again, rubbing her fists along the top of her thighs, and Dawn looked at her with concern.

"Did you bump your head when you fell in the lake yesterday?" she asked.

"Oh, sod off." Rosie flopped back against the cushions but then looked at her sideways. "You really don't remember?"

"I've honestly no idea what you're talking about."

"I meant to pop a kiss on your cheek. But then you turned –"

Dawn raised her eyebrows.

"– and you kissed me."

Dawn stared for a long moment and then fell about laughing. "That's your best one yet, Rose – you really had me going there for a sec, I—" She broke off at the dreadful scowl on Rosie's face. "Wait, really?"

"YES!" Rosie slammed her hands down on the couch. "You bloody kissed me! Why the hell would you do that?"

"I..." Dawn leaned backwards, shaking her head in consternation.

Rosie was working herself up to a state. "You wouldn't give me a bloody blanket, and then I had to squeeze onto the *bloody* couch next to you – so I didn't *bloody* freeze to death – and then when I'd finally got comfortable, I felt a bit bad for being grumpy and went to pop a *bloody* kiss on your *bloody* cheek and—"

Dawn's face went white. "Oh."

"Yes, thank you – *bloody* thank you!" Rosie exclaimed, seeing comprehension flutter at last. "You did!"

"Oh God I did," Dawn whispered.

Rosie ran out of words, resorting to an expansive, open-handed you see! motion instead. Dawn stared at her with her jaw hanging slack, and colour crept up her cheeks.

As the silence stretched almost awkward, Rosie exclaimed, "WHY DID YOU DO THAT?!"

Dawn dropped her gaze beneath her ire and mumbled, "I… don't know Rose, I was… half-asleep…"

Rosie flung herself back onto the couch, gesturing vigorously. "Threw me for a bloody six, that did – and the most ridiculous part is – honestly, now, Dawn – it was sort of nice."

Dawn, who'd been sinking lower under her indignant fury, stiffened. "Wait – what?"

"I mean, I know it's *weird*, being how intimate it was," Rosie clarified, "but it was… sort of… nice."

Dawn's face turned thunderous. "*Rose.*"

It was Rosie's turn to blush. "What? I didn't start it!"

"Did you stop it?" Dawn challenged.

Rosie opened her mouth, closed it again. She'd been too surprised, too absolutely shell-shocked by the intimacy of it, to do much more than freeze until Dawn had pulled away.

"Well, there you go," Dawn snapped, mutinous. "Takes two."

Rosie wavered, and some of the heat left her voice. "But why. I'm serious, Dawn – this is serious, now – because it wasn't just a friendly peck – you *really* kissed me. Why would you do that?"

"I don't know!" Dawn spluttered, her pitch rising. "I suppose I just, well, I don't know – you know – a bit of whiskey, half-asleep – all cuddly and cosy after a long day – you know?"

"I *don't* know!" Rosie shot back, leaping up again to pace her agitation. "That's the point!"

"Oh, shut up about it – just shut up, will you!" Dawn squeezed her eyes closed, trying to drown out Rosie's accusations.

"I can't shut up about it," Rosie insisted. "I can't just do that – I want to know why!"

Dawn pressed her spine back against the couch, desperately hoping she – or Rosie, preferably – would fall through the floor so the conversation would be over. "I don't know, I don't know, I just don't KNOW!"

"Come on, Dawn, for Christ's sake – why would you do that to me, why would you – I bloody dreamed about it, after – I couldn't sleep, Dawn, I—"

Rosie broke off, watching Dawn shrink deeper into her seat – vulnerable beneath the onslaught of a tête-à-tête she wasn't ready for first thing in the morning – and something triggered inside her. In one fell movement, she closed the distance between them, caught her fingers desperately through Dawn's silver hair, and pressed a fervent kiss to her lips. Dawn stiffened in surprise, but then relented and let her.

At last, Rosie pulled back, her arms supporting her weight against the top of the couch behind Dawn's head. An inch away, she whispered, "Why did you do it?"

Speechless, Dawn gazed into her bewildered blue eyes.

# CHAPTER EIGHT

For a heartbeat, Rosie stayed where she was, hovering over Dawn, but then she reared up and spun away. "*Stop it*, Dawn!" she cried, fisting her hands into her tousled blonde locks as she backed away. "Just bloody stop it!"

Dawn sat frozen, blinking incredulously, and then crowed, "That was *you*!"

"There's a *line*, here, Dawn – we can't cross it – I won't cross it!"

"You just bloody did!"

"Well, I bloody take it back!"

"Now, hang on, Rose, what the hell is the matter with you? It was just a kiss, – it's not like we haven't kissed before."

Rosie tugged at her hair, pulling her head back in frustration. "That was at university, Dawn – for a laugh – forty bloody years ago! This is different!"

Dawn's astonishment settled to annoyance. "Stop it, Rose, stop it, now. You've worked yourself into a state."

Rosie gave an explosive exhale, agitatedly massaging her head. "I know, I'm sorry, I'm sorry – I don't know what's wrong with me."

"Come and sit here," Dawn commanded, giving the couch

a sharp pat beside her. "Come and sit, now that's enough."

Rosie obeyed; her hands still tangled through her hair. Gingerly, she perched on the edge, and Dawn reached out to pull her arms down before she was scalped. But Rosie leaned violently away from her touch, and Dawn's mouth opened – gaped – shut again beneath a heavy frown.

"*Rose.*"

"Sorry…" Rosie mumbled, fidgeting. "Sorry."

Dawn sat quietly mutinous for a few moments, waiting for her to calm down. At last, Rosie tucked her trembling hands firmly into her lap, and Dawn fixed her with a glare.

"All right, now?"

Rosie sniffed. "Yes."

"Good."

Dawn got up and left Rosie sitting glumly on the couch, heading to the kitchenette to finish making the tea she'd started before Rosie's abrupt trip down insanity lane. She glared daggers at Rosie's ridiculousness the entire time she was filling their mugs and then stalked back over to give her one. "I've added a sugar," she huffed. "You bloody need some sweetening up this morning."

Rosie dropped her gaze, feeling foolish, and curled her fingers around the warmth.

"Look, Rose," Dawn began, trying for patience now that she'd had a second to think about things, "I didn't kiss you on purpose last night – I was almost completely asleep, hardly even remembered this morning – so I think we can safely say that was just an automatic reaction from me being married for thirty-odd years. You were in my space, and when you moved" – she shrugged – "I moved."

Rosie opened her mouth to protest, but Dawn cut her off with a sharp look.

"And that's the end of *that*. Now, as for that lovely kiss you planted on me just now, that was all *you* – no, shut up, let me finish – look. You've recently been through a nasty divorce, and maybe your emotions are a bit all over the place, but I think you've got yourself all in a tizz about nothing." Rosie bowed her head, cheeks burning, and Dawn lightly squeezed her arm. "It's all right, Rose."

Rosie looked up, blinking against a tear. "It's not all right. I've made an utter tit of myself."

"Yes," Dawn smiled, "you have."

"Can we just…" Rosie took a deep breath and lamely waved a hand.

Dawn nudged her shoulder in solidarity. "Yes. Let's."

Rosie nodded and took a great swig of her tea before leaning back against the couch.

"Maybe I did bump my head yesterday," she sighed.

"No," Dawn disagreed. "You've always been a bit mad."

"Oh, thanks," Rosie snapped, and Dawn grinned to see some of the tumult leave her expression.

"You damned fool," she said, with a wry shake of her head.

Rosie's lips puckered. "You do bring out the worst in me."

"Bugger that. You manage to make a tit of yourself just fine without my intervention."

"Can't argue that, actually," Rosie sighed. "Over the course of the twenty years I've not seen you, my life has gone to hell."

"Now, Rose," Dawn chastised, shifting on the couch to face her with a serious expression, "don't be so hard on yourself. Everyone's life goes to hell after forty."

Rosie laughed. "Well, that's inspiring."

Dawn smiled, surreptitiously noting that her friend's face had returned to a normal colour. Patting Rosie's hand with sympathetic affection, she pushed to her feet and made her way towards the bathroom. "Now, will you hurry up and get ready?" she called over her shoulder. "You'll not like me if we miss breakfast."

"Is that a threat?"

Dawn stuck her head back around the door frame, hazel eyes flashing. "It's a bloody promise!"

Still, it took copious amounts of badgering on Dawn's part until Rosie was finally ready to face the day.

"I'm going to wake you two hours early, tomorrow!" Dawn cried as she finally bustled her out the door. "Your curious, and that's a friendly word, relationship with time will be the bloody death of me!"

Rosie shrugged expansively. "We've still got ten minutes before breakfast is finished."

"THAT WAS TWENTY MINUTES AGO!" Dawn shouted, giving her a hearty shove in the direction of the lift.

Rosie grinned impishly, dragged her heels, and let Dawn bully her down to the dining room. There, they almost scraped a decent meal as the staff were clearing the buffet away, and Dawn slung cusses at Rosie the whole way along the meagre counter. Rosie jovially sparred with her – telling her that fried foods were no good for her anyway – until, with a mostly-continental plate, Dawn stalked off to a table near the window. Rosie plopped down opposite to tuck into a delectable selection of ham, cheeses, and fruit.

"Could have had a proper Full English if we'd gotten here TEN MINUTES EARLIER," Dawn growled, tearing viciously at a bread roll.

Rosie passed her some butter. "Had our pick of the tables, at least."

"Because they're all bloody empty!"

Rosie sighed happily and turned her gaze out the window. "Would you look at that view, though? Can see the lake and everything, from here."

Mutinous, Dawn deliberately turned her back on it and attacked her plate.

"We'll take a walk around that later, I reckon," Rosie continued, ignoring Dawn pointedly ignoring her. "Do you think—"

A commotion near the door interrupted her, and both women swivelled in their seats to see what all the shouting was about. Young Liz came through the doorway backwards with her hands upraised. "Mr Smith, please! The dining room is for guests only!"

Behind Liz, a large, powerfully built man in his sixties stormed in on a tide of crackling energy, and Rosie's blood ran cold at the unwelcome sight of her ex-husband.

"I want to see my wife!" Richard commanded, barging past Liz.

Grey-faced, Rosie shrank in her seat as he spotted her. Adjusting course, he marched across the room – but Dawn suddenly blocked him halfway across the floor. Rosie hadn't even seen her move, and she stared with her mouth hanging open as Dawn met him head-on.

"Jesus," Richard faltered, coming to a halt as he realised who barred his way. "Dawn?"

"How *dare* you!" Dawn hissed, jabbing her finger into his chest. "How *dare* you show your face in here?"

He recovered and attempted to circumnavigate her. "Step aside. This is between me and my wife."

But Dawn lifted her rigid finger until she almost caught it up his nose; she might be diminutive next to him, but her ire made her gargantuan.

"*Ex*-wife," she corrected, dangerously soft. "You are not welcome here, Richard. Turn around, and slink back through that door – now."

His face darkened, and he seemed to grow larger for a moment – but then he caught the eyes of several hotel staff who had gathered to watch the whole exchange. The aggression in his stance wavered, and he raised open palms instead. "Look here, it's not what you think, I've come to apologise."

Dawn pouted. "Aww… your latest fling run off, has she? Found another man with more money and bigger balls, has she?"

"Bugger off, Dawn," he growled.

Dawn barked a sharp laugh. "Get out, Richard, before I slit your throat with this butter knife." She brandished one, suddenly, and he took an involuntary step backwards.

"Jesus, Dawn. Calm down, for God's Sake, would you just—"

"Get. Out." Dawn set her stance and bristled, leaving no doubt that she absolutely would come good on her threat, ludicrous as it might sound.

Richard blinked, and then whispered derisively, "Psycho." But he fisted his hands at his sides, turned on his heel, and stalked back the way he had come. Dawn stood her ground as he retreated, the butter knife upraised like a sword.

Richard paused in the doorway, and his parting words dripped malice. "Don't invite trouble, Dawn."

He left, then, and Dawn – undaunted – threw the butter knife after him. "If I see your face here again," she shouted, "I'll peel it off with a spoon!"

Rosie, statuesque witness, listened to his angry footsteps echoing behind him through the lobby. After a few moments, there came the muted slamming of a car door, shortly followed by the churn of gravel and a roaring engine, and – at last – a deathly silence.

## CHAPTER NINE

After a long moment, Rosie exhaled and got shakily to her feet, clutching the edge of the table for support. "Holy shit," she whispered, staring at Dawn.

"Slimy prat," Dawn fumed. "Showing up here out of the blue – how bloody dare he."

"Thanks, Dawn," Rosie said quietly. "I wasn't ready for that."

"I know," Dawn said, her face softening. She held out her arms, and Rosie fell into them. "It's all right, now," she soothed, patting her back, "he's gone."

Rosie sighed and buried her face against Dawn's shoulder. "He'll be back, though. Now that he knows where I am. God, I haven't left the house in over a year – how on earth did he find me here?"

"I've no idea," Dawn replied with a shake of her head. "Dodgy bastard. Don't you worry, we'll let the staff know that he's not welcome."

"He already isn't," Liz chimed in quietly, coming over to them. "Nice take with the butter knife, Mrs Clermont. Are you all right?"

Dawn nodded. "Yes, thank you – when did he get here?"

"About twenty minutes ago," Liz said, looking apologetic. "He wasn't supposed to come in – guest privacy policy – but he wouldn't be deterred. We told him we couldn't disclose any information about who was staying, but he was adamant to see Miss Bishop, here. He called her Mrs Smith, though."

"I'll bet he did," Rosie snapped. She drew herself up suddenly, freeing herself of Dawn's embrace so she could stand tall on her own two feet. Squaring her shoulders, she let anger build within her to fortify herself. "I'll just have a word with my daughter, I think."

Dawn exchanged a glance with Liz as Rosie turned smartly out of the dining room, and then dashed after her. But she fell behind on the stairs as Rosie surged forth on a tide of bright bravado and found her already furiously dialling from the handset when she finally caught up. Thankfully, Rosie hadn't shut the door, and Dawn swept in to stand over her with her hands on her hips.

"Now, Rose," she cautioned. "I doubt poor Mary has anything to do with this – she's always been very protective of you."

"I just want to ask," Rosie said, folding herself possessively around the phone so that Dawn couldn't reach it.

Mary answered her mobile before Dawn could say anything else.

"Your *bloody* father has just been here!" Rosie exploded. "Did you tell him where I was?"

The outraged outpouring from the other end of the line made Dawn fold her arms in an I-told-you-so fashion, even though she couldn't quite make out what Mary was saying. Rosie listened for a good long while and, at last, sheepishly hung up the phone.

"Well?" Dawn demanded.

"Mary seems to think he likely went to the house and found the brochure that I may, or may not, have left on the kitchen counter…"

Dawn raised her eyebrows. "Regardless of the brochure being out or not, how the hell did he get in?"

"I'm fairly sure he still has a key—"

"He bloody shouldn't! Rose – listen, now – it's your house, now. He's no business barging in there, and certainly not stalking you to the middle of Cumbria!"

Rosie looked up with a trapped expression, worrying at her lip between her troubled thoughts. "I can't believe he followed me out here – I didn't think he'd… This is why I never left the house… I knew he'd be angry if he came back and found me gone, but I didn't think – God, what am I going to do?"

"First of all," Dawn said, eyes flashing, "don't you dare feel bad for getting on with your own life. Christ, Rose – I've never seen you look so… small. What on earth did that bastard do to you?"

Rosie choked on a nervous laugh. "Nothing. He didn't do anything, Dawn – he just… he's always had a bit of a temper – work stress, you know – and I don't blame him, really, I mean, I'm not the easiest to – and I'm getting old – and—"

Dawn swooped across and caught her by the shoulders, shaking her to silence. "Don't you dare – don't you *dare*, Rose! Stop it, now – just bloody stop it. I will *not* stand here and listen to you demeaning yourself because Richard's an *arsehole* who somehow convinced you that his woes are all your fault. That YOU somehow screwed up!"

A blush crept up Rosie's cheeks, and she dipped her head to spare herself Dawn's violent gaze.

"I mean it, Rose. That's bullshit. I may have missed a few years of your life –"

"Too many," Rosie mumbled.

"– but I can see from a mile away that he's the one who's out of line. This is not your fault, how *dare* you defend him!" Dawn paused, and her face darkened to thunderous. "Christ, if I'd realised…"

Rosie attempted a weak smile as Dawn sputtered to silence. "You really would have attacked him with that butter knife?"

Dawn's eyes glittered. "I'd have done a lot worse. I might, still."

They regarded each other for a moment, reaching for the funny side, but then Rosie's sense of humour failed her. She gently tugged herself free of Dawn's clutches and shuffled to sink onto the couch. Leaning back, she stared listlessly out the window.

Dispirited, she murmured, "God… how did I fail so badly in my marriage?"

"You didn't *fail*, Rose," Dawn said vehemently, coming to perch beside her.

Rosie fixed her with a sideways glance. "I'm divorced, Dawn – that's the literal definition of failing at marriage."

"Well, yes – but that doesn't mean that *you* failed. Marriage is hard, and Richard's a dickhead."

"Wish you'd told me that thirty-two years ago."

"I can't be expected to know *everything*, now, can I? He was all right in the beginning – before his ego got too big for his boots. Look, Rose, the truth is that sometimes it just doesn't work out. But Richard is a fool – you're bloody brilliant, and you could do a lot better than him."

Rosie sighed. "I don't think he'd agree. I wonder what the hell he was thinking, coming here? He told me in no uncertain terms that he never wanted to see me again. Oh, Dawn… I really don't know if I can face him…"

"You don't have to," Dawn said, squeezing her hand. "Call Mary back, ask her to ring him up and threaten him with a restraining order. An attack on his reputation should throw him off good and proper."

Rosie blew out unevenly. "And in the meantime?"

"Stay where I can see you."

Rosie managed a shaky smile. "He's always been rather wary of you."

"And I'll give him a bloody reason to be if he bothers you again," Dawn replied darkly. "Here, pass me that key card – I want to go down and make sure he really did leave. I'll have a word with the staff, too."

"Well, I'm sure Liz will have your back – did you see the look on her face?"

"Girl after my own heart," Dawn said with a sinister smile. She made to get up, but Rosie clutched at her fingers.

"Don't be long, will you?"

"Won't be a minute," Dawn promised, freeing herself. "You sit tight – put the kettle on, and ring Mary again."

Rosie nodded, feeling inexplicably ill as Dawn quietly shut the door behind her. She got slowly to her feet in the resounding emptiness left in Dawn's wake and meandered to the kitchenette as instructed. When she'd flicked on the kettle, she shuffled to the door and tugged on the handle to make sure it really was locked. There, she rested her palm flat against the veneer for a moment. Pressing her forehead to her knuckles, she let out a shaky breath. Softly, she asked herself, "What's the matter with you, you twat?" But her self-abrasion didn't stop the upsurge of fear that hitched in her chest. Echoes of smashing crockery chimed in her mind, the splinter of a dining chair as it crashed into a wall, and the vision of herself, pressed into a corner with her hands over her ears, waiting desperately for it to stop. Indeed, he'd never touched her physically, but there are other kinds of scars.

A loud click from the kettle summoned her back to the present, and she pushed away from the door to make the tea. But as she poured shakily into two mugs, a surge of guilt prickled. She should have talked to him, at least. Seen what he wanted. She felt a bit bad that the shock of seeing him so suddenly – and somewhere she'd least expected – had knocked her so. Maybe he'd had something important to say, maybe he'd come to explain his rebuttal, to make amends…

And she'd let Dawn threaten him with a bloody butter knife.

"Oh, God," she whispered, clutching at the counter for support as she realised how unfair she'd been. They'd spent thirty-two years together, and she hadn't even given him the time of day. Sure, she'd been angry at his casual dismissal of their long marriage – smarting, over the lies he'd fed her, and more furious still at herself for believing them – but they'd been happy, once. They'd made a good team, hadn't they? Done well, hadn't they? He was certainly successful – well-respected, soundly liked; always the first one to be invited to important events. She, on the other hand, wasn't so good with people, and perhaps hadn't been the best accessory to the life he'd worked so hard for. It was no surprise, really, that he'd grown tired of her; at least when they were young, she'd been blessed with beauty. She'd looked the part if nothing else. But as she'd grown older, her looks had faded, and her shy, sometimes defensive personality had come to the fore instead. It was easy to forgive the perceived aloofness of a beautiful young woman – not so much an acrimonious old crone.

She sighed. If only she'd had his flair with people – or Dawn's, for that matter. Dawn could hold her own in any company; something Rosie had always admired and sometimes envied. Her lip twitched into a small, sad smile as she remembered herself in the centre of yet another gala, lost beneath the crush of a crowded room and completely out of her element. Dawn would have been the soul of the party – the degree of gorgeous liveliness by which all others measured themselves.

Absently, she stirred the tea, and then, as if sensitive to her thoughts, Dawn reappeared. She let herself in and closed the door, her eyes immediately sweeping the room for Rosie. Spotting her – and the distraught look etched onto her face – she crossed with quick strides to join her.

"He's gone, Rose," she reassured. "The gatehouse confirmed he roared off down the lane, and they could hear the engine howling for bloody miles."

Rosie nodded slowly, but she did not look up from the teacups.

"Hey, now," Dawn murmured, "what's the matter?"

"I... should have heard what he had to say," Rosie replied softly. "I owe him that, at least."

Dawn's eyes widened and then creased beneath a dark frown. "You owe him nothing, actually. Just because he's feeling lonely and sorry for himself, doesn't mean he can suddenly come snivelling back to you – don't do this to yourself, Rose."

When Rosie didn't respond, Dawn guided her gently away from the kitchenette and back towards the couch. Retrieving the tea, she settled next to her and reached for her hand, watching the turbulent storm of emotion flitting across her face. Rosie shrunk into herself, trying to hold a tenacious tear at bay.

Softly, Dawn prompted, "All right. Talk me through it, then."

Rosie swallowed, took a moment, and then lifted her chin. "I… let him down. That's why he gave up on me and went running to another woman, a younger, more modern woman. I've become more reclusive with every year that's gone by, less able to be the glamorous partner he needs in his world – less… willing, I suppose… to help him keep up appearances. That's all he needed from me. He's worked so hard, Dawn – but I just couldn't do it any more. I got old, and tired. A little bitter, maybe. I wanted to retire, buy a small home by the seaside somewhere, maybe, just live quietly for a while. It's what I wanted, but… it was selfish to ask him to give up his career for that. It took him so long to build it. Honestly, I'm surprised that he stayed with me as long as he did, and I'm not sure I deserved it."

She bowed her head beneath the weight of her confession, and Dawn waited in silence until she looked up again. When she did, Dawn caught her gaze and held it with an unusual depth of seriousness.

"Rose," she said quietly, "I'm going to say something now, and I want you to listen – really listen, all right?"

Caught upon a strange wave of cold apprehension, Rosie hesitated, but Dawn appeared to be waiting for her approval – and not about to let it go without a scuffle. At last, she relented with a tiny nod, and Dawn took a deep breath.

## CHAPTER TEN

D awn shifted on the couch to face Rosie more squarely. "All right, here it is, then. Do you know why we haven't seen each other in twenty years?"

Rosie raised an eyebrow, confused by the sudden turn of topic. "Life gets... busy." She shrugged. "It's easy to drift apart."

"We managed to see each other almost every day for the twenty years prior," Dawn reminded her. "Thick as thieves since university."

"What's your point, then?"

"My point is that we didn't see each other anymore because I didn't... want to."

Rosie's face clouded, betrayal catching a burr straight through her heart. "You what?" Somehow, the admission hit far harder than anything Richard had ever done. She snatched her hand free of Dawn's, and Dawn sighed.

"It wasn't you I didn't want to see, Rose. It was the person Richard had turned you into. He exhibited you like some kind of trophy, put you on display for all the world to see – just another notch in his sterling career. And you let him. Every year he climbed the ladder, he flaunted you harder, paraded you up and down in front of his cronies, and it was... hard... to witness the erasure of you that came with it. But I know" – she paused for a quick, uncertain breath – "I know you loved him, Rose, and I didn't want to question your happiness."

Gathering herself, she pressed on. "But to hear you now, going on about how you didn't deserve him, somehow *failed* him, after everything... To see you so *diminished* – Rose, I couldn't do it." She broke off and swallowed, hard, but her words clogged up in her throat. Bowing her head, she gave a rueful sniff and swiped at a budding tear.

Rosie stared at her for a long moment, a veritable war of emotions flashing across her face. "So, you just abandoned me?"

"What?" Dawn jolted upright with a startled look. "No! That's not it, I—"

Rosie smiled tiredly. "I'm having you on, Dawn. Everything you just said is perfectly accurate. Painfully so. You've painted an exact portrait of my life in a handful of words, and I love and hate you for it." She swallowed an unhinged laugh. "God, I've been such a fool for so bloody long... I've wasted more than half my life trying to keep Richard happy – and I've only just now realised how stuffing miserable that's made me."

"Better late than never," Dawn said, trying for a smile, too. "You should know, these last couple of days is the most *you* I've seen you for a very long time. And I've missed *you*, Rose."

Rosie gave a heartfelt sigh. "I've missed me, too."

She held out her hand in solidarity, and when Dawn took it, she squeezed her fingers tight. "Thanks for giving up on me."

Despite Rosie's forgiving smile, Dawn blushed. "I tried to talk to you – really I did – but there were so many bright lights in your life I sort of faded out."

"I'm sorry," Rosie said quietly. "I'm sorry that I didn't listen. Maybe if I had, all those years ago, life wouldn't have chewed me up and spat me out quite so savagely."

"You do look a bloody wreck," Dawn said with a sniff.

"A far cry from the devastating beauty that used to fawn along on Richard's arm?"

"Absolutely worlds away."

Rosie's eyes twinkled. "Good."

"You're still beautiful though, Rose."

Rosie broke into laughter, holding out her arms to look sarcastically down at herself. "I'm on the wrong side of sixty, thickened out in all the wrong places, and I have enough wrinkles to be classed as an elephant." She winked, then, and added, "But I do appreciate you being nice, for a change."

"I mean it," Dawn said. "You've always been the most beautiful person I know – despite your savagely prickly exterior."

Rosie scoffed. "How do you do that? Honestly, I've never met anyone so adept at dishing double-edged compliments."

"Learnt it from you," Dawn smirked. She paused to give Rosie a once-over. "Well, thankfully you seem to have tipped back towards sanity – for the time being, at least."

"Until you drive me up the wall again," Rosie huffed.

Dawn smiled, relieved by the acid in her tone. "I'll take that as a challenge, shall I?"

"You hardly need to *try*. You've a rare talent."

Dawn chortled and then turned back to more present matters. "Did you ring Mary back, by the way?"

"No, not yet."

Dawn reached for the handset and held it out. "Well?"

Rosie scowled. "Let me drink my tea first, at least. It'll be ice cold in a minute." She leaned past the outstretched phone to salvage her cup instead, and Dawn tilted her head.

"Would you like me to do it?"

Rosie spluttered. "If you're suggesting that I'm avoiding calling my own daughter to ask her to threaten my ex-husband – her *father* – with a restraining – don't be ridiculous, Dawn."

Dawn raised an eyebrow, waiting.

Rosie let out an explosive huff, and her glower darkened. "Fine. Yes. You do it."

Dawn used the mouthpiece of the phone to hide a knowing smile, cleared her throat, and hit redial on the handset. When the ringing tone sounded, she switched it to loudspeaker, raised a challenging eyebrow at Rosie, and waited for Mary to answer.

After a moment: "Hello? Mum?"

"Mary? Hi, it's Dawn."

Silence.

"Can you hear me, Mary? It's Dawn."

More silence, and then: "...*Dawn?*"

Dawn threw Rosie a dirty look. "Yes, Dawn. Maybe you don't... remember me..." – she swallowed as if the suggestion were bitter – "it's been a while. I'm an old friend of your mum's."

"Old is right," Rosie muttered, but Dawn shushed her.

Mary's response was guarded. "Dawn? Mum – I swear if you're having me on with one of your bloody impressions, I—"

She broke off at Dawn's cheerful laugh. "Your mum's never been that good with impressions."

There was a small moment of static as Mary digested that, and then: "Bloody hell – *DAWN*?! Good Lord, it's good to hear your voice!"

Rosie leaned over the phone. "Oh, for heaven's sake, Mary, no need for theatrics. It's just Dawn. It's not as if somebody bloody famous or important has appeared to walk among us—"

"Yes, *thank you.*" Dawn pushed Rosie aside. "How are you, Mary? It's been a lifetime."

Mary laughed exuberantly. "Bloody has! Where did you crawl in from?"

Dawn groaned. "You sound just like your mother. Listen, now, I'm actually calling because Rose here is too scared to ask you" – she ducked out of reach as Rosie lunged for her – "if you'll call Richard and drop him a tiny promise of a restraining order if he doesn't quit his weird antics of showing up uninvited."

"Oh." Mary's tone darkened. "Yes, of course I will. That's a good idea. Was he out of line again?"

"He was a little pushy, a little angry," Dawn said. "Gave your mum here a bit of a shock with his sudden appearance. But he backed off easily enough – just Rose thinks he'll be back now that he knows where she is."

Mary sighed in agreement. "More than likely. Dad can be stubborn, and… unpredictable. Don't worry, I'll ring him and have a quiet word. We're still on good terms – well, mostly. Not that I see him much – I don't like that kind of energy around my boys."

"Thanks, love," Dawn said. "In the meantime, I'll play bodyguard for your mum, here."

"I've no doubt you'll be able to keep Dad at bay – he's never liked you, anyway."

Dawn snorted. "I'm not his biggest fan, either."

"I know," Mary said, her smile evident in her voice. "Now, I have to go, but listen – Mum, that means you, too – try to stay out of trouble, all right? I've a long memory, and I shudder to think what you pair will get up to unsupervised."

"*Mary*!" Rosie glared at the phone with a wounded expression. "How could you say such a thing?"

"Mum, please. As if I believe a word of your indignance." Mary's tone dropped to a caveat. "I mean it – *don't* get kicked out of there. I'll not be impressed if I have to make an unscheduled two-hour trip to fetch you."

"We've made it this many days without incident, Miss," Dawn chimed innocently – and Rosie could practically hear Mary rolling her eyes. She laughed, and then, saying her goodbyes, hung up. Dawn put down her side, too, and flashed an impish grin at Rosie.

"So," she said, lifting her eyebrows, "what kind of trouble should we get into first?"

Rosie groaned and got up to make a fresh cup of tea.

# CHAPTER ELEVEN

Contrary to Dawn's suggestion, they did not, in fact, find any trouble for the rest of the morning – and Dawn had even agreed to a sensible stroll around the nearby lake that afternoon. Indeed, as she traipsed gamely along at Rosie's side, skirting brambles that reached claws from the untrimmed edges of an overgrown path, she hadn't suggested anything untoward for hours. Instead, she pointed out brilliant butterflies against the grey sky, and chattered brightly as she shouldered against Rosie every now and again.

But finally, Rosie stopped and turned to face her with a threatening expression. "You're making me nervous," she said. "I can practically hear your brain ticking."

Dawn widened her eyes. "Whatever do you mean? I'm just enjoying the scenery."

"And surreptitiously forcing me to adjust course every now and then."

A slow, smug smile spread over Dawn's lips. "I'm surprised it's taken you this long to notice."

"It hasn't, you plonker. You're painfully obvious about it."

"Oh."

"But we're well off the beaten track now," Rosie continued, "and I'm rather concerned that you actually have no idea where it is you're leading us."

"Cheers for that vote of confidence. If you must know, I'm following Liz's instructions."

"*Liz's* instructions?"

"You'd be surprised how interesting that kid is. She knows a lot about this area, actually. Grew up here, and all."

Rosie rolled her eyes. "Just like you to get cosy with the locals."

"You should try it sometime," Dawn said, unperturbed. "You might just learn something."

"And what, exactly, are we learning?"

"About a secret waterfall – Liz told me how to get there."

Rosie lifted her suspicious gaze back the way they had come, following the patchy path until it was lost to trees. The Inn was miles behind, and completely out of sight. "Did she happen to mention how far it is?"

"Oh, ye of little faith. We're almost there, we just have to leave the path in a minute, and then—"

"*Leave* the path?"

"Yes, Braveheart. The clue was in secret waterfall. C'mon, help me look for the marker."

Dawn scanned their surroundings, moving carefully forward between thickening brambles. Scowling, Rosie stalked after her but came to an unceremonious halt as a thorn lash caught around her ankle. She yelped, and Dawn scooted back to see. Cautiously, she loosened its claws, fighting to unhook them from Rosie's trouser leg.

"Stay still!" she admonished as Rosie squirmed. "I told you not to wear cotton slacks. Should have gone with jeans – much tougher."

Rosie gritted her teeth. "All right, Rambo – would you just get on with it, please?"

Dawn finished extricating Rosie's ankle, and then, pushing the vine safely aside, lifted Rosie's trouser leg to see. Tiny spots of blood welled, and one had almost managed a trickle.

"Oh no!" Dawn exclaimed.

"What?" Rosie cried, frantically craning her neck.

"Some of your acid's leaking out."

"Oh ha, HA," Rosie growled, batting Dawn's paws away. With a huff, she rearranged the folds of her slacks in an attempt to cover her legs better and then glared up with a mutinous expression.

"Tuck them into your socks," Dawn suggested.

"Sod off."

Grinning, Dawn scampered off to resume her search. Finally, she whooped and pointed enthusiastically at a small pine with a rough arrow shape etched into its bark.

"Aha!" she crowed. "Here we are! This is where we head due north."

Rosie squinted dubiously at the faded marker. "Do you have any idea which way is due north?"

"You're taking all the fun out of this, Rose. It's supposed to be an *adventure*." Dawn set off determinedly in the direction the arrow pointed, using a long stick to push nettles aside with all the flair of a dashing daredevil.

Behind her, Rosie snarked, "Think you're some sort of Victorian explorer, do you?"

"Absolutely," Dawn slung over her shoulder. "Too bad I don't have those fabulous khaki pantaloons and a pith helmet, maybe…"

She surged ahead, and Rosie muttered, "You're definitely taking the 'pith' making me walk this far."

She cussed under her breath as the angry plants snapped back to challenge her after Dawn's twig-aided passage. They trekked on for what seemed an age, Rosie growing increasingly irritable, until, at last, Dawn stopped so suddenly that Rosie walked straight into her.

"Do you hear that?" Dawn hissed, holding up a hand.

Rosie's eyes bulged, and she swept the thick undergrowth as if a wild beast might leap upon them at any moment. "Hear what?"

"Water!" Dawn gave a happy huff, swinging her stick violently at the snatching weeds as she blazed onward.

Rosie made a derisive sound deep in her throat, eyed the bushes once more – just in case they did, in fact, harbour ravenous monsters – and then hurried to catch up before Dawn abandoned her completely. A tiny stream soon came into view, burbling between mossy banks as it trickled around gigantic tree roots, and Dawn adjusted course to follow it upstream. Closer to the water's edge, the brambles backed off and gave way to a carpet of marsh marigolds and blue forget-me-nots, and Dawn stopped to point out a lemon-yellow butterfly flitting between the flowers. Rosie's mood lifted considerably as she paused to watch it, and Dawn had the good grace to wait until it fluttered off across the water.

As it disappeared behind a thicket, Rosie offered, "I think they call that one a Brimstone."

Dawn smiled. "I like its wings. Sort of... leaf-looking, aren't they? Pretty." She looped an arm through Rosie's. "Shall we? I'm sure the waterfall is close now."

Rosie gave a sarcastic salute. "All right, Doctor Livingstone, lead the way."

Together, they meandered around mossy tree trunks, keeping an eye out for more butterflies. A large holly bush made them detour briefly away from the stream, and when they returned to the bank, they finally reached the culmination of their search.

There, Dawn stumbled to a halt, and Rosie dissolved into laughter.

"*That's* the waterfall?"

Scowling, Dawn stalked to stand over the tiny feature with her hands on her hips. It was about two feet high; a slim, silver trickle that bounced joyously despite Dawn's judgemental glare.

"Well," Rosie quipped, "now we know why it's a secret – no one cares!"

"I'm going to kill that Liz!" Dawn muttered. "All that bloody walking – *this* is what we get?"

Still giggling, Rosie said, "Do you know what the best part is?"

"What?" Dawn snapped, unamused.

"We still have to walk *back*."

"Shut up – just shut up – you're enjoying this far more than necessary!"

Rosie clamped her mouth closed, fighting her mirth, and Dawn flopped heavily down onto a fallen log. She gave a dejected sigh – and then the whole rotting tree trunk gave way beneath her, dropping her into a yelping mess of compost and pine needles. Rosie couldn't aid her for several long seconds, unable as she was to breathe for the sheer force of her laughter. Dawn, stuck on her arse – covered in forest floor and glaring up with a new level of savagery – was too much, and Rosie doubled over the stitch in her side.

But eventually, she managed to compose herself enough to help Dawn up, and gingerly brushed her down to remove the worst of the muck.

"Are you all right?"

"No thanks to you!"

Dawn pushed her away and set to dusting down her own clothing, and Rosie moved off to one side, watching with a stupid grin still plastered across her face. But after a moment, she realised Dawn wasn't smiling – in fact, she seemed close to tears. Her own mirth melted like snow before a rainstorm, and she reached gently for Dawn's shoulder.

"Hey," she said softly, "what's the matter? Did you hurt yourself?"

Dawn stopped her vigorous brushing of dirt spots on her trousers. She lifted her chin and drew a careful breath. "I'm fine – nothing my posterior padding can't handle."

"What is it, then?"

When she didn't respond, Rosie caught hold of her other

shoulder and gently turned her, ducking down to make eye contact as Dawn bowed her head. "Dawn, what's wrong?"

Dawn gave a wonky smile and gestured lamely. "It's just... this is my life, Rose. A series of promising events that end in stupid disappointments." She blew out sharply to halt a threatening sob. "Like this *stupid* waterfall... honestly... I'm not even sure why I'm surprised."

"Oh, Dawn..."

Rosie gathered her quietly into her arms, and small, tired tears leaked down Dawn's face.

Tucking her chin into Rosie's shoulder, she whispered, "Why is life so shit, Rose? Nothing bloody works out, anymore."

Rosie held her tight – holding her together – and Dawn wilted into her embrace, clinging to her as if she were the only thing of substance left in a fading world. They stood for an age, quietly keening for things lost, or missed – all perfectly wrapped up in the guise of a substandard waterfall.

"I'm sorry," Rosie whispered at last.

"What for?"

"Just... everything."

Dawn nodded weakly against her chest and heaved a hefty sigh. Finally, she pushed back and stared up at Rosie with watery eyes. "Stupid, isn't it?"

"No," Rosie said, reaching to adjust her beanie for her, "it's not. There'll be other waterfalls, though. More spectacular ones."

Dawn sniffed and glared at the tiny stream. "Next time we'll visit the one in Africa."

"Africa?"

"I saw a program on telly about one called Victoria... something."

"Falls?" Rosie suggested sardonically.

"Yes, that's it. Victoria Falls. Puts this piddling thing to absolute shame – and I've always wanted to go to Africa."

Rosie smiled. "All right. Tell you what – if we ever find our way back to the Inn – we'll make plans and I'll take you there for our next adventure."

A small glimmer of hope shone between Dawn's drying tears. "Will you really?"

Rosie's mouth quirked. "I'm quite sure I'll regret agreeing to an adventure with you in *Africa*, of all places… but yes. I will."

The ghost of a grin fluttered on Dawn's lips. "Will you do the gorge swing with me?"

Rosie narrowed her eyes. "*Gorge* swing?"

"It looks like marvellous fun – they put you in a harness and chuck you off the side of a cliff."

Rosie spluttered. "What did I *just* say about regretting – off a cliff?! Sodding hell! – you're bloody mad, you are!"

Dawn pouted – extremely effectively, given her recent tears – and put on her best puppy-dog eyes.

"NO!" Rosie howled, violently shaking her head. "Absolutely over my dead body will I be thrown off a bloody cliff!"

Dawn let her lip wobble. "But Rose…"

"No, Dawn – no! I've changed my mind about Africa – you just – get back in your log, damn you!" She manhandled a protesting Dawn back towards the rotten trunk and leaned her threateningly over the abyss.

"All right!" Dawn cried. "We won't do the bloody gorge swing!"

With a huff, Rosie let her up.

"Can we still go see the waterfall, though?"

Rosie sighed expansively. "*Yes*, dear. We'll go see the bloody waterfall in Africa. No cliffs, though."

Dawn gifted her a bright smile, and the tentative hope in her eyes was too much for Rosie to bear. She caught Dawn up in a fierce hug. Soft against Dawn's ear, she accused, "You'll be the bloody death of me."

"There are worse ways to go," Dawn said. When Rosie rolled her eyes heavenward, Dawn squirmed free of her arms. "C'mon, Rose – let's get back and start planning!"

Rosie threw her head back, balled her fists, and allowed herself a small tantrum, and Dawn – tears forgotten – hooted a laugh as she disappeared back around the holly bush.

In her wake, the quiet pressed in around Rosie. She snapped her lips firmly together, lest the forest beasts heard her and came to see about dinner, and then, with a resigned sigh, scuttled off in Dawn's wake.

## CHAPTER TWELVE

Rosie's face reddened as she found herself ensnared by yet another bramble, and she kicked viciously at the vine with her free foot. "Dawn? Dawn! Would you bloody wait!" *Damned slacks*! "Dawn!" She looked up, trying to see further down the overgrown path, but there was no sign of her companion. As she cast her gaze more frantically, a small, cold fear fluttered pale wings beneath her ribs. "Dawn? Seriously, it's not funny – don't you leave me here!"

"I'm right here," Dawn said, from behind her shoulder.

Rosie jumped with a hiss, ensnaring herself even more firmly in the brambles, and Dawn steadied her with a gentle hand.

"Hold still, let me get you out of that." She set to, working steadily to free Rosie's leg again. "I'd only gone around that bush there to see if it's easier to get through than this way. I'm never far away, you damned fool."

Rosie muttered darkly under her breath – more from fear of abandonment and the rapid anti-climax of relief when she'd realised Dawn was actually still right there, than anything else – and kept her leg still while Dawn worked.

"I'm banning you from taking these slacks to Africa," Dawn continued brightly. "I've heard there are vicious thorns there, too – and I'm not coming back for you if a lion's after us."

Rosie turned green. "A lion?"

"Sure," Dawn said, sitting back with a satisfied huff as she unhitched the last tangle. "Where do you think lions are *from*?" She caught the look on Rosie's face, and added, "And crocodiles, leopards, snakes – ooh, giant spiders—"

"Stop it, now – stop it!" Rosie exclaimed, glancing fearfully about as if they might suddenly appear in the middle of the English countryside.

Dawn grinned, pulled her carefully out of the briar, and vowed, "I won't let any of them get you."

"Oh, sure. Easy to promise that in the middle of bloody *Cumbria*. Be serious, now – how much further until we get back to a big, fat glass of wine?"

Dawn squinted down the path, back up again. "Um…"

Rosie sucked in a savage breath. "Do *not* tell me we're lost."

"We're not – we're not. I'm just… not a hundred per cent sure how *far* we are. Hard to judge time when you keep wasting it playing in the bramble patch."

Rosie swung at her, but Dawn ducked out of the way, grinning. "I'll leave you in the next one!" she warned against Rosie's glare.

She scampered off to scout their course, leaving Rosie to pick her way carefully around the next snaking tendrils. Rosie glowered, and was so focused on the thorns that she didn't notice the slightly slumped earth beneath her feet as she progressed – until it collapsed beneath her. With a yell, she went down in a shower of roots and debris, jarring hard against the bottom of an abandoned badger tunnel deep as her midriff.

"Dear God," Dawn exclaimed from above as the dust settled. "What on earth am I to do with you?"

"Stay back!" Rosie snarled, waving her away from danger.

"It's collapsed quite a way," Dawn pointed out. "Here, if I sit on the edge, like this" – she dropped onto her backside and shovelled earth with her feet, levelling the slope towards Rosie – "I'm pretty sure we'll have you out in a heartbeat."

Rosie folded her arms and waited until she was done, watching her every move with a judgemental expression. At last, Dawn decided the footing was secure enough to attempt a rescue, shimmied down a bit, and held out her hand. With her aid, Rosie tried to shuffle out, but hissed as she put weight on her right ankle. It buckled, dropping her to fist her hands in the sod, and she wheezed against the pain.

"Bloody hell, Rose! Are you all right?"

Rosie looked up to meet Dawn's concerned expression. All trace of merriment had drained from her face, and it was pinched instead with fear.

"I'm fine," Rosie said, in an attempt to placate her worry, "just bumped my ankle, is all. We'll go slowly, okay?"

Dawn chewed at her lip as she nodded, and then wormed down into the hole to support her better. Together, with much stopping and starting, they managed to crawl over the lip, and then Rosie rolled onto her back against the damp leaf litter and stifled a groan. Dawn hovered, her gentle brown eyes darting beneath furrowed brows, until Rosie had caught her breath. Carefully, she helped her up to standing and supported her as she listed over her injured leg. Rosie's knuckles whitened as she clung to Dawn's shoulder, and Dawn caught an arm around her waist to keep her upright. "Bloody hell – can you walk?"

Rosie gasped a laugh. "I'm actually… not sure."

Tentative, she pushed weight onto her sore leg. She yelped, but it held firm as she limped a step forward, and she glanced sideways at Dawn.

"Well, not completely crippled."

"Not bloody far from it," Dawn said, frowning. She adjusted her grip around Rosie's waist, and Rosie looped her arm more firmly over her shoulder. "One step at a time, then. This is just like the time you fell off the roof at that hen's party—"

"*You* fell off the bloody roof! I had to carry you to the bloody car!"

"I know," Dawn grinned. "Just checking your memory's still intact after your trip down the rabbit hole, Alice."

"You should bloody carry me now, I feel," said Rosie airily. "Tit for tat."

"I would," Dawn said, urging her forward another step, "but you know, my back's not what it used to be, and you're not quite as svelte as you were…"

Badgering, sparring, cajoling, they made it about half a mile before Rosie said she had to rest. Dawn spied a solid-looking log, tested it with her own weight, and then helped Rosie to sit for a bit. Around them, the day turned slowly to dusk, and Dawn shifted on her heels as she hovered. It was another mile still back to the Inn, by her rough guestimate – hell of a far to limp. She knew she should probably go for help, but she was unwilling to leave Rosie on her own; instead, she perched beside her on the log, noting her grey face with a deep, unsettling concern.

"I'll be all right, in a minute," Rosie said, braver than she felt. "I just need to rest for a bit."

Dawn nodded. "Take as long as you need, Rose – the path's not going anywhere."

"No, but daylight is." Rosie chewed at her lip as she scanned the clouds scudding low over the horizon and ushering them into an early evening. "Maybe you should—"

"I've already thought of that, and I'm not going anywhere. We'll go slow, take lots of breaks. We'll get there."

Rosie managed a small smile and nodded. She reached for Dawn's hand and held it tight, gathering her courage. Dawn slipped her free arm around her shoulders and pulled her into a one-sided hug.

"We'll get there," she repeated, and Rosie clung to her conviction.

But it was full dark long before they'd reached safety, and Rosie was flagging.

"C'mon, Rose," Dawn gasped softly, "just a little farther…"

Rosie gritted her teeth and concentrated on one painful step after the other, trying not to tug on Dawn's shoulder more than she could help. Her friend was tired, too – Dawn stumbled next to her and paused to readjust her grip.

"Wait, Dawn" – Rosie listed sideways at the sudden loss of momentum – "there's a bench, here, look. Just… pop me down."

Dawn obliged, dropping next to her with a hearty groan. "God, who knew a mile was so bloody far?"

"Listen, now," Rosie said, stretching her ankle gingerly out in front of her, "I think—"

"If you're going to tell me to 'go on without you'," Dawn interrupted, "let me remind you that this is not a bloody movie. There are no medals for ridiculous chivalry in real life."

Rosie closed her mouth.

"We'll wait here a bit," Dawn continued doggedly, "catch our breath and then carry on. It can't be too far, now."

"That's what you said an hour ago."

Dawn sighed. "I know. But I'm hoping this time it's true."

Together, they looked down the dark path, just starting to silver with faint moonlight that streamed through shattered clouds. Somewhere, a vixen barked – high and sharp – and Rosie jumped. Dawn caught an arm tighter around her waist. "Only a fox," she murmured.

Rosie tucked close beneath her sheltering embrace, but suddenly something rustled through the undergrowth, and Dawn's grip tightened painfully. Rosie stifled a yelp against her digging fingers, and then they both froze, listening hard. Nearby, leaf litter scrunched, twigs cracking beneath something far larger than a fox.

"What is it?" Rosie hissed hoarsely.

Dawn shushed her; whatever it was, it was moving towards

them with slow, careful strides. They squinted, but the moon dipped behind a cloud and plunged them into full darkness. Dawn shot to her feet and tucked Rosie behind her, trembling as she reached for her nerve. The clouds scudded onward again, freeing the moonlight – and across the way, a man-shaped silhouette turned suddenly to face them. Dawn hitched a breath, setting her stance in front of Rosie – she might be tired from their long trek, but she had no intention of going down without a fight. The man was half-hidden against a tree shadow, hard to see clearly; it was too dark, and there was still too much distance to tell who it was. Dawn swallowed, an earlier threat echoing in her head. It couldn't be Richard… could it?

"Dawn," Rosie whispered.

Dawn lifted her hands, fingers pressed together like blades, thumbs tucked in –

"Dawn."

– that one karate class she took that one time might come in handy tonight. Behind her, Rosie shifted, and the man took a tentative step in their direction. Dawn unleashed an almighty battle cry, chopping a violent warning with her hands.

"*DAWN.*"

"*What*, Rose?" Dawn flung over her shoulder, not taking her eye off the shadow for an instant. "I'm a little bit busy here if you couldn't tell!"

"For the love of—" Rosie leaned forward and caught hold of her coat. "You pillock – it's Pip!"

"It's – what?"

"Would you calm down? It's *Pip*."

From across the way, Pip lifted a hesitant wave. "Hi, Mrs Clermont. We're just out looking for you."

"We?" Dawn shot back suspiciously; karate fists still upraised.

A torch beam swung between the trees off to their left, briefly flashed over them, and then dropped low on approach to reveal Liz's worried face behind.

"Ahem, yes," Pip said. "Me and Liz."

"Liz and I," Rosie corrected under her breath.

Dawn dropped her hands and harrumphed. "What the hell happened to your torch, you creeper!"

Pip held it up apologetically. "It's dead. I told Liz I'd stick to the path and make do with the moonlight, while she swept through the forest a bit."

"Good Lord!" Liz said as she neared. "Are you two all right? You've been gone for ages!"

"*Really*?" Rosie exclaimed, widening her eyes. "Gosh, I'd never have said it was more than a few minutes, at most—"

"Madame Muck here is a touch grumpy," Dawn interrupted with a dark scowl. "Stumbled into a ruddy badger hole and sprained her ankle."

"*I'm* grumpy? You're the one who – ouch!"

Liz looked up in surprise from where she'd crouched to look at Rosie's offending limb. "I'm sorry, I…" She broke off with a puzzled frown. "Wait… I haven't even touched it, yet." Raising an eyebrow at Rosie, she gently probed with delicate fingers. "Have you been walking on it?"

"No," Rosie snapped, flinching. "I flew here. Of *course* I've been bloody walking on it! Did you want us to sleep in the bloody woods?"

Unperturbed, Liz put on her most dazzling smile. "No fear, Miss Bishop – I've a medic kit here, we'll get you bandaged up in a jiff." She tucked the torch under her arm and whipped out a compression bandage, looking up at Rosie with an impish expression. "The Inn's not too far, actually – you were almost there."

With practised ease from the mandatory first-aid training that came with her job, she strapped Rosie's ankle and then sat back to scrutinize her handiwork. "There," she said. "I don't think the sprain's too bad, to be honest – that should be much more comfortable now."

"Good, now that that's done." Dawn loomed over Liz with her

hands on her hips. "Listen here, you, that *bloody* waterfall—"

Rosie interrupted with a savage oath. "Is this really the time?"

"Shut up, Rose – that bloody waterfall, Liz – I'm extremely unimpressed with you, sending us on such a wild goose chase!"

Taken aback, Liz's eyes widened. "Wild goose chase?"

"Dawn, I want to go home. Would you just—"

"Yes, bloody goose chase! Four-mile hike for a two-foot-high piddling rivulet!"

Liz tilted her head quizzically. "Two-foot high? The secret falls is closer to twelve… Did you turn left at the second marker after the pine arrow?"

A dangerous silence fell. Rosie sucked in a breath, preparing to explode, and Dawn stammered, "S-second… marker?"

Rosie lunged. "DAWN! I'm going to KILL you!"

But she toppled as her ankle gave way, and Dawn swung out an arm to catch her.

"Christ, Rose! Can you do it *after* we get back to the Inn?"

Rosie huffed, hanging on to her as she fought to regain her balance. "Fine – *only* because I need your bloody help to get there." With Dawn holding her steady, she carefully put her weight onto her bandaged ankle. It held, and she heaved a small sigh of relief. "Thanks, Liz. That's actually a lot better."

"Will you manage the rest of the way back?" Dawn asked.

Rosie hobbled forward, nodded uncertainly, and Dawn slipped an arm valiantly back around her waist again to offer her support.

"Do you want some help?" Pip said, from where he was hovering off to one side.

"We're fine," Rosie snapped.

Pip backed off with his palms upraised, and Liz gifted them an impressed grin as she shone her torch to light the way home.

## CHAPTER THIRTEEN

A t long last, the lights of the hotel winked into view, and Pip and Liz went on ahead to prepare some supper and two large glasses of wine. Dawn slowly helped Rosie across the final stretch of rolling lawns.

"C'mon, Rose," she said through gritted teeth. "Almost there, old girl."

Rosie hissed. "If you call me that… one… more time…"

But she was too exhausted to finish her threat. The front steps loomed, and Rosie cussed breathlessly all the slow way up, hanging onto Dawn with the last of her reserves. As they stumbled through the doors, they were met with an outburst of cheers and applause, and they lurched to a halt. It seemed like half the Retreat guests had turned out to witness their safe return, and Rosie put on her fiercest scowl to greet them. "What are you looking at?" she snarled at the crowd, clinging to Dawn with one hand and brandishing a fist with the other.

Dawn tugged her onward, and smiles followed them despite Rosie's noxious glower.

"We're gaining a bit of a reputation, I think," Dawn said wryly.

"We've always had a reputation," Rosie snapped. "We're just bloody living up to it."

Dawn summoned the lift and bundled Rosie in despite her protests – "It's three flights, Rose, don't be ridiculous" – and the silver contraption soon spat them out at the top. Only the long hallway now stood between them and a well-deserved rest – "This is close enough, Dawn, damn it, just let me sleep in the corridor" – and Dawn bullied Rosie onward the last few steps.

Finally, they stumbled through the door to their room, and Dawn pushed Rosie all the way to the couch. There, she let her rest at last with her foot propped up and turned for the covered plates that Liz had already brought up and left for them. They picked at the food – too tired to delight in what should have been an indulgent meal after a long day in the wilderness – and drowned their sorrows with the wine.

Dawn stretched languorously after draining the last of hers, but then a knock at the door forced her to her feet once more.

"Who the bloody hell is it?" Rosie called.

Dawn let Ed in – another guest on the Retreat, who happened to be a recently retired doctor – and he shuffled forth with a calm smile. "Only Ed, come to check on your ankle."

Rosie turned to glare over the back of the couch. "Ed?"

"Miss Bishop," he said by way of greeting, holding up a battered medical bag. "Mind if I take a quick look?"

Rosie sat back with a huff, watching suspiciously as he did just that. She'd never been a fan of doctors – and hadn't liked Ed since day one as a result – but his soft hands and warm voice allayed her fears. Still, she grumbled heartily as he removed Liz's bandage and performed a series of flexion tests, and Dawn watched, restless, as Ed nodded to himself and muttered observations. When he'd finished his examination, he flourished an icepack and issued Dawn strict instructions for keeping it on for twenty minutes at a time, every couple of hours. He also showed her how to put the compression bandage on properly, so that she could remove and reapply between icings, and told her the foot must be kept elevated. When he was satisfied that Dawn had appropriately absorbed all he had to say, he gifted her a tube of ointment to help with potential bruising, and then rose and smiled kindly down at Rosie.

Rosie glared. "Oh! I've seen that face before – how bad is it, then?"

Ed stroked his scruffy beard. "Honestly…? I wouldn't even class it as a level one sprain. It's more a jolt, really – a bit of bruising, at most – but it'll be tender from your trek, of course. A little ice, a little rest, and you'll be up and about by tomorrow."

"Thank you, Doctor," Dawn cut in, before Rosie could offer an acerbic comeback. She accompanied Ed to the door, nodded along as he issued last-minute suggestions, and then quietly shut it behind him.

When she returned, Rosie stared up at her with a murderous expression. "What the hell does that quack know? I'm sure this is bloody broken—"

"Ed's all right, Rose. He's been a doctor a long time, and I'm quite sure he's not out to get you. He seems to think rest will bring it down quick – it's all the walking that agitated it." Dawn adjusted the ice pack, moving it briefly out of the way to have a closer look. "You know, I think the swelling's less already."

Rosie craned her neck to see but did not agree despite the obvious. "Did he at least leave something for the pain?"

Dawn held up a small box of pills, and Rosie spluttered. "*Paracetamol?* Am I twelve?! What the hell is that going to help?"

"It's not that bad of an injury, Rose, honestly."

Dawn put the pills down and slowly got up to fetch a glass of water, and Rosie curbed her comments as she watched her friend's tired, shuffling movements. When she returned, Rosie accepted two paracetamols without complaint and dutifully swallowed them, and then Dawn put the compression bandage back again. When it was secure, Rosie breathed a sigh of relief and moulded her face to a softer expression.

"Thanks, dove. And for, you know, carrying me home."

Dawn gifted her a tired smile. "Couldn't leave you in the woods, now, could I?"

"If I'd died out there, I'd have come back to haunt you for the rest of your life."

"And I'd go mad – I don't like you *that* much."

Rosie smiled, sheepish. "You look knackered. Shall we call it a night?"

Dawn nodded and sluggishly pushed to her feet once more. She helped Rosie across the room, settled her into the closer of the two beds, and arranged the covers around her propped-up foot. Rosie opted to lie on her side – she'd never been able to sleep well on her back – and Dawn fussed until she had her comfortable.

"Will you lie here and talk to me for a bit?" Rosie asked as she made to turn for the other bed. "I can still hear demon-foxes in my head."

Dawn chortled. "I think you'll find those were just regular foxes."

But she flicked off the ceiling lights and slipped under the covers opposite Rosie, tucking her arm under a pillow to face her. With her free hand, she brushed a strand of hair from Rosie's cheek.

"It's all right," she said. "I won't let the demon foxes get you."

"Protect me with your karate, will you?"

Dawn's lips curled impishly, soft-shadowed in the dim lighting, and Rosie's gaze drew down unbidden. Distracted, she stared.

As the moment stretched, Dawn's smirk faltered. "What?"

Rosie tilted her head with a thoughtful frown. "You've a very… expressive mouth."

"I – what?"

"Your mouth. It's very expressive."

"What's that got to do with—" Dawn started to say, but froze as Rosie brushed her bottom lip with a feather-light fingertip.

Fascinated, Rosie traced the curve – and remembered that same quirky smile taunting her from the edge of a dare, decades ago. Dawn kept perfectly still, watching her, until she blushed and withdrew her hand.

But Rosie's eyes remained vivid above the heat of her cheeks. "Do you remember that night, at the party?"

"Rose. There have been millions of parties over the years."

"The Barton Mixer."

"Oh. Yes – that was the night you met Richard."

"Was it?" Rosie said, watching Dawn's lips forming words without really hearing them. "You wore cherry gloss, that night."

"Did I? That was forty years ago, Rose. I don't remember."

"I do," Rosie said softly. "We drank a lot of champagne. The party got rowdy, and the boys had us on for a bet we wouldn't kiss. Fifty quid, remember?"

Dawn's smile broadened as she recalled. "Oh, yes. Easy money – we made them give us fifty *each*, after."

Rosie's eyes drifted up, unfathomable sapphires in the dark. She met Dawn's gaze and held it. "You wore cherry gloss."

Dawn held her breath, found herself unable to blink. "Did I?"

Very gently, Rosie nodded as the memory tugged at her, and hesitated for only a fraction before she leaned forward. Dawn's surprised lips were malleable and forgiving beneath hers – there was no cherry gloss tonight, but still, she tasted of heaven. The soft moment stretched for a long heartbeat, and then Rosie quietly pulled away.

With her eyes still closed, Dawn murmured, "You really must stop kissing me. I'm… starting to like it."

Rosie ducked behind a coy smile, and Dawn mumbled something unintelligible as she pulled her back within range. Her gentle fingers curled through Rosie's hair, and then she showed her just how expressive her mouth could be.

But at last, she caught Rosie's lower lip between her teeth and nipped it, releasing her from the moment.

"Stop it, now, Rose," she murmured. "I'm exhausted. The least you can do after making me carry you twelve miles is let me sleep."

Rosie bridled. "*Two* miles! And you've no idea what exhausted feels like – *I'm* the one who broke my bloody ankle!"

"Bruised." Dawn rolled onto her back with a groan. "Go to sleep, damn you."

"Aren't you going to your own bloody bed?"

"Don't be ridiculous – I couldn't move another single inch today."

With a sigh, Rosie gingerly shifted her ankle and wiggled closer. She patted the blankets down and fidgeted for a long moment, but then settled as Dawn held out an arm for her to cuddle beneath. Finally, with Dawn's heartbeat sweet in her ears, Rosie shut her eyes and gave in to a deep fatigue.

# CHAPTER FOURTEEN

Perhaps it was discomfort from her ankle or the echoes of foxes screaming in her dreams, but Rosie did not sleep well that night. She woke often, lay staring at nothing for long aeons, and struggled to keep track of her wandering mind. In between, she dreamed that she was lost, desperately trying to get… somewhere… and that she was alone.

The idea terrified her.

Strange, haunting emotions plagued her – vague visions of faceless things, goading her as she stumbled through the dark. Her gasps came unevenly each time she woke, but each time she did, Dawn's steady breathing soothed her. Time and again, she tucked in close to keep the fears at bay, but finally, in the grey light of almost morning, echoes of dream-Richard's voice forced her to full consciousness.

*Nothing will ever make YOU happy.*

Rosie shifted her ankle with a hiss, pressing her hands against her eyes to combat her ex-husband's lingering sneer. Beside her, Dawn stirred with a drowsy glower.

"Rose, what the bloody hell is the matter with you… I'm

trying to sleep."

When Rosie didn't respond, Dawn blinked to reasonable awareness and rolled to face her. Noting Rosie's pale face in the dark, her glower faded. "Are you all right? Is it the ankle?"

"That does keep waking me," Rosie admitted, "but I'm grateful... really. I've been having weird dreams."

"Mmm. Paracetamol is known for its hallucinogenic qualities."

Rosie scoffed, and Dawn gave her a sleepy grin.

"Go on, then. What were you dreaming about?"

"Foxes. The dark. Richard..." Rosie trailed off, and Dawn waited. "I was lost. Trying to reach somewhere. Or something? I'm not sure. It was all mixed up – shapes and faces, blurry and yet extremely distinct."

"Well, that's oddly vague and specific," Dawn yawned. "I'm so glad kissing me before bed has given you nightmares. Reassuring, that."

"What? It has nothing to do with *that*."

"Hasn't it?"

Rosie snapped open her mouth to respond but then closed it beneath a sudden upsurge of uncertainty. Dawn winked and rolled out of bed.

"Want some tea?"

Before Rosie could say anything, Dawn flicked on the wall lamps and padded to the kitchenette, stifling a shiver against the early morning air. The hotel kept the heating on to counteract the lingering chill of spring, but Rosie always insisted on sleeping with a window open. Claustrophobic, she said. Dawn humoured her – that's what duvets were for, anyway. Humming under her breath, she made tea and scooped a couple of chocolates from her secret stash at the back of the cupboard, all the while ignoring Rosie's indignant summoning from the bed. At last, she returned to find that Rosie had managed to prop herself up on her own against the headboard, with a dreadful glower plastered across her face.

Dawn thrust a cup into her clawed fingers before sitting down with a grand air of serenity. Rosie scowled through the mist billowing from her mug and pursed her lips until they hurt.

After a long, tense moment, Dawn innocently asked, "D'you want another Paracetamol?"

Rosie nearly spilt her tea. Dawn unleashed a delighted cackle at the sheer outrage etched onto her face, and Rosie attempted one-handed to push her off the bed. She failed dismally, being half-crippled and also weighed down by a hot beverage, and Dawn sat back with a gleeful sigh when Rosie ran out of steam.

"Drink your tea, now," Dawn said, raising an eyebrow. "In a minute, I'm going to ice your ankle again."

Rosie grumbled but did as she was told. By the time she'd finished, and Dawn had treated her sore leg and strapped her up again, it was full daylight outside. Dawn left her brooding over a fresh cup of tea and commandeered the bathroom. When she was done, Rosie managed to prop herself up in the shower long enough to wash away the misadventures of yesterday, and Dawn changed her sodden bandage again after she'd dressed.

"Shall we go down for breakfast?" Dawn asked at last.

"Throw me out the window," Rosie grumbled. "It'll be quicker."

"I would, but then you'll miss out on all the fun."

Rosie's glower darkened. "What fun?"

With a mischievous grin, Dawn helped her to the door, and Rosie positively snarled when she saw what awaited her. "NO, Dawn. I am NOT going to be seen on *that*."

"Oh, c'mon," Dawn sniggered, closing the door behind them to bar Rosie's escape. "It'll be a laugh."

"Why in the hell did they send *two*, anyway? Bugger-all's wrong with you!"

Dawn scooped a note out of one of the front baskets and flourished it. Clearing her throat, she read: "'Mrs Clermont, please make use of this complimentary mobility scooter to supervise Miss Bishop. We are concerned that she might wander off and find even more trouble if left to her own devices. Sincerely, Liz.'"

"WHAT!"

"She's a point, there."

"She bloody does not! I'll bloody have that Liz up by the scruff of her neck, I'll—"

"You'll never catch her."

"Oh?" Rosie clambered onto her scooter. "Watch me."

She fired it up, testing it in a small circle around the hall, and Dawn's smirk widened.

"You're a natural on that, Rose."

Rosie rode over her foot. "Get on yours, dammit – if I'm to look like a tit, you have to, too."

Muttering under her breath, Dawn wiggled some feeling back into her toes and settled onto the second scooter. Rosie circled her and then came up alongside.

"Can you even handle that thing?"

"I'm sure I'll manage," Dawn scoffed. "Race you to the end of the hall?"

Before Rosie could consider the challenge, Dawn lurched forward, and Rosie's yelp of indignance was the portent to a slow-motion drag race the length of the corridor. Dawn kept her lead thanks to her fractional head start, and as the wall loomed, she slowed to gloat. But Rosie's competitive streak kicked in – *lose?* On a *mobility scooter?* – and she powered forward to pass Dawn at the last second.

"Rose—!"

Bang.

Rosie collided with the wall at a blistering eight miles per hour. Her scooter ground sideways and scratched a long swathe into the wallpaper before shuddering to a halt, and Dawn, after an initial breathless fear in case Rosie had hurt herself – again – fell about laughing.

"Jesus Rose!" she wheezed, wiping at tears. "I forgot how bloody ruthless you are!"

"I won, didn't I?" Rosie smirked.

"MRS CLERMONT!"

"Uh-oh." Dawn spun with a guilty face as Liz came striding down the hallway.

"This is the absolute worst case of supervision I have *ever* seen! What on earth am I to do with the pair of you? Honestly, Pip is about a hair's breadth from throwing you both out of here!"

"Pah!" Rosie exclaimed. "*Pip*? I'd like to see him bloody try!"

Dawn turned an audacious grin on Liz. "C'mon, Lizzie – here, have a go."

Liz faltered, vacillating despite herself. Dawn stepped off her machine, slow and deliberate. The youngster looked from one to the other, and Rosie raised an eyebrow in challenge. Liz's attempted severity melted, shortly replaced by a rebellious grin.

"Oh, go on, then," she said.

Dawn stood back with a flourish, and Liz hopped onto her scooter.

"Race, Miss Bishop?" Liz taunted. "We're starting evens, though. Top of the hall and back again – Mrs Clermont can judge the winner."

"You're on!" Rosie said, unpeeling her scooter from the wall and bringing it alongside.

"Start us off, Mrs Clermont?"

"I think, at this stage of the game, Liz, you should be calling me Dawn."

Liz beamed. "Excellent – start us off, Dawn!"

"Right, then." Dawn cleared her throat and held up a hand. "Ready? Set—Rose!"

Rosie was off, but Liz had the reactions of a cat and was upon her immediately. Neck and neck, they trundled the length of the hall, until Rosie prematurely pulled her scooter around to head back again.

"Ha!" she cried as she turned a slow circle before Liz did. "You're done for!"

"Am I?" Liz shot back. She hefted her scooter forward onto the front wheel and swung the back around.

Jaw agape, Rosie almost crashed into the sidewall. Dawn whooped from the other end, and before Rosie knew what was happening, Liz had pulled in front. Cussing, Rosie leaned low over the handlebars and used her good foot for extra leverage but couldn't quite catch Liz before she crawled past Dawn. Liz hopped triumphantly off her scooter before it had even stopped moving, flicked it off, and flourished a bow at Rosie.

"I'm sure that's not allowed!" Rosie growled as she pulled to an undignified halt.

Liz tossed her flaming hair and winked. "Had to make up for your jumping the gun."

"Fair!" Dawn declared. "Bloody brilliant, Liz – where'd you learn to do that?"

"I'm a Formula One scooter driver in my spare time," Liz said without missing a beat.

"Cheat!" Rosie snarled. "I demand a rematch!"

"Sore loser, Miss Bishop?"

"Don't egg her on," Dawn warned. She rescued her scooter and plopped firmly back onto it before any further racing could ensue. "That's enough for one day, I think. Now, what are we going to do about the wallpaper?"

Liz followed her gaze to the blemish Rosie had left on the wall, twisted her lips thoughtfully, and then hauled over one of the decorative sideboards from further down the hall to squat in front of it. Dusting her hands, she said, "No problem. You were never here."

Dawn cocked her head at Rosie. "I told you this girl is the right sort. One of us, she is."

Rosie's scowl darkened. "If she really was, she'd have known to let me win."

## CHAPTER FIFTEEN

Despite an admirable amount of moaning and moping, Rosie was hobbling around unassisted after a couple of days and had long abandoned her mobility scooter. Dawn kept a careful eye on her progress throughout, debating if risking her ankle was safer than risking any more of her boredom-inspired petulance. At last, on the third morning – after listening to Rosie practising different groans across an entire octave – Dawn decided she'd had enough.

"Right," she announced, "today we're going out!"

"I don't *want* to go out," Rosie whined, from where she was lying on the bed, pretending she had nothing left to live for.

Dawn shrugged. "Suit yourself. I'm going, though."

She collected her coat and a key card and made for the door.

"*Where* are we going?" Rosie called.

Dawn paused in the doorway but did not turn around. "There's a car show on today."

Rosie sat up. "There's a *what*?"

"You heard me."

She sauntered out, and Rosie flung herself off the bed. "Wait, Dawn! I love cars!"

With a loud 'ow' punctuating every hurried step, she dashed for her coat and a scarf and raced out, too. Just beyond the door, she almost collided with her quarry, and Dawn automatically steadied her as she lurched to a halt.

"Oh!" Rosie exclaimed. "I thought you'd gone."

"Would I go without you? C'mon, bus leaves in a few minutes."

Rosie made a rude noise. "Always the bloody *old-age* bus. Why can't we just drive ourselves, like normal people?"

"Do you have a car here?"

"Well… no."

"There you are then."

They took the stairs to accommodate Rosie's dislike of the lift, and Dawn was willing enough to go at Rosie's pace – she'd already told Pip they'd be going, so she knew the coach would wait – but Rosie eagerly descended the triple flights with barely a limp.

At the bottom, Dawn made a derisive sound. "You know – you appear to have made an *astounding* recovery since I saw you hobble to the bathroom this morning."

Caught cold, Rosie stopped and made a show of testing her ankle. "I suppose it is a *bit* better."

But as she continued onward, her limp became suddenly more pronounced again, and Dawn stifled a snigger. She drew level and gave unsuspecting Rosie a shove – and Rosie's ankle bore up just fine as she took an extra step onto it to catch her balance.

Dawn laughed. "I *knew* you were having it on!"

Rosie scoffed and surged ahead. "Honestly, Dawn, I don't know what all the fuss is about. Would you hurry up? We'll miss the bus."

Shaking her head in amusement, Dawn followed her out.

In the coach, they took their usual seats right at the back. The trip was a little longer than usual, just over half an hour through the winding lanes, and Rosie glared impatiently out of the window the whole way. But at last, the narrow roads opened out into a village that sported the sign *BIDLEY*, and they passed between quaint stone houses to reach a large, open field decorated with rows upon rows of cars.

"Goodness," Rosie said, plastered to the window as they parked, "would you look at them all?"

The coach had hardly ground to a halt before Rosie was dashing out with Dawn following gamely behind her. The rows stretched endless, offering a new delight at every turn, from vintage classics to the latest sports cars, and they'd made almost a full circuit before Dawn tugged Rosie to a standstill in front of a TVR Cerbera.

"Holy Mother of God," Dawn whispered, staring at it. "What I wouldn't do to own one of these…"

"Mmm. I could see you driving that," Rosie said. She eyed Dawn critically. "Yes – very mid-life-crisis-y."

"Pfft. A girl's gotta have dreams, Rose. Go on, which one would you pick?"

Rosie narrowed her eyes and swept them down the line. Marching over to a black convertible Alfa Spider, she put her hands on her hips and said, "This one."

"Ooo," Dawn said, coming to fawn over it. "Good choice! Would you just look at this leather interior?"

Rosie did, indeed, look. "Perhaps I'll buy one. We could cruise along the M4, maybe catch the ferry to Ireland and tour up the Wild Atlantic Way."

Dawn giggled. "With ludicrously large sun hats and gaudy scarves – that's a dream, all right. Quite sure these are out of our budget, though."

Rosie smiled, wicked. "Actually, Richard had to pay me out a whopper in the divorce, and I still get dividends. Half the company was mine, after all. We can get a Spider. Or a Cerbera. Or… both."

Dawn crowed with devilish amusement. "Ha! You sneaky

fiend – serves him right!"

Rosie grinned, and then pursed her lips, thinking. "The weather's a bit shite in Ireland though. Tell you what, instead of wasting our pennies on cars, how about we make that trip to Africa? At least it's sunny there."

Dawn sighed dreamily. "I'd love to go to Africa."

"We will," Rosie promised.

Arm in arm, they strolled down the line, perusing more magnificent, streamlined feats of engineering. The pale sunlight kept them soft company, holding the promise of later drizzle at bay, and they meandered onward until Dawn decided she was hungry. Then, they found a little bench off to one side of the field, and Rosie settled happily onto it to watch the comings and goings of the day.

"I'll wait here and keep our spot while you grab us a bite," she suggested.

"Suits me," Dawn agreed. "It's busy out, and I'd like to have somewhere to sit for a bit. What do you fancy?"

"I want one of those chip-on-a-stick things we passed, and a cappuccino maybe from the cart next to it."

"And some doughnuts, for after?"

"Yes – those dinky ones that they make while you're watching."

"Sugared?"

"Of course."

Intent on her mission, Dawn turned back the way they'd come and made a beeline for the food stands. Rosie settled with a sigh, tilting her head to let the weak sunshine get at her face as she listened to the laughter of excited children floating between the exasperated calls of their stressed parents. It was a colourful day, bright spring flowers bobbing gently in the breeze, and she paused in her thoughts to hear the world sing.

But then the sun disappeared, and a shadow loomed over her.

"Hello, Rose."

The violence with which her heart leapt, in reaction to that single utterance, almost toppled her off the bench. Her eyes flashed open, her breath caught in her chest, and she shrank back – for it was a voice she recognised, but it had none of the warmth of Dawn's.

"Mind if I join you?" Richard continued.

She wanted to scream: *I mind! I mind – dear God, I mind!*

But the words stuck in her throat, as they had for years, and Richard took her silence for permission. Perching genially beside her, he took a deep breath of the spring air and then turned to face her with a doleful smile. "I've been trying to catch a moment alone with you all morning."

*All morning?* Rosie swallowed bile, but her silence remained stubborn, and Richard dropped his gaze.

"Listen, Rose – I'll make this quick before that bull terrier of a friend of yours comes back. I've had a lot of time to think lately. I know I've done some stupid things and letting you go was the stupidest of all. I know you don't care for my confessions, but I have to admit that I'm just a shadow of a man without you." He caught one of her clammy hands beneath his own and took a deep breath. "I've a killer contract coming up, real rising star, and I can't blow it. I need you, Rose. I need your shrewd instincts, to help me close this deal. The company hasn't been the same since I lost you."

*LOST me? Dear God – if you ever wanted to shout and scream and lose your shit, Rose, now's the time!* But her tongue remained thick in her mouth, her breathing fast and shallow, and she was unable to do more than listen.

"There's an important gala coming up," Richard continued, "an introductory sort of situation. I have to meet this kid and convince him to sign, and I'd really like it if you were there with me. I could use your finesse, you know, when it comes to getting a good read on things. You always were a great judge of people."

*Except for you.*

"I know it's a lot to take in, Rose, and I know things have been a bit rocky between us. But I want you to know that I'm really sorry. I'm an arse, and I should have treated you better; you're the most phenomenal woman I've ever met. I'll regret to the day I die that I lost sight of that." He squeezed the hand she couldn't quite pull away. "I don't expect you to just up and forgive me, of course – I'm not so callous – but I'm asking you to perhaps consider this one favour, for old times' sake. You were the light of my life, and though I slipped now and then, it was always you who pulled me back. I screwed up, Rose, and I'm really sorry."

With a morose sigh, he released her at last and got quietly to his feet. Straightening his tailored jacket, he offered her a confident smile beneath his parting words. "Promise me you'll think about it, eh, Rose? It's just one evening. A King is nothing without his Queen."

*A king is – God, say something, Rose! TELL HIM TO SOD OFF.*

He turned, then, lifted his collar up, and tipped his hat to her before striding back into the car show. Rosie watched him until he was lost to the melee; she felt a little faint, and there was an erratic fluttering in her chest. *Was she old enough for a heart attack? Probably.*

When the crowds had swallowed him up, she shut her eyes again and concentrated on her breathing, counting long breaths in and out again in an attempt to steady her trembling. After a few minutes, she'd almost succeeded in restoring some semblance of calm, but then a light touch on her shoulder made her yelp.

"Jesus, Rose!" Dawn said, desperately rebalancing her wares as Rosie's jolt knocked them akilter. "What the hell's the matter?"

"Richard…" Rosie whispered, staring down at the masses. "He was here."

Dawn froze, coffee dripping from a lopsided cup. "What?"

Rosie noticed and reached to rescue it, helping herself to a large, steadying sip. "While you were at the food stands. I think he's been following us half the morning – he said he was waiting to catch me alone."

Dawn sat down beside her, looking her over with a dark frown.

"Are you all right? What in the bloody hell did he want?"

"He asked me to a gala," Rosie said, bemused, "amongst a whole wash of other bollocks about how sorry he is."

"A gala?"

"To meet and potentially sign some young talent, apparently."

"What the hell has that got to do with you?"

Rosie barked a strained laugh. "Absolutely bloody nothing."

"What else did he say?"

"Nothing particularly interesting. He wasn't here very long; wandered back off between the cars."

Dawn scanned the thronging field beyond their vantage. "Which way did he go?"

"Leave it," Rosie said with a shake of her head. "There's a million people here now. Let's just... take a walk or something."

"All right," Dawn agreed tightly, "but if I see him on the way, I'll not be held responsible for my actions."

"Drive over him with that TVR, will you?"

"Bus, more like. Wouldn't want him smeared all over that nice car."

They finished their spiral chip-on-a-sticks and then, with a doughnut and half-drunk cup of coffee each, meandered around the outskirts of the field to the exit. Mercifully, there was no sign of Richard, and they left the car show behind them in favour of the village.

"Good Lord." Dawn pointed as they passed a riot of daffodils commandeering an entire verge. "The cheek of them!"

"Hideous, aren't they?" Rosie smiled, pleased by both their charm and the pleasant company they reminded her of.

The village wasn't exceptionally large, and they'd roamed through most of it before they came to a small stone church. In the shaded park surrounding it, they found a bench and settled to admire the view.

"I think I could retire to a small village like Bidley," Dawn said with a contented sigh.

"You're already retired," Rosie reminded her. She leaned comfortably against Dawn's shoulder. "But I could easily imagine you living somewhere like this. Hell, I could even imagine you living in this church."

"People don't *live* in churches."

"Priests do. And Vicars."

"They bloody don't. They live at the Vicarage. But no – that sounds entirely too pious for me. I might prefer a little of the coast, actually – sand and sunshine instead of fields and cow pats."

Rosie laughed amiably. "It would be lovely to live by the seaside. I really wanted to, but Richard always had other plans."

"Speaking of which…"

"Do we have to talk about that? Honestly, I was having such a lovely moment."

"He's following you round half of England, Rose. I think this presents a bit of a problem."

Rosie sighed, stifling a shiver. "He obviously called Mary's bluff on the restraining order. He wasn't really out of hand though, Dawn. Very polite – apologetic, even."

Dawn turned to face her with a murderous expression. "I hope you're not bloody falling for that smarmy hogwash."

"What? Don't be ridiculous. All I wanted was for him to go away." Rosie shifted uncomfortably. "It was the weirdest thing, though… I couldn't seem to say a word the whole time."

"Oh, *no*, Rose – you didn't say anything? God, that means he'll think there's hope. He'll never bloody leave you alone now!"

"I think you might be overreacting," Rosie sniffed. "I hardly said yes to his ridiculous bloody request."

"But you didn't say no?"

"Well…"

Dawn gave an exasperated huff. "You mark my words, Rose, he's not going to let it go. Men like Richard need a firm 'sod off', with a firm kick up the arse to drive it home."

Rosie brooded, not quite wanting to admit that Dawn was

absolutely right. She should have said no – *why* didn't she just bloody say no, right there and then? What was it about him that rendered her speechless, even when she wanted to scream the country down? He'd always taken her silence for permission, and there was no reason why this time would be any different.

"Tell you what," Dawn said, watching the play of emotions across her face, "next time he turns up, *I'll* give him a kick up the arse."

"Quite sure that counts as assault," Rosie mused. "Might be jail time."

Dawn scoffed. "Absolutely bloody worth it."

"I hope it doesn't come to that," Rosie quipped, but her smile was a little strained.

## CHAPTER SIXTEEN

Later that afternoon, as they made their way back to the coach and left the drama of Richard behind them, Dawn kept the conversation light.

"I'm telling you, Rose," she said as they reached the car park, "I know a thing or two about wine, honestly. I've tasted enough to sink the Titanic."

"Apart from the fact that the Titanic has already sunk, I'm not doubting you. But I do think that Chilean wine is better than French wine," Rosie replied.

"When have you ever *tasted* a Chilean wine?"

"I got a bottle at Tesco the other week—"

"*WHAT?* Let me stop you right there, Rose. If you're basing your wine connoisseur-ing on a bottle you got from *Tesco* – I just… I have no words. In fact, due to your complete lack of anything resembling refinement, I'm going to have to organise a wine tasting for you as soon as possible."

"How about tonight, then?"

Dawn missed a step. "*Tonight?* Rose – where am I possibly going to get a selection of fine wines at such short notice, and in the middle of bloody Cumbria?!"

"You could try Tesco."

"Oh, sod off."

Rosie shot her a sideways glance as they boarded the coach. "I could really use a drink, though."

Dawn huffed and harried her up the step. "Fine. I'll see what I can do – but don't blame me if the wines are substandard. Oh!" – her eyes widened suddenly as she remembered something – "It's Liz's day off today. I can send her off to find some for us."

"How do you even *know* it's Liz's day off?"

Dawn sagely tapped her nose as they took their seats. "I keep abreast of useful information."

"That poor girl is not going to want to spend her day off running about to get wine for two crazy women."

"I'll invite her to join us. Then she won't mind at all."

Rosie laughed. "What part of 'two crazy women' did you miss? I highly doubt Liz will be charmed to spend her evening off with the likes of us."

"Maybe not with *you*," Dawn harrumphed, "but I'm cool as they come. And she'll put up with you, too, if I vouch for you."

"I think you're rather overestimating your own powers of persuasion."

"Mmm. We'll just see, won't we."

The coach pulled into the car park at Greenside and Dawn and Rosie debarked and made for their room, still bickering about whether or not Liz would oblige their whims.

"We should just order room service champagne or gin or something," Rosie said as they traipsed up the stairs. "Leave that poor girl alone."

"It can't hurt to *ask* her," Dawn replied, unwilling to relinquish her stance.

Rosie rolled her eyes and opened the door to their room – but stumbled to a halt before she'd quite stepped through. Beside her,

Dawn froze, too.

"Christ," Rosie whispered.

"What the bloody hell is this?" said Dawn at the same time.

Slowly, Rosie pushed the door wider, and they stared, for, on every available surface, from wall to wall and including every square inch of floor space, flowers filled the room. Exotic bouquets, roses, lilies, even the odd orchid – it seemed most of Earth's flora species were represented.

"Oh, look," Dawn said sarcastically, wading through to the TV stand, "there's a card." Picking it up, she read, "*A King is nothing without his Queen*." She flipped it over, but that was all it said. Baffled, she turned to Rosie, who had gone white as a sheet. "Oh, no, Rose! *Don't* tell me these are from Richard! What did I tell you about just bloody saying NO."

Weak-kneed, Rosie crumpled onto her backside amidst the riot of colour. Dawn strode back to her, kicking blooms unceremoniously out of the way before dropping down beside her. Reading the card again, she scoffed.

"What is he, fifteen?" She tipped her head sideways at Rosie and cracked a grin as she fanned the embossed message. "*A King* – dear Lord – you know, Rose, *this* is what desperation looks like, honestly. Ten-out-of-ten." She clasped her hands together and batted her eyelashes. "Oh, gosh! I'm sure you're just *gasping* to take him back, now."

Rosie's expression turned murderous, flushing colour back into her grey face. "Shut up. You're so full of it!"

Dawn's impish smile widened. "Am I?" She snatched a wayward daffodil from the closest arrangement and pressed it over her heart. With a pitiful expression, she mimicked Richard in falsetto. "Oh, Rosie! I'm so sorry for everything I've done!" The daffodil danced near her cheek, offsetting her twinkling eyes. "Here's five billion flowers because nothing says I love you like dying plants – oof!"

Rosie lunged for her, crushing her taunts beneath a yelp

of surprise. "Shut up!" she snarled, batting the daffodil head downward and catching Dawn's shoulders with white knuckles. "Shut up, now!"

Dawn froze under the heat of her gaze, bemused and a little contrite. "Sorry, Rose, I was just—"

"Would you stop talking?" Rosie hissed, squeezing her eyes tight shut against a violent trembling. It was too much; Richard, the flowers – Dawn and her damned daffodils – all of it. She shook with it; she was too unstable, too consumed by emotions she didn't understand, to deal with any of it. Her eyes flashed open, meeting Dawn's perplexed gaze, and she drowned in it.

"Rose…"

Dawn's voice fluttered through her, and her gentle hand settling on Rosie's arm set her heart to racing. Rosie found herself staring; in the midst of myriad flowers sent by her insane ex-husband, she'd never seen anything quite like Dawn at that moment. Her dark eyes were bottomless, creased with disquiet, and her lips moved with gentle elegance as she expressed her concern. Low and throaty, Dawn's voice seeped through her once more. "Rose, are you all right?"

"No," Rosie whispered. "I'm not all right. I'll never be all right again."

"That's a tiny bit ridiculous," Dawn admonished, attempting a small smile. "Of course, you will. It's only a few flowers – nothing we can't toss out the window."

"It's not the flowers," Rosie murmured, so quietly Dawn almost didn't hear. "It's not Richard, either." It was true – that door, somehow, had firmly slammed shut.

"What is it, then?"

"Daffodils."

"Daffodils? You're not making any sense, Rose."

"None of it is."

Dawn gave an exasperated huff. "Now you've completely lost me."

Rosie plucked the daffodil from her fingers and held it up. After a moment, she lifted her focus from its bright yellow head to Dawn's confused gaze. "This might be insanity."

"I'll say. Richard has lost his stuffing mind."

"For the last time, Dawn – I'm not talking about bloody Richard."

Dawn graced her with a long-suffering blink. "What are you talking about, then?"

"You."

"Me? I didn't send you a truck-ton of unwanted flowers!"

"No, but you gave me daffodils."

Dawn frowned. "You're starting to piss me off now, Rose – why are you being so bloody cryptic?"

Rosie fixed her with a steady gaze and carefully considered her next words. "When I was locked up in my house, drifting aimlessly between disinterest and despair, I saw a clump of daffodils on the verge opposite my kitchen window. They reminded me so strongly of something. Someone. *You*, as it turns out – though I didn't realise it at the time. Still, something in my subconscious must have stirred when I saw those bright, brave little flowers – and when Mary suggested this ludicrous trip, the daffodils beyond the window were the reason I said yes."

She shifted, put the daffodil down, and took Dawn's hands in her own.

"I hadn't realised how much I'd missed you until you walked into the room that first day. And then, when I couldn't find you the following morning, it frightened me… in a way I've never felt frightened before. I have a great deal of… affection… for you, Dawn. And I'm so very afraid to lose you."

Dawn squeezed her fingers. "I'm not going anywhere."

"Not now, no. But what about after this trip? We only have a few days left, and then… well, then what? We'll go back to our sad, lonely little lives, and not see each other for another twenty years?"

"We might be dead if it's another twenty years."

"I'm serious," Rosie said. "I don't even know where you live anymore."

Dawn laughed, then – sad and fragile – and patted her hand. "To be honest, neither do I. My home was repossessed a few weeks before I won this trip. That's why I've been so hellbent on making the most of this holiday – it could be the last one for a very long time. I've been staying with my sister the past few weeks, but that's a temporary arrangement."

"Your house was repossessed?"

Dawn dropped her gaze and swiped at a stray tear. "Yes, I – uh – I couldn't afford the mortgage anymore. Jack's medical bills… We couldn't wait, you see - he was deteriorating so rapidly. So, we had to go private. I gambled everything, Rose. And I lost. Everything."

"Oh, Dawn…" Rosie pulled her into a hug, her own wayward thoughts and fears abruptly eclipsed by her concern for her friend. "We'll think of something. You can come and stay with me if you want, 'til you get back on your feet, at least."

Dawn lifted her head and sniffed loudly. "I might have to, anyway – someone's got to bloody protect you from Richard's insane advances."

Rosie followed her gaze around the room, and the absurdity finally sank in. Slowly, a cheeky grin crept onto her lips. "But Dawn… a King is nothing without his Queen, you know."

Dawn smirked back. "But a Queen is perfectly fine on her own. C'mon, let's get up, now – my legs are starting to go numb." With a groan, she pulled free and climbed to her feet. "God, my knees aren't what they used to be…"

"Mine neither," Rosie agreed, reaching for the hand-up Dawn offered.

Side by side, they surveyed the riot of flowers in their room.

"What will we do about this mess, then?" Rosie asked.

Dawn tilted her head with a wicked smile. "Straight out the window, I reckon."

Rosie laughed, and Dawn marched over to throw the windows wide. In a few moments, stalks and petals were raining down onto the lawn three stories below amidst chaotic laughter and a lot of snide remarks.

"No – wait – not the card!" Dawn yelped, snatching it out of Rosie's fingers a second before she let it fly, too. "I want preserve this ludicrous memory."

Rosie giggled, and Dawn surveyed the handful of daffodils they'd rescued and put into a jug on the kitchen counter – and dusted her hands in satisfaction.

"Right," she said. "Now that *that's* dealt with..."

She stalked over to the phone and snatched it up to dial furiously.

"*Now* what are you doing?"

Dawn looked up with a bland expression as if it were obvious. "Calling Liz about that wine."

Rosie scoffed. "You've left it far too late."

Dawn retorted confidently, "We'll just see, won't we."

## CHAPTER SEVENTEEN

As the day faded into evening, Dawn opened the door to admit Liz – and a hostess trolley loaded with wine.

Rosie glowered. "So, you did come."

"Why wouldn't I?" Liz asked with a puzzled frown. She unpacked a few bottles onto the counter, turning them so that they could make out the labels.

"Told you," Dawn winked at Rosie. She moved over to peruse the selection of wines and threw a sidelong glance at Liz. "Rose here thought you'd be mortified to hang out with two 'crazy women' on your evening off."

"What?!" Liz cried. "Firstly, you're my kind of crazy, and secondly, I absolutely adore your joie de vivre!"

"Joie de vivre?" Dawn repeated with a smirk. "*Us?*"

"Don't you *have* any friends?" Rosie snapped at Liz. Part of her was irked at Dawn being right (as usual) and another part – a little more imprecise, perhaps – was disappointed that it wasn't just her and Dawn this evening.

Liz ignored her and flourished her wares for Dawn. "I got it all, Dee – eight of the finest bottles Tesco had to offer."

Dawn choked, clawing white-knuckled at the edge of the counter.

"HA!" Rosie crowed, instantly amused. "I bloody *told* you Tesco had decent wines!"

"Is something the matter?" Liz asked, staring at Dawn with a concerned frown.

Rosie's eyes sparkled; her momentary irritation forgotten. "Not at all – I *do* like this girl, Dawn."

"Oh, piss off," Dawn muttered. But she valiantly set about sorting the bottles into some sort of order, and then fastidiously opened them all.

"I hardly think we're going to drink eight whole bottles," Rosie commented wryly, watching.

"Your lack of class is showing," Dawn shot back. "We're supposed to have just a little sip of each, to taste and compare."

"What about the rest of it?"

Liz chipped in with a smirk, "We'll drink it after."

Rosie's grin broadened, and Dawn rolled her eyes heavenward.

"Heathens, the pair of you! Sit down, now, and pretend you have some panache."

With impish expressions, Rosie and Liz did as they were told, and Dawn poured a drop of the first bottle into each of the three waiting glasses.

Rosie eyed hers. "Is that it?"

"TASTE AND COMPARE."

"All right!"

Rosie and Liz composed themselves, and Dawn lifted her glass, swirling it and holding it up to the light. Pressing her nose into it, she sighed in delight, and Rosie smothered a snort of amusement. Dawn took a small sip, rolled it over her tongue to explore the flavours, and then looked over at the other two expectantly.

"Well?" she said.

Rosie forced her face straight and sipped at hers, and Liz followed her lead.

"What do you think?" Dawn persisted.

Rosie frowned thoughtfully and put on her poshest voice. "Well, *dah-ling* – I'm getting the impression that it could be rather a full-bodied vintage, but I really can't say due to the fact that my glass is mostly empty."

Liz snorted wine out of her nose.

Dawn sighed expansively. "The sacred art of wine-tasting is utterly wasted on you pair."

"Utterly," Rosie agreed. "How about you just choose us the nicest bottle of the lot and we'll drink that one first?"

Dawn allowed herself a pained grimace but reached for an Argentinian Malbec. "Rinse your bloody glasses, at least."

Grinning, Liz scooped them up and went to rinse them along with her wine-spattered face. All clean, she returned them to Dawn, who reverently poured them each a proper glass.

"That's better," Rosie said, lifting hers to have a sip. "Ooo – actually – that's bloody fabulous!"

Dawn raised her eyebrows. "Full-bodied enough?"

"Positively voluptuous."

Dawn pulled a face, and Rosie winked salaciously at her. Between them, Liz grinned.

"You two are so cute! You're the literal definition of my couple goals."

Rosie choked on her wine. Recovering, she wiped her mouth with the back of her hand and snapped, "I'm sorry… *couple*?"

Liz's grin widened and she held her hands up in supplication. "Whoa. Aren't you?"

Dawn snorted a laugh. "Rosie bloody wishes! I could see how you think that, though, Liz – anyone would, judging by how useless Rose is without me."

"I am not useless!" Rosie huffed. "I finished this glass of wine all by myself, didn't I? Pour us another one, Dawn, for Christ's sake."

Dawn got up to oblige and winked at Liz. "See?"

Rosie wasn't ready to let it go. "It's just wine, Dawn." She turned to Liz. "I'm curious now – humour me, now, since you think you know everything – what are you, some kind of lesbian expert?"

Liz smirked, somewhere between impish and sheepish. "Well, you could ask my girlfriend."

"Oh!" Dawn smiled. "How sweet! What's her name?"

"We don't care, Dawn."

"Her name's Lucy."

"Aww… Liz and Lucy – what a lovely ring. Don't you think it's lovely, Rose?"

"No."

"Tell us about her, Liz."

"No, don't."

Liz's smile softened, and her eyes took on a gentle shine. "She's the most wonderful girl in the world; beautiful, smart, funny – biggest heart you've ever seen."

Rosie threw her head back with a hearty groan. "Ugh. Young love makes me ill."

Dawn raised an eyebrow. "That's just because you're old and bitter."

"I am not."

There was a moment of silence, and then Rosie huffed loudly. "Didn't you bring a board game or something, Liz?"

Liz hopped off her stool. "As a matter of fact, I did." She rummaged in the cart, announcing each as she pulled them out. "Here – I've got Thirty Seconds, Trivial Pursuit, *aaand*…" – she retrieved the last box – "Oh, Monopoly."

Dawn yelped. "Oh, *God* no – put that Monopoly one back right now!"

Liz faltered halfway to depositing it on the counter. "You don't like Monopoly?"

"Rosie here will burn the building down if she loses."

"I will *not*!"

Dawn fixed Rosie with a flat expression.

"Fine," Rosie huffed. "Let's not play Monopoly – unless you're willing to give me a pre-loan and also Boardwalk and Park Place to start?"

"Put it away, Liz!" Dawn howled.

Grinning, Liz tossed the box unceremoniously back into the cart. "So, one of the other two, then? Or there's also cards…"

Rosie leaned forward. "What kind of cards?"

"Um…" Liz crouched to reach into the bottom of the cart. "Two standard packs and… oh, Uno."

Rosie cocked her head at Dawn. "Uno cards pair well with wine-tasting, yes?"

"Uno cards pair well with everything," Dawn agreed with a grin.

Liz nodded and pushed everything else to one side. She shuffled the cards and began to deal, and Rosie slapped Dawn's wrist as she reached for her growing pile. "You can't touch the cards until the dealer's finished!"

"Why the hell not?"

"It's bad luck, obviously."

Deliberately, Dawn picked her hand up before Liz dealt the last card and raised a challenging eyebrow at Rosie. "We'll just see, shall we?"

Rosie's mouth twisted into a grim line. "We shall."

"Ready?" Liz asked, flipping the first card – a green seven. "You're first, Dawn."

"Excellent," Dawn smirked, hitting Rosie immediately with a draw-four.

Rosie spluttered. "Challenge! You can't bloody play a draw-four if you've got cards of that colour in your hand!"

Dawn exposed her cards, slow and sadistic. There wasn't a green one to be seen. "You were saying…?"

"You started without a single green bloody card *and* a draw-four? That's ridiculous!"

"What can I say," Dawn said, poker-faced, "I'm just lucky."

"Lucky is bloody right," Rosie grumbled, taking four cards.

"What colour, Dee?" Liz asked, flaring her hand in readiness.

"Red."

"Excellent."

She played a red three, and then Dawn followed up with a reverse card that changed the direction of play. Liz's smile turned diabolical as it became her turn again; with a flourish, she hit Rosie with a draw-two.

Rosie gifted her a murderous glare. "Really?"

Liz thrust her chin out, grey eyes sparkling with mischief. "Really."

Rosie pouted and reached for two more cards. She tucked them into her already over-flowing hand with a mutinous expression. "Why the hell did we invite you – I'm telling you, Dawn, I hate this girl."

Dawn laughed. "Just shut up and play, Rose."

After four rounds of stunning losses, Rosie declared that she wasn't playing any more. Dawn and Liz, two-for-two, decided to retire gracefully, and Liz leaned over to top up Rosie's wine.

"Sorry, Rosie," she grinned.

"It's bloody 'Miss Bishop' to you, you impudent sprog – and you're *not* sorry."

"Quite right, Miss Bishop," Liz winked, "I'm not. I rather enjoy besting you if I'm honest."

Dawn laughed. "Ooh, them's fighting words! Careful, Liz – you'll kick her into overdrive."

"Pfft. I'm not afraid of 'Miss Bishop', here."

Rosie composed her face into a pristine expression and thumbed her wine glass thoughtfully. "Are you working tomorrow, Liz?"

"What? Uh – yes, I am. Why?"

"Oh, no reason… Only that there's about four hundred wrecked flowers that need picking up on the lawn in the morning."

"There – what?"

"Gift from my ex-husband. I'm feeling generous though, so you can have them."

"You threw them out the window?"

"It was Dawn's idea," Rosie breezed.

Liz rounded on Dawn. "You threw four hundred flowers *out the window*?"

Dawn raised an eyebrow. "You do see what she's doing, don't you, Liz?"

Liz hesitated, and her irritation melted to confusion. "What?"

"She's trying to turn us against each other," Dawn chuckled. "Oldest trick in the book, Rose."

With a sly smile, Rosie tipped her head at Liz. "Working on her, though."

Liz's gaze flashed from one to the other, and then she groaned and clutched at her head. "God, I've had far too much wine to keep up with your psychological warfare."

"Of course," Rosie nodded sagely. "It's well past your bedtime, I'm sure."

"Oh, ha, HA. Don't you old ladies usually get to bed at about six?"

"Careful, now. Using that word *old* could get you killed."

Liz grinned. "I don't doubt it. But actually, it probably is past my bedtime – I'm on early shift tomorrow, so I should get home. Someone's got to pick up all the flowers, after all."

Dawn smiled genially. "Sorry, Liz – seemed like a clever idea at the time. I'll pop down and help you, in the morning."

"No need," Liz said affably. "I'll find a couple of the lads to give me a hand. You're the guest – and my favourite one, at that – so there's definitely no need for you to trouble yourself." She turned to Rosie, her smile widening. "D'you want us to pack them up and send them somewhere, Miss Bishop? Maybe crumple them a little bit, first? Charcoal a few?"

An exuberant laugh tore from Rosie's lips. "Do you know what, Liz…? You can call me Rosie, after all."

# CHAPTER EIGHTEEN

As Dawn returned from locking the door behind Liz's retreat, she mused, "She's lovely, isn't she? Nice of her to bring all the wine. Still got some left. This one's good – it's a Chilean Syrah."

"I'm glad *you're* still sober enough to read the bloody label." Rosie leaned over to squint at the bottle Dawn had just poured from. "Wait – that's a bloody no-name Shiraz!"

Dawn giggled. "At this point, I think we've had enough to pretend."

Rosie thought about that for a second, and then declared, "Fair!" She hefted her glass high, slugged from it, and then announced, "Finest bloody Chilean Syrah I've ever tasted."

Dawn cheered and offered her a wonky toast, and Rosie leaned forward with her glass outstretched. More than a little tipsy, she almost toppled off her stool – sending Dawn into a full fit of hysterics that echoed on Rosie's own lips. For a prolonged moment, laughter reigned, and wine sloshed from teetering glasses to coat the countertop.

"Oh, bollocks!" Dawn wheezed, waving fruitlessly as if that

might magic the mess away. "Pass us a cloth, Rose, quick!"

Clutching at a stitch in her side, Rosie managed to weave across to the kitchen drawer and fish one out. She tossed it towards Dawn, but it opened up mid-flight and lost all momentum, fluttering down into a pathetic heap in the middle of the floor. Dawn sobbed with mirth as she watched it fall, and Rosie found that her legs simply would not support her amusement any more. With a sort of slow-motion rolling movement, she slumped down sideways until she was lying flat on her stomach, and then, determined not to leave her task unfinished, wormed her way across the tiles to retrieve it. Dawn guffawed, beating a fist helplessly against the melamine.

"Stop, Rose!" she gasped, overcome. "Jesus Christ, *stop!*"

But Rosie adamantly continued her sluggish mission, inch by inch, until she reached the cloth — and Dawn was howling with laughter and begging for mercy by the time she finally made it all the way across. Face down, she collapsed at the base of Dawn's stool and valiantly held up one hand to deliver her trophy, but Dawn, destroyed, couldn't quite make her arms work to take it.

They both were unable to move for nearly a full minute and shook with silent, heaving laughter. But being stationary helped, and at last, they calmed enough for Dawn to mop the table and Rosie to roll over onto her back.

"You're such an idiot, Rose, honestly!" Dawn grinned down at her. "Who the hell fetches a cloth like that?"

Rosie quirked an eyebrow. "You know, Dawn, I did the best I could with what I had. You try crossing a room when your legs have dissolved."

Dawn wiped at her streaming eyes. "Get up here, you damned fool."

"No, I can't," Rosie said with an expansive sigh. "I don't have any legs."

"Idiot," Dawn said. But she got off her chair to help Rosie up.

With much bitching, she manhandled Rosie into a standing position and turned her to sit back down on one of the stools.

"No!" Rosie exclaimed. "Not these damned uncomfortable things – couch, please."

Shuffling, cursing, grumbling, Dawn obliged. When they were within range, she spun Rosie and dropped her all at once, so that she flopped down with a thud.

"*Nicely!*" Rosie scolded.

Rolling her eyes, Dawn went to fetch the wine. "Don't spill on here, now," she warned as she handed Rosie a glass, "there's no way in hell red wine will come out of these beige covers."

"I'm not a child."

"But you are *ridiculous*."

Rosie gave her a cheeky wink. "Oh, do sit down, Dawn," she said, flapping her free hand against the cushions. "You're hovering like an overwrought hen."

Muttering, Dawn sank down next to her – and spilt her wine.

"HA!" Rosie crowed.

"Oh, calm your tits!" Dawn scoffed, brushing at the red spot on her shirt. "It's on me, not the bloody couch."

Rosie chortled and sat back, carefully cradling her own glass. After a moment, she mused, "What do you make of that Liz, bloody thinking we're a lesbian couple?"

"Well," Dawn responded impishly, "you *do* keep kissing me."

"That doesn't make us *lesbians*," Rosie snorted. "That's just a bit of fun. I've never had a lesbian fantasy in my life."

Dawn sat forward; her interest piqued. "What, never?"

Rosie fixed her with a blank expression. "Oh, and I suppose you have?"

"Well… yes, I suppose. I mean, I've… thought about it."

"Being with another woman?"

"What else does a lesbian fantasy entail?"

Rosie turned to face her. "Really?"

"Yes – I mean, not enough that I've ever… sort of… *acted* on it, but…" Dawn paused, giving the question her full attention. "I suppose as the years have gone by, and society has changed, it's become more and more integral, more *noticeable*. People don't bat an eyelash, anymore."

"Which they bloody shouldn't, anyway," Rosie said, surprising herself with her own vehemence. "Nothing wrong with love, however it comes about."

Dawn nodded, brooding into her wine. "Exactly. But when we were growing up, it wasn't... acceptable. So, it was very hush-hush, and I never really thought about it. Hardly even knew it existed – I don't think I even *met* any lesbians until I was at least forty."

Rosie tilted her head in thoughtful agreement. "Fair point."

"But when I sort of... consciously realised that there are women who love other women. I don't know. It... sort of makes you curious, don't you think?"

"Does it?"

"Doesn't it?" Dawn countered.

Rosie pensively pursued her lips. "Well, now that we're talking about it... I suppose it does. Just a little, mind."

Dawn giggled. "Just a little? C'mon, Rose – are you honestly telling me you've never noticed another woman? Never... wondered?"

"To be fair, I've spent most of my adult life married, so I've never—" She broke off, suddenly very aware of Dawn's impish expression, the one so unique to her marvellous face.

"You've never?" Dawn prompted.

Her dark eyes glittered intently, and Rosie swallowed a gulp of wine. "I've never thought about it," she said, just managing to stop herself from adding *until recently*.

Dawn thumbed at her wine glass. "I have. Not seriously, mind you – just a little curiosity. Sort of what it might be like." Her lips perked into a mischievous grin. "I always imagined I'd be into blondes, to be honest."

"I think I'd have preferred brunettes."

"Oh, you have a preference, now?" Dawn teased. "I thought you hadn't considered it?"

"I hadn't," Rosie said, quite truthfully. "Well, not consciously, anyway."

"Not consciously?"

Slowly, Rosie nodded. "Yes. But… dark hair has always drawn my eye. So, brunettes."

"Damn," Dawn smirked. "That's me out then. I'm grey as the bloody sky in winter."

"Now you are, yes."

"Should have had me before I greyed out!" Dawn laughed.

Rosie smiled, indulging in the game. "You were a lovely brunette – but I actually think I prefer this silvery look you have going on. It's rather gorgeous, especially when you wear that adorable beanie of yours."

Dawn batted her eyelashes. "Are you flirting with me, Miss Bishop?"

"Is it working?"

"You're pretty shit at it, to be honest."

"Pfft. That's only because I'm not using the full force of my flirtatious abilities on you."

Dawn crowed and almost spilt her wine again. "Flirtatious abilities? *You*…? That'll be the bloody day!"

Rosie put on her most indignant expression. "I can flirt!"

Dawn gave her a sympathetic look and patted the cushion next to her. "Come here, Rose. Let me show you what it means to flirt – because I'm quite sure you have no bloody idea. Come on, now, come here."

Mutinous, Rosie scooted closer.

"Put your glass down and pay attention, now. This is an important life skill I'm about to teach you."

Rosie faced her and sat stiff, adamant that no matter what Dawn did next, she would be utterly, unaffected. "Go on, then," she said.

"Oh, I do love a challenge," Dawn replied, putting her own glass down. "Are you ready?"

Rosie rolled her eyes. "As I'll ever be."

A slow, impish smile spread across Dawn's lips, and she took a breath to begin – but Rosie interrupted immediately.

"Don't do *that*."

"What?"

"That" – Rosie circled an accusing finger at her mouth – "smile-thing you do. Absolutely no good comes from that expression."

Dawn's smile widened, wicked. "You're not afraid, are you?"

"Afraid?" Rosie scoffed. "Of *you*?"

Dawn's grin positively glittered, and she moved forward until she was mere inches away. Beneath the heat of her gaze, Rosie involuntarily leaned back, but Dawn followed her retreat until she was pressed against the couch arm with nowhere else to go.

"You're cheating!" Rosie hissed in an incensed whisper, shrinking beneath Dawn's proximity.

"You *are* afraid!" Dawn smirked, delighted. Softly, she brushed a strand of Rosie's hair away from her cheek. "I can see it in your eyes." She trailed a finger along the fine cheekbone beneath one and stared. "You have beautiful eyes, Rose... I've always imagined I could see my soul reflected in them."

A small, thoughtful frown creased Dawn's brow, then, and her finger glided down towards Rosie's lips. Rosie's mouth parted ever-so-slightly beneath the electricity of her touch, and Dawn hesitated.

"You know... I've always, sort of wondered."

"What?" Rosie croaked, acutely aware of her fingertip, the spinning of her brain, the couch pressed against her back.

Dawn seemed about to say something but then shook her head.

Softly, Rosie goaded, "Now who's afraid?"

Dawn bit at her lip. "It's... not something I can take back."

"Let's hear it, then."

"I've always sort of wondered... what it would be like with you," Dawn finished. She blushed, then, and made to draw her hand away, but Rosie caught it and held her fast.

Her voice floated, barely a whisper. "Is this your version of flirting?"

Dawn, dark eyes unfathomable above the heat of her cheeks, clutched at what the whole point of the joke had been. She gave a nervous laugh and said, "Is it working?"

Absolutely still, Rosie whispered, "It might be."

"It's just the wine," Dawn replied. Almost a plea.

Slowly, Rosie shook her head, and Dawn squeezed her eyes shut.

"But… if it's not the wine…"

For a long moment, they vacillated, but then Rosie pulled her unresisting form down, and Dawn gave a tiny gasp as their lips met. Ignited by a hunger she couldn't begin to fathom, she tangled her fingers through Rosie's hair and kissed her in earnest, and Rosie met her with reckless abandon. But as the heat built between them, Rosie pulled back with a groan and pressed a hand to her spinning head.

"I told you," Dawn said, flatly. "It's the wine."

Rosie's blue eyes flashed open, and her heart bucked at Dawn's hurt expression. Quietly, she reached for her and pulled her down to lie beside her. "No," she disagreed softly. "The wine is making my brain swim, but that's only irritating me that I can't appreciate this moment properly."

A tentative smile crept back onto Dawn's lips. "I do hope *that's* not just the wine talking."

Moving slowly enough to accommodate her throbbing head, Rosie leaned up to kiss her and prove her point.

"Satisfied?" she asked.

"For the moment," Dawn replied.

Rosie dropped back down. "You and I are going to talk about this tomorrow."

"Should I be worried?" Dawn asked, tucking in beside her.

Rosie looped an arm around her to keep her close and opened one eye. "*Are* you worried?"

A soft, shy smile stretched over Dawn's lips. "Actually, no. I'm a little… curious, perhaps… as to what comes next."

Rosie wiggled deeper into the couch, content to sleep there once more. "Your bloody curiosity will be the death of me."

"You started it," Dawn grinned.

Rosie returned a sleepy smile. "I did – and to be honest, I'm not sorry at all."

## CHAPTER NINETEEN

Rosie woke still tangled up in Dawn's arms, and the warmth of her body stretched the entire length of her side, soft and safe and undeniably *real*. Afraid to move, Rosie blinked against a raging headache and tried to make sense of what had happened last night, and Dawn shifted beside her.

"Are you awake?" Dawn whispered

"Mmm," Rosie responded.

Dawn paused for a breath, and then asked, "Are you... all right?"

"All right?" Rosie murmured. She turned her head, searching the depths of Dawn's beautiful brown eyes for some clue as to how the hell to answer that. "If you're referring to my hangover, then no."

Dawn grimaced. "You know I'm not talking about that. I'm talking about what happened. Between us. Are you regretting?"

Rosie frowned and trailed tentative fingers down Dawn's cheek. "The amount of wine we drank, yes. What happened, no. But Dawn..."

"Mmm?" Dawn breathed, leaning into her touch.

"What is this? What does it mean?"

Dawn smiled softly. "Why does everything have to be black and white with you, Rose? Why can't it just be shades of grey with a dash of the unknown?"

"Because that *scares* me. Christ... it's *you*, Dawn."

"So?"

"So!" Rosie half sat up, indignant. "That means there's forty years of friendship riding on this malarkey! What if – what if it... ends badly?"

"And what if it's wonderful?"

Rosie stuttered to silence. Quietly, Dawn wrapped her into the safety of her embrace and, helpless against the surge of butterflies in her chest, Rosie melted into her. With a strange sense of desperation, she held tight – as if Dawn might fade away at any moment.

Softly, Dawn murmured, "It's all right, Rose."

"What if it's not?" Rosie said, her voice wavering with barely contained emotion. "I've been so scared of this moment for so long now—"

"Wait a minute." A teasing smile played across Dawn's lips in the dark. "Are you telling me you *planned* this?"

Rosie managed to scoff. "Of course not."

"But you've thought about it?"

"Yes, damn it – all right? – I've thought about it. Since the bloody minute you walked into the bloody room at the start of this *bloody* trip, I've thought about it!"

Dawn leaned back to look at her, and a soft curiosity enlivened her dark eyes. "Care to elaborate?"

"I don't know," Rosie said, shaking her head. "I don't know what I'm saying, really..."

"Well, what *do* you know?" said Dawn. "Let's start there."

A small frown creased Rosie's brow, and she cleared her throat. "I *do* know that your sudden appearance gave me butterflies – and I'm not usually prone to butterflies, Dawn."

Dawn smiled wryly. "Which is odd, considering your fascination with them. Go on, what else?"

"That morning after the first night, when I couldn't find you…" Rosie's voice dropped to the merest whisper. "I've never been so terrified. I thought… I thought maybe I was losing my mind, that I'd imagined you – and I've never missed you so much in my entire life as I did at that moment. The thought of you being gone it…" She gave a helpless shrug. "And after, when we fell so easily back into the stride of our friendship – I can't believe how long I've lived without you. Everything about you, you're just… You *matter*, Dawn – more than anyone else in the world."

"Not a hard thing to achieve, to be fair," Dawn quipped. "There's hardly any competition what with your lack of friends."

Rosie scowled. "Stop it – I'm serious, now – this is serious. The last time I *noticed* you like this—" She broke off behind her second accidental confession, and Dawn raised an eyebrow.

"This isn't the first time?"

Rosie dipped her head and blushed. "No," she sighed. "The first time was when you walked into my flat a million years ago and introduced yourself as my new flatmate."

Dawn's eyes widened. "Really, Rose? God, why didn't you ever say anything?"

Rosie scoffed, and her awkwardness fled. "What was I supposed to say? 'Oh, hello, my name is Rosie, and, holy tits, you're beautiful'? That'd have gone down a treat, I'm sure."

Dawn snorted. "Mmm. Could have been quite awkward if I'd told you that you made my heart beat a little faster, too."

"You what?"

"Probably why we didn't get on so well in the beginning," Dawn winked. "Caught off-guard by the magnetism."

"No, *that's* because you were loud and overbearing and obnoxious."

"Or because you were a stuck-up, posh prude without a single interesting hobby." Dawn grinned. "Seriously, though, since we're being honest – it's true that I noticed you, too. You're a wonderful person, Rose – inside and out. Always have been. I've never met anyone quite like you – and I think I have enough years of life experience now to say that with some authority, since I've met *quite* a few people."

Rosie's face darkened. "But it doesn't matter, Dawn. It didn't then, and it shouldn't now. I'm not *gay* – and neither are you."

"Does there have to be a label?" Dawn asked.

Rosie floundered. "Well, no, but…" She shook her head, trying to clear the mess of wayward thoughts competing inside her mind.

"We've always got on famously, haven't we?" Dawn said. "I've loved you dearly for years, you know."

"Well, yes – but it's always been platonic."

"Has it?"

Rosie's pitch rose a couple of notches. "Hasn't it?"

"Certainly doesn't seem that way anymore," Dawn smirked. "Good Lord, what have you made of me, Rose?"

"ME!" Rosie approached a shriek. "Don't you peg this on me, you plonker!"

"You kissed me first," Dawn pointed out.

"YOU KISSED ME BACK!"

"And you *liked* it."

Rosie spluttered, cornered. She could hardly deny *that*.

"See," Dawn said with a twinkle in her eye. "C'mon, Rose… Is it really so terrible if two people, who have already loved each other for so many years, maybe fall in love?"

Rosie's mouth opened and closed, soundless. After a moment, she whispered, "Is that… what this is?"

Dawn smiled in solidarity with her confusion. "I don't know."

"What *do* you know?" Rosie snapped, vacillating between possibility and panic.

"I know that I enjoy your company," Dawn said, "and that your sense of humour matches mine *perfectly* –"

"I'm not sure *that's* a good thing."

"– and being around you is fun and easy. I feel the most... *me*... when I'm with you – and that's a rare thing, Rose. It's true that I've never really considered myself to have any inclination towards being attracted to women, but... I don't know – seeing you again was like being hit with a cricket bat. Seeing you, standing in the doorway, with your beautiful blue eyes and signature obnoxious expression, well... I *noticed*." Dawn paused to clear her throat. "And it rocked me. I felt like I'd been searching for something for twenty years to fill a void I didn't quite know I had, and then suddenly... there you were. But I didn't dare say a bloody word, for fear of what you'd think of me."

Rosie stared at her with a terrified expression, unable to quite believe her ears in hearing her own feelings come directly out of Dawn's mouth.

Dawn dipped her gaze, a little mortified by her confession. "I know, it's crazy."

Rosie frowned until Dawn looked up again. "It *is* crazy. We're sixty, Dawn – old women don't bloody lark about like lovesick teenagers!"

"Yes, we're sixty," Dawn agreed, searching Rosie's startled blue eyes for the truth of her thoughts, "and definitely not lovesick teenagers. This is entirely something else – I don't quite know what, but—"

"It's madness, is what it is," Rosie insisted.

Dawn's mouth quirked. "We've always been a bit mad, Rose. Luckily, your madness matches mine."

"I'm not sure that's *lucky*," Rosie huffed. "You do bring out the worst in me, you know."

"I know, but it's fun."

Rosie sighed, surrendering, and pulled her close. "What am I going to do with you?"

Dawn grinned wickedly. "I suppose we'll find out, won't we?"

Rosie pushed her off the couch, and, laughing, Dawn managed to roll sideways onto her feet. "C'mon," she said with a wink, "we'd better get down to breakfast."

"Why do all things end with your stomach?" Rosie asked, scowling as she heaved herself upright.

"Because there's a chocolate croissant downstairs with my name on it."

Rosie tilted her head back with an exaggerated moan, and Dawn's impish smile suddenly faded to a curious expression. Distracted by the soft stretch of Rosie's neck beneath the sweep of her blonde hair, she moved closer.

Rosie froze mid-theatrics. "What are you doing?"

"I just… want to try something…" Dawn murmured.

"What?" Rosie asked, narrowing her eyes.

"Hold still a second."

Tentative, Dawn laced her arms around Rosie's waist, and Rosie stiffened. She was acutely aware of the light pressure of Dawn's hands against the small of her back, and her heart fluttered, erratic. Dawn hesitated, but then, on a small tide of bravado, leaned in and pressed her lips to the side of Rosie's neck. Rosie tipped her head sideways in involuntary response, and a tiny groan escaped her. Her hands caught fistfuls of the back of Dawn's shirt as Dawn trailed slow, fiery kisses down the sensitive skin to her collarbone. Powerless against the roaring in her ears, Rosie arched her back to press up against her.

"Stop it," she gasped, pulling Dawn closer in an attempt to crush the flutter inside her. "Christ, Dawn, stop…"

Dawn, her breaths coming a little short, trailed kisses back up Rosie's throat and along her tilted jaw, and Rosie couldn't quite contain the moan that tore from her lips.

Dawn abruptly pulled back. "Jesus," she whispered, squeezing her eyes tight shut against the flood Rosie's mewling ignited.

Weak-kneed, Rosie clung to her, heart hammering like it might break free of her ribs. She hid her face against the inset of Dawn's shoulder as tried to catch her breath, doing her best to calm her traitorous body.

After a long moment, Dawn commented, "*Well*. That was a little more intense than I'd anticipated."

Rosie lifted her head and glared. "I think that's quite enough experimenting for one day, *thank you*."

Dawn grinned. "I'm not going to argue, there. Who knew I'd have such an effect on you?"

Rosie made a derisive sound and pushed her off. "For the love of— Go! Go and get changed!"

Smirking, Dawn snatched up a set of fresh clothes and high-tailed it to the bathroom. In her wake, Rosie perched on the side of the couch and drew a series of careful breaths. She ran a finger absently along her throat, tracing her still-burning skin, and frowned at her inadvertent responsiveness to Dawn's advance. She hadn't felt like this since – well, she couldn't remember when actually. She'd long thought herself well past the ability to be turned on? Was that the term she wanted? But her assumption was definitely wrong. A small smile stretched; it was the strangest, most unexpectedly delightful thing.

Dawn reappeared, fresh and dressed for the day. "What are you smiling about?" she asked as she breezed into the kitchenette.

Rosie quickly composed her face back into its customary glower. "I'm not."

"If you say so," Dawn smirked, digging in the cupboard for a chocolate.

"Oh, shut up," Rosie snapped, getting up to find something clean to wear. "And don't eat that – we're going for breakfast in a minute."

She rifled through her small cupboard with unnecessary vehemence, and Dawn watched her with surreptitious amusement. Finally, Rosie found a top and slacks she fancied, tucked them viciously under her arm and – with a dirty look in Dawn's direction – made for the bathroom.

With an air of indignant finality, she slammed the door shut, and Dawn laughed around a mouthful of chocolate.

## CHAPTER TWENTY

As they left the room to head down to the breakfast buffet, Rosie growled, "Not a word about any of this, Dawn."

"Who would I even tell, Rose?" Dawn replied with a wounded expression.

"I mean it," Rosie snapped. "Don't get funny."

Dawn snickered, then masked it beneath an unconvincing cough as Rosie glared at her. "I won't, Rose," she said, holding her hands up.

Rosie judged her sincere enough to proceed. "All right," she said as she hesitated in the dining room doorway. "Just act normal."

Dawn pushed past her. "We haven't broken any laws."

Rosie yelped and scampered after her as she strode across to the buffet.

"Morning!" Dawn said brightly to the servers behind the counter. "I'll have one of everything, please!"

Rosie grabbed a plate, too, but kept her gaze averted as she moved down the line. Vaguely, she pointed at a couple of things and tried not to draw too much attention to herself.

"Morning, Rosie!" Liz said from beside her elbow – nearly

making her jump out of her skin. "Sorted out your flower problem!"

"What? Oh, thanks," Rosie mumbled, avidly staring at a pile of fritters.

"Would you like one of those, Miss?" prompted the server opposite her, who'd given up waiting for her to ask for one.

"Hmm?" Rosie looked up, accidentally made eye contact, and blushed. Hurriedly, she mumbled, "Oh, no, thank you," and retreated to find a table.

Liz watched her go with a bemused expression, then shrugged and scooted to catch up with Dawn. "Hi, Dee!"

Dawn smiled, loading her plate with delicious, sugary things. "Morning, Liz – did you win with the spectacular mess on the lawn? Sorry, again, about that."

Liz tucked a swathe of fiery hair behind one ear and winked conspiratorially. "Spic-and-span out there. Not a petal to be seen." She dropped her voice, then, and added, "Hey – is something the matter with Rosie? She doesn't seem herself, this morning."

Dawn glanced over to where Rosie had found a small table out of the way and sat doggedly staring into her meagre food. "Give us another one of those," Dawn said to the youngster over the counter, "for her, over there." She jerked her head in Rosie's direction, and the server obliged with a polite smile as Dawn turned back to Liz. "She *isn't* quite herself, this morning, actually. Didn't sleep too well – lots on her mind, maybe."

Liz nodded sympathetically. "I'm sure. Can't be easy having your ex-husband keep hassling. What's his problem, anyway?"

Dawn's easy smile vanished – she'd forgotten about Richard, over the course of the events since yesterday evening. "He's just a wanker," she clipped. "No cure for that, I'm afraid."

"Shame," Liz said, glancing towards Rosie. "She's lovely, really – even though she hides it spectacularly well – and she doesn't deserve the likes of that bastard. Hope she finds someone to treat her better."

"She will," Dawn replied, stoic.

Liz gave her a bright smile. "And in the meantime, she's got a great mate like you looking out for her." She glanced at the growing line of guests along the counter. "Right, I better get back to work – just popped over to say hi! See you later, Dee!"

She skipped off before Dawn could utter another word, and Dawn grabbed one more chocolate croissant before heading over to Rosie. She deposited her plate and pulled up a chair next to her, and Rosie threw her head up with a murderous expression.

"Sit on the other side of the table!"

Dawn paused, and then exaggeratedly fluttered her eyelashes. "But how am I supposed to hold your hand underneath it, then?"

Rosie gave an explosive huff and got to her feet. Dragging her chair around, she sat stiffly opposite. "Stop it. People are giving us funny looks."

"They are now, yes," Dawn said, unperturbed. "Thanks to the scene you just made with the chair."

Rosie scowled into her food. "Let them bloody look, then."

Dawn perused the room. "Aww, they're over it already. Obviously, we're just not that interesting."

Rosie said nothing, viciously impaling a piece of sausage with her fork, and Dawn watched her for a long moment.

"Relax, Rose," she said at last, "nobody's any the wiser. Here, I brought you a blueberry muffin – since you completely bypassed them in your rush to come and hide in the corner."

"Oh." Rosie's glower softened. "Thanks – I love blueberry muffins."

"I know. Listen, now, Rose. It's all right to be feeling out-of-sorts – God knows, I am—"

"You're out-of-sorts?" Rosie looked up, surprised.

"Honestly, Rose…" Dawn smiled. "This is new and nerve-wracking for me, too, you know."

Rosie frowned, disbelieving. "You don't look out-of-sorts in the slightest."

"That's because I have excellent self-control – perhaps I should give you some pointers?"

"Don't patronize me."

Dawn laughed softly. "C'mon, finish your breakfast and let's get a move on before we're late."

Rosie narrowed her eyes over her muffin. "Late for what?"

Dawn huffed in exasperation. "There's a whole itinerary pasted on the fridge, Rose."

"Is there?"

"Honestly, I give up with you."

Rosie smirked despite herself and went back to her breakfast. As they indulged in the really rather excellent food, Rosie slowly relaxed, and by the time they were finally done, her anxiety had almost completely faded. At last, Dawn scraped back her chair, pocketed the last chocolate croissant to nibble on during the coach ride, and ushered Rosie out the door.

Wet gravel crunched underfoot as they crossed the driveway, and they adjusted their scarves against the snap in the air. It was drizzling, but not enough to dampen their enthusiasm.

"Where to this time?" Rosie asked amiably.

"Beatrix Potter's house," Dawn said. "Thought it might be nice to take a look at that."

Rosie smiled. "I do love Peter Rabbit."

Dawn let her precede down the aisle of the coach, and they settled themselves onto their usual seats at the rear. "More of a Tom Kitten fan, myself."

"You've always been a cat person."

"Are you insinuating that I'm an old cat lady?" Dawn said, affronted.

"Do you *own* any cats?"

"No," Dawn chortled. "I'd love to, though."

The coach was quite empty today, and, as it rumbled away from Greenside, Rosie surreptitiously reached for Dawn's hand.

She cradled it in her lap, her own fingers loosely tucked through Dawn's, and Dawn caught her eye.

"What?" Rosie said, as if she were oblivious to what she'd done.

"Nothing," Dawn smiled. She leaned back contentedly and watched the slow progress of rivulets questing down the window. "Shame about the weather today, isn't it?"

"The *weather*?" Rosie snarked. "*That's* what you're going with? Mmm – very discreet, you pillock."

Dawn laughed. "It *is* bloody shite, though."

"Proper English, today."

"Bloody *lovely*."

"It's sort of… cosy, though," Rosie offered.

Dawn shifted ever-so-slightly so that her shoulder was pressed against Rosie's, and her sigh was agreement enough.


They spent most of the drive in comfortable silence, content to watch the misty landscape beyond the windows, and were almost disappointed when the coach finally pulled into a tiny car park. There, they were ushered off, and the coach – so as not to block anyone into the little space – trundled away to park somewhere else and wait for them. Their small group was checked in at the booking office, and then Dawn and Rosie let the others pull ahead on the two-hundred-metre stroll to Hill Top House itself. All along the road verges, daffodils lifted their defiant heads to the dreary day, and Rosie spared a smile for them as she nudged Dawn to notice their exuberance. At the top, they passed through the garden gate onto a slate-flagged pathway that led to the front porch.

"Shame we didn't come in another month or two," Rosie said, looking about. "It's a bit early for most of the flowers, I think."

"The primroses are pretty, though," Dawn said, pointing to a multicoloured patch of them.

Herbaceous shrubbery lined the edges of the path, and ahead, a guide was explaining how the gardens were a haphazard mixture of flowers, fruits, herbs, and vegetables, carefully restored in just the way Beatrix herself had planted it, more than a hundred years ago. Rosie pointed out a beehive nestled under a large, slate slab in the garden wall, and they admired the attention to detail in the Gardener's efforts to maintain the feeling of authenticity.

"It's such a lovely garden," Dawn said, as they drew towards the building. "We really must come back and see it in summer."

A large wisteria dominated the front of the house, with rose bushes guarding the door and a Japanese quince over the porch, and the guide mentioned that in a few weeks, they would put forward a riotous display of blue, white, pink and red.

"It's smaller than I thought it'd be," Rosie commented.

"It's sweet, though," Dawn said as they entered the house. "I'd happily live somewhere like this – peaceful and out of the way." She stopped just inside, blinking. "Although, it's a little dark in here, isn't it?"

"Struggling without your glasses, are you?" Rosie quipped.

"Perhaps I'll borrow yours," Dawn shot back.

But their vision adjusted, and the guide informed them that the house was exactly as it had been when Beatrix Potter herself had lived there. Everything inside had been carefully chosen by the writer to decorate her sanctuary, and she'd done a grand job of bringing her personality to life in each room. Dawn and Rosie followed the group around the house, straggling at the back.

"I don't think this is *exactly* how it was when Beatrix lived here…" Dawn commented to Rosie in a low voice.

"What do you mean?"

"Well, for starters, I'm quite sure I've never been in anyone's house that's this *clean*."

Rosie choked back a laugh before it could echo through the quiet rooms. "Shut up, you nitwit – you're going to get us into trouble!"

Dawn grinned impishly as the guide looked over to where they were standing, and then pretended to be wholly absorbed by the decorative plates mounted on the kitchen wall as he came back towards them.

Mistaking the sincerity of her interest, he followed her gaze and said, "Those were painted by Beatrix's father, Rupert Potter."

"Ooo, lovely," Dawn said, nodding with appropriate fascination.

Rosie snorted into her sleeve to hide her laughter and had to pretend she was having a coughing fit. Dawn patted her back in an exaggerated fashion and pouted at the guide.

"She's fine," she said, shaking her head sympathetically. "Allergies, you know."

A confused frown crinkled the guide's face for a moment, but then he reinstated his polite smile and moved on with the tour. When he was safely out of earshot again, an explosive snigger escaped Rosie.

"Shh!" Dawn scolded, elbowing her. "Don't irritate Teacher!"

Rosie batted her away to a safe distance and forced herself to look at something – anything – other than Dawn's mischievous grin. But the pictures on the wall were no match for the ludicrous faces Dawn was pulling behind the guide's back, and Rosie failed utterly to compose herself. A snort-laugh precedented a spiralling descent into manic laughter, and then the guide returned smartly with a disapproving frown etched onto his surly face.

"Oh, bollocks!" Dawn hissed, grabbing Rosie by the arm. She tried to tow her to a safe distance, but Rosie was overcome, tears streaming and knees too weak to move.

"Is there a problem, ladies?" the guide said. His mouth was sour – as if he'd honestly never seen anything so ridiculous in all his long years, and certainly hadn't the patience for it. Rosie, looking up with ill-timing, doubled over beneath a fresh wave of giggles.

"No, no – no problem," Dawn said, widening her eyes to a picture of innocence. "Sorry, she's just – not feeling too well today."

"Mentally?" The guide tilted his head, unimpressed.

"Wow," Dawn smirked at Rosie, "this guy missed sensitivity training day." She drew herself up. "I'll have you know, Sir, that manic laughter is not a disorder! How very dare you speak to my friend like that!"

"I'm very sorry," the guide said – clearly not sorry at all – "but you are disturbing the rest of the group. I'm going to have to ask you to step outside and perhaps take a moment to compose yourselves."

"C'mon, Dawn," Rosie gasped, tugging weakly on her sleeve. "I could do with some bloody air."

Dawn gave the guide one more miffed expression – as if the entire thing were his fault – and then towed Rosie out of the house. They tumbled through the door into the gardens, face first into a blast of damp, chilly air that rouged their cheeks and filled them with exuberance, and their impish laughter echoed.

"Stuffy old git," Dawn chortled.

"He was rather, wasn't he?" Rosie cackled. She looped an arm through Dawn's, and they meandered down the garden path.

"There's that lovely pub just down the road," Dawn said. "Shall we go have a look?"

"What pub?"

"The one just past the booking office – saw it on the way in."

"Trust you to notice the bloody pub," Rosie said with a roll of her eyes, but she gestured flamboyantly for Dawn to lead the way.

## CHAPTER TWENTY-ONE

With their coat hoods pulled up against the cold drizzle, they ambled back down towards the car park, turned left beyond, and found the Tower Bank Arms right where Dawn had said it would be. Over the front door, a small wooden portico boasted a quaint antique clock, and Dawn grinned as Rosie pointed it out.

"Ooo, goody! Just in time for the lunch menu!"

Rosie rolled her eyes. "I was pointing out the *clock*, not the time. It's only been two hours since we had breakfast – surely you're not hungry again already?"

"Not for a full meal, obviously," Dawn said with a wink. "Just dessert. Something hot and sweet would go down a treat, day like today."

Rosie, feeling the cold a bit, couldn't disagree. They stepped inside, and a smiling waiter came to greet them.

"Table for two, ladies?" he said.

"Yes please," Dawn smiled back. "By the fire if you can."

"Of course, this way."

When their server returned with a pair of menus, Dawn gleefully ordered a warm chocolate brownie with berries and double Jersey ice cream.

"Ice cream?" Rosie said, distastefully. "Too bloody cold for ice cream."

"The brownie's warmed," Dawn said, "so the ice cream is just sauce."

"I'll have the sticky toffee pudding," Rosie said to the waiter. "With cream, not ice cream."

Dawn pouted. "I'd have eaten your ice cream."

"You're getting your own," Rosie pointed out.

"What are we getting to drink? Fancy a milkshake?"

"C'mon, now – that's *too* much bloody cream. I wouldn't mind a coffee, though."

Dawn handed the menus back to the waiter and gifted him a dazzling smile. "Two coffees, please – dash of whiskey in each."

He grinned back. "Coming right up."

As he disappeared into the kitchens, Rosie turned a disapproving expression on Dawn. "Dash of *whiskey*?"

"Just to warm up, Rose."

"It's eleven in the morning! That's what the bloody fire's for."

But the waiter returned with their cheeky coffees, and Rosie drank hers without complaint. Shortly after, the desserts came, and Dawn enjoyed hers with enough exaggerated sound effects to make Rosie blush.

"Will you stop it?" Rosie said, stifling a giggle. She glanced furtively around the room before wolfing her own dessert to hide her discomfort.

"Mmm...' Dawn moaned. "Oh, mmm – oh, GOD, that's to die for."

Rosie went bright red, caught between being mortified and finding it ridiculously funny. "Stop it, Dawn – people are starting to look at us funny!"

Dawn gifted her a chocolate-coated grin. "I can't help it if this brownie is just the most sinfully delicious thing I've ever tasted."

Rosie abandoned her sticky toffee and hid behind the wine list, sniggering. "This is why I never go out with you in public!"

"What! I'll have you know, I'm the *pinnacle* of respectability in public."

Rosie lowered her wine list half an inch. "Except when there's chocolate involved."

"Got me there," Dawn agreed sagely. She took another giant mouthful around a promiscuous moan, just as Rosie caught the eye of an amused man making his way towards them. Immediately, she bridled, and her face darkened to a thunderous scowl.

"What are you staring at?" she snarled at him. "Can't a girl bloody enjoy a bit of dessert in peace around here?"

But the man's eyes twinkled and, unperturbed, he continued his approach until he stood over their table. "Madams," he said, his voice polite and quiet around an effortless smile, "meant no disrespect – I was merely coming to see how your meal was. I'm Brian, the manager – and may I just say" – he turned his brilliant smile on Dawn – "I don't believe anyone has ever enjoyed one of our brownies with quite such gusto."

Dawn beamed – but couldn't say anything for the mouthful of brownie still puffing out her cheeks – and Rosie relaxed enough to answer in her stead. "The desserts were rather lovely," she said with a tentative smile. "I'm sure you couldn't tell, but my friend here, especially, enjoyed hers."

Brian gave a genial nod, and asked, "May I get you anything else?"

Rosie raised her eyebrows at Dawn and then tilted her head at Brian. "I don't suppose we can get another of those brownies to go?"

His smile broadened. "Of course. I'll get one boxed up for you."

"Thank you – and then we'll have the bill, please," Rosie said.

Brian strode off to see about it, and Dawn reached for Rosie's hand over the table. "*Ohmygod*" – she swallowed the last crumbs – "a brownie to go?!"

"You're welcome," Rosie smiled. She rescued her hand from Dawn's sticky clutches. "God, you've got chocolate *everywhere*."

Smirking, Dawn made a show of licking her fingers one by one, and Rosie rolled her eyes and shooed her from the table.

"For heaven's sake – go and wash up. They'll never let you back on the bus looking like that."

Dawn sauntered off to do so, and Rosie paid for their lunch when Brian returned with the bill and the takeaway brownie. By the time Dawn returned, Rosie was standing with her back to the fire and waiting to go. She turned to link an arm through Dawn's and giggled as she noticed a smudge on her friend's cheek. Grabbing a serviette off their table, she attacked Dawn's face with it.

"Hold still, you," she admonished. Dawn yelped and struggled, but Rosie held fast until not a spot of chocolate remained.

Dawn scowled as Rosie finally released her. "Damn it, Rose! Maybe I was saving that for later!"

"Sure you were," Rosie laughed. "C'mon, now, hurry up – we'll miss the bus back in a minute."

Dawn leaned back as Rosie pushed her towards the door. "Do you have my brownie?"

Rosie groaned. "Do you even have to ask?"

"Thanks, dove," Dawn grinned, giving in suddenly to Rosie's pushing. Rosie missed a step at the abrupt lack of resistance, but Dawn caught an arm through hers and steadied her along. "Don't drop that brownie," she warned.

Rosie made a rude noise and wobbled the box, but they made it outside without incident. A blast of cold air hit them upon exit, and they stopped to fasten their coats properly, hoods up against the biting wind.

"God, that's turned nasty," Rosie said between chattering teeth.

"Hasn't it?" Dawn agreed.

Leaning into the wind with their heads down against fat, splattering drops, they quickened their pace back around to the car park. Mercifully, the coach was ready and waiting, and they hustled inside, dropping heavily into their seats at the back as it pulled away.

"I hope my brownie's all right," Dawn said.

Rosie groaned wholeheartedly. "I'm starting to regret asking for the bloody thing. Honestly, if I hear one more bloody word about this bloody—"

The coach lurched around a corner, and she dropped the box. Dawn yelled, leaping frantically for it as it plopped against the floor. White-faced, Rosie watched her trembling hands retrieve it, and they both held their breath as Dawn lifted the cover. The brownie was a little battered, with chocolate icing smeared across the lid of the box, but it was intact. Dawn gave a heady sigh of relief.

"Honestly," Rosie said crossly as she settled her shaking hands into her lap, "anyone would think I dropped a *child*, the way you're carrying on."

"You're comparing a chocolate brownie to a *child*?"

"With your bloody reaction, it might as well have been!"

"You're completely off the mark, Rose – I'd never have dived so fast if it wasn't chocolate."

"God." Rosie gave an explosive huff and thumped back against her seat. "You are impossible."

Dawn smiled knowingly. "The brownie's fine, Rose."

Rosie bit at her lip and glanced sideways. "Is it?"

"Yes, dear. No harm, no foul."

"I'd have been miffed if it'd come out the box."

"I know – would've completely ruined your heroic moment of getting it for me in the first place."

Rosie scowled in an attempt to contest a faint pink tinge colouring her cheeks. "It was an afterthought, Dawn – I'm honestly not that concerned about it."

Dawn shouldered against her with a bright smile, cradling the brownie on her lap. Content to let Rosie deny being thoughtful, she turned her gaze out the window for the ride home and watched the rain falling in earnest beyond the glass. Rosie settled, too – after surreptitiously checking the box was indeed secure in Dawn's hands – and stifled a shiver as the temperature dropped by degrees. With a groan, she shifted in her seat, stretching her legs a little to loosen her sore joints.

"What's the matter?" Dawn asked.

"Just the old knees, you know," Rosie said with a rueful smile. "Always more noticeable when it gets cold – all this chilly rain, my bloody knees are stiffening up."

Dawn nodded sagely. "My back's a bit achy, too. But we'll be home just now, and then we'll have a piping hot bath and curl up on the couch with a duvet."

"I'd kill to watch an episode of Flog It."

Dawn gave a genial smile. "Didn't they axe that show?"

Rosie grimaced. "Don't remind me."

"How about a horror movie, then?"

"A *horror* movie? Are you out of your mind?"

"C'mon," Dawn grinned, "it'll be fun."

Rosie snorted. "It will not."

"We'll find something mild," Dawn continued, warming up to her idea. "Just a couple of jump-scares, maybe – nothing too violent—"

"I'm going to show you *violence*, in a minute," Rosie said darkly. "Starting with a freak accident happening to that brownie of yours."

Dawn's eyes flew wide, and she clutched the box protectively to her chest. "You wouldn't!"

"I dropped it once," Rosie warned. "I can drop it again." She sat forward, menacing. "No. Horror. Movies. Or the brownie gets it!"

"All right!" Dawn giggled. "No horror movies – we'll just see what's on the telly, shall we?"

"That, we can do."

Dawn grinned and cuddled her brownie close.

# CHAPTER TWENTY-TWO

When they reached their room, Dawn carefully unpacked the brownie into a small bowl, and Rosie stared wistfully into the kitchenette.

"Are you going to share that?" she asked.

"Heavens, no," Dawn replied, returning with the morsel held reverently out in front of her.

"Why have you got two spoons, then?"

"I wanted you to *feel* as if you're included in this experience," Dawn said. She handed Rosie one, plopped down onto the couch beside her, and lifted the bowl to inhale the heavenly chocolate scent. Rosie leaned over to catch a whiff, but Dawn pivoted ever-so-slightly so that she couldn't reach it.

Rosie sat back with a small sigh and stared sadly down at her empty spoon.

"Don't pull that face," Dawn accused, frowning. "You *know* how I am with chocolate." Rosie's lip trembled, and Dawn's scowl darkened. "Damn it, Rose. Just one bloody taste, then." She held out the bowl and averted her gaze as if she couldn't bear to watch.

Rosie caught the edge and helped herself to a huge scoop.

Dawn glanced sideways, and her mouth tightened to a grim line at the size of the helping. The spoon hovered for a long moment, and Rosie licked her lips so excessively that Dawn had to look away again. Rosie grinned at her stricken sigh but then gave her a nudge. "Here you go. Do you really think I'd eat your brownie?"

A tremulous smile stretched across Dawn's pale lips, and Rosie handed her the spoon.

"I just wanted to see if you'd give me any," she smirked as Dawn practically inhaled the offering. "I'm not honestly going to deprive you."

Dawn sighed and mumbled through a mouthful of chocolate, "S'true love, Rose."

Rosie scoffed, reaching for the remote. "Don't get funny."

She flicked through the channels until a muffled yelp from Dawn stopped her on a movie with a large, grumpy-looking green ogre dominating the screen.

Dawn swallowed quickly, and then exclaimed, "Let's watch this! I *love* Shrek."

"It says it's Shrek Two."

"Even better! That's my favourite one – the fairy godmother reminds me of you."

Rosie snorted. "There's nothing fairy-godmother-y about *me*."

"Wow," Dawn said, hoisting an eyebrow. "The resemblance really is uncanny."

Rosie pursed her lips, unconvinced, but settled comfortably next to Dawn and resigned herself to watching the animation. It was better than a bloody horror movie, anyway. Dawn polished off the rest of her brownie, dumped her bowl on the side table, and then sat back with a contented sigh. After a moment, she yawned, stretched magnificently, and casually dropped an arm around Rosie's shoulders.

Rosie gave a long-suffering blink. "Did you just…?"

Dawn's eyes flashed mischief, and she gave Rosie's shoulder a cheeky squeeze. "Slick as greased lightning, babe."

"That was the *most* painfully obvious manoeuvre I have *ever* had the misfortune to witness."

Dawn grinned. "Secretly, you think it's adorable."

"Shush, now, and watch the bloody movie." The waspish expression on Rosie's face was almost undermined by the smile tugging at her lips. She leaned into Dawn's side and turned her gaze rigidly to the TV – to avoid letting on that she did, indeed, find it extremely endearing. Dawn sighed, content, and as the film commanded their attention at last, she toyed idly with a strand of Rosie's hair.

After a moment, Rosie tilted her head. "That's rather nice."

"Hmm?"

"That. Whatever you're doing to my hair. It's nice."

"Oh," Dawn said, and her fingers came to an awkward halt as she became aware of their movement. She lifted her arm down from Rosie's shoulders. "I hadn't realised I was doing anything, to be honest."

Rosie's bright blue gaze accosted her, and Dawn inexplicably blushed.

"Well, don't stop," Rosie said. Her voice was low – a challenge.

Dawn swallowed. "It's… a bit of an awkward angle…"

Rosie tilted her chin. After a long beat – in which she appeared to be weighing up her options – she half-raised an eyebrow, shifted over, and pulled her legs up onto the couch. With an air of finality, she reclined and placed her head firmly onto Dawn's lap.

"Better?" she asked, closing her eyes as she settled.

Dawn sat perfectly still for a moment, but then, tentative, twined her fingers through Rosie's tresses – and elicited a soft groan from Rosie's lips. Dawn shuddered in involuntary response, and Rosie's eyes flashed back open.

"What's wrong?" she demanded.

Dawn took a shallow breath, staring down with a beseeching look. "I don't think" – she swallowed – "I don't think you can do that, Rose. Not anymore."

Rosie frowned. "What do you mean?"

"I *mean*, my heart just about stopped when you did."

"Did *what*?"

Dawn ran her fingers through Rosie's hair again – drawing forth another involuntary moan – and she inhaled sharply. "*That*, Rose. You can't do *that*."

"I can't help it," Rosie purred playfully as she tilted her head back. "Mmm... God, that's lovely..."

"Stop it," Dawn whispered.

Another soft flurry slipped from Rosie's lips, and Dawn's hands tightened through her hair. The pressure of her grip made Rosie look up again – and finally notice the faint heat across her cheeks, the slight parting of her lips. Rosie's teasing response died in her throat, and she found herself locked beneath the confounded intensity of Dawn's gaze.

"Oh, um – sorry," she whispered, suddenly self-conscious. She tucked her chin in to stifle her blushing, but prone as she was, she had nowhere to hide.

Dawn's fingers clutched tight a moment more, but then she relinquished her grip and cleared her throat. "You're going to miss the movie."

Rosie couldn't seem to move, transfixed as she was by the depth of Dawn's hesitant gaze. Neither of them paid any attention to the TV.

"Bugger the movie," Rosie whispered. She sat up and swivelled closer, and a startled gasp escaped Dawn as she stopped half an inch away.

They sat perfectly still, each gauging the other's resolve.

"Well?" Rosie said at last.

Dawn sighed forward, claiming her unresisting lips in a delicate kiss. Slowly, it intensified, and Rosie shifted to push Dawn down against the couch. They reclined together, but the edge was too close, and Dawn listed dangerously sideways. She latched onto Rosie, who tugged her to safety before she could fall.

"Sorry," Rosie sniggered.

Dawn tucked herself more firmly onto the couch with a wry expression. "Dumping me on the floor *might* just ruin the moment."

Rosie grinned. "Shut up."

She laced her hands through Dawn's hair, smothering protests beneath her questing mouth, and, despite her momentary indignance, Dawn melted into her embrace. The kiss deepened, gently experimental, until Dawn absently twined one leg around Rosie's. Startled by the contact, Rosie jerked her head up.

Dawn stiffened beneath her. "Sorry," she whispered meekly.

Softly, Rosie shook her head. "Surprised me, is all."

A small smile curved Dawn's lips, and Rosie leaned down to kiss it, unresisting this time as Dawn's calf slipped back between her own. Slowly, Dawn's hands wandered, exploring across Rosie's shoulder blades, down her spine and up once more into her hair. Rosie quivered beneath her touch, but Dawn was careful to keep it light above the fabric of her clothes, modest in its adventures. Gaining courage, Rosie ran her fingers the length of Dawn's side, tracing her outline over the top of her shirt. The moment quietly stretched through most of the movie, until, at last, Dawn pulled back to stifle a yawn.

Rosie smirked. "Boring you, am I?"

"Wearing me out, more like," Dawn smiled. She cupped Rosie's cheeks, soft in the semi-dark. "You're beautiful, Rose."

Rosie dipped her head and blushed, disbelieving. "Hardly. I'm *old*. And tired."

"That makes two of us," Dawn quipped.

Rosie yawned, too, and then pushed upright with a groan. "God, I'm not made for canoodling on the couch, anymore."

Dawn laughed and sat up beside her. She rolled her shoulder, numb from leaning on it, and had to agree. "Next time, what say we make use of the bloody bed?"

A slow smile stretched over Rosie's lips. "Next time?"

Dawn cocked her head and raised an eyebrow. "Hate to tell

you, but this is only the beginning."

"Is it, now?" Rosie challenged, indulgent.

Dawn winked salaciously but then got distracted by a musical number starting up on the TV. "Ooo! This is the best part, Rose!"

"Isn't that bloody movie finished yet?" Rosie grumbled.

Dawn shushed her, captivated by the diabolical fairy on the screen as she waved her wand and took the stage. Though not quite finished, the film wasn't far from it and had reached the part where Shrek was about to attempt a heroic breaking-and-entering into the palace to get to his wife. Rosie watched as the Fairy Godmother donned a sparkling red gown, reclined across the top of a grand piano, and began to sing.

"Oh!" Rosie exclaimed as she recognised the tune of Bonnie Tyler's 'I Need a Hero.' "I bloody love this song!"

"Isn't that fairy just fab?" Dawn grinned. "God, look at her go!"

Rosie's lips quirked, mildly impressed. "She's got a pretty good voice; I'll give her that."

Dawn elbowed her. "A lot like someone else I know. Ooo! You should sing this at that karaoke thing day after tomorrow."

"What karaoke thing? *Don't* tell me you've signed me up for that – you know I don't enjoy singing in public."

"I didn't sign you up for anything," Dawn scoffed. "It's the farewell ball on the last night of the Retreat – there's dinner and a DJ and dancing and everything... Did you even *look* at the itinerary?"

"*What* itinerary."

Dawn got up and marched over to the kitchen. She snatched up a piece of paper with a clatter of falling magnets. "For the hundredth time – *the one that's on the fridge!*"

Returning, she waved it in Rosie's face, and Rosie took it from her with a bemused expression. "Has that really been there the whole time?"

Dawn unleashed an explosive groan and flopped back down beside her. "Yes, dear. I've told you more than once."

Rosie, now immersed in the activities list, said, "Hmm?"

Dawn rolled her eyes and leaned over Rosie's shoulder to point to the last night, where it clearly stated there was to be a farewell ball. "Here, see. Did you even bring anything to wear?"

The expression on Rosie's face was answer enough.

"Right," Dawn declared, in a tone that brooked no argument, "shopping trip it is!"

Rosie unleashed an explosive groan. "*No*, Dawn! I hate shopping!"

# CHAPTER TWENTY-THREE

Early the next morning, as shrubbery flashed by and fields and woodland coalesced into a single streak of variegated green, Rosie gritted her teeth and clutched white-knuckled at the headrest of the seat in front of her.

"Christ, Liz," she growled, "would you bloody slow down?"

"Only doing eighty," Liz responded cheerfully, putting her foot down.

Rosie shook the headrest, trying to elicit assistance from Dawn up front, but Dawn only laughed and watched the world whizz by.

"Bloody speed-freaks!" Rosie groaned, sinking back as deep as she could into the tattered seat. "This is only a Vectra, you know, not a stuffing Ferrari!"

"God, imagine if it *was* a Ferrari," Dawn grinned. "We could really fly, then!"

Liz giggled, and Rosie glowered, clinging to her seatbelt for dear life.

"Nearly there, Rose," Dawn offered genially. "Only a couple more miles."

"Of hell," Rosie growled. "You forgot the 'of hell' bit."

Dawn turned her attention back to Liz. "Thanks for driving us, kid."

"Yes, *thanks*," Rosie snarked.

"No problem," Liz said. "Pip wasn't going to let the bus go for just two of you, and I have a few supplies to pick up in Ulverston anyway. They've got a couple of decent clothes stores, so you should find what you're looking for."

"Don't see why I can't just go in slacks and trainers," Rosie muttered.

"Because it's a *formal* ball, Rose," Dawn reminded her, for the umpteenth time.

"I don't *do* formal," Rosie huffed. "I've had just about enough of that in my life, thank you very much."

"It's not *that* kind of formal."

Rosie leaned around the seat. "Make up your mind, is it formal, or isn't it?"

Dawn turned to blink at her. "It's formal, but it'll be *fun*. It's not one of those pretentious galas you've spent half your life attending."

Rosie flopped back again, grumbling, and they hurtled around a corner and down a narrow lane bordered by terraced buildings in myriad pastel colours. The car skidded to an unceremonious halt at the end of a cobbled road, demarcated by bollards and riotous flowerpots, and Liz offered a bright smile.

"Here we are! This is the end of the High Street. Take a gander down there, and I'll meet you back here in, say, an hour?"

"I don't think we need a whole bloody—"

"An hour is perfect, Liz, thanks," Dawn said, getting out of the car. She opened the door for Rosie and tugged her out, and then gave Liz a jaunty wave. "See you in a bit."

Liz grinned and roared off, swerving around an oncoming post van at the last second.

Rosie watched her departure with a foul expression. "How long do you reckon it'd take to walk back?"

"C'mon, Rose," Dawn smirked. "It wasn't *that* bad."

Rosie raised an eyebrow. "To be fair, she's probably a better driver than you are."

Dawn's smile vanished. "What! I am an *excellent* driver, thank you very much."

"If a billion speeding tickets in your pocket counts as 'excellent driving' then yes, I'll have to agree."

Dawn scoffed and took her arm, and they strolled across the cobbles, taking in the scenic town. It was fairly early, so the streets were quiet but for the soft chatter of shopkeepers opening up their stores, and they proceeded as if the day had been made just for the two of them.

"Oh, look here, Rose!" Dawn said as they passed a florist sporting a stunning window display – but it wasn't the blooms that had caught Dawn's attention.

She nodded up at the sign and Rosie smiled as she read it. "'Floral and Hardy'...? Huh. That's... actually excellent."

"Clever, isn't it?" Dawn agreed.

"Isn't there a Laurel and Hardy Museum here somewhere, too?" Rosie asked.

"Yes – but that's not the point of our visit."

"Well, no," Rosie muttered, "but it could be..."

Dawn tugged her onwards. "Not today, m'dear. Today is for dress shopping."

Rosie groaned. "I hate dress shopping."

"C'mon – if you're quick about picking something out, we can stop by the museum."

Rosie perked up at that, and practically towed Dawn into the first dress shop they spotted. "That one," she said immediately, gesturing vaguely at a laden rack.

"There's about forty on there," Dawn scoffed, pulling her further in and smiling at a friendly-looking rep. "Excuse me – hello – yes – we're looking for a dress for my friend here, an evening gown, please."

The attendant – a tall, androgynous young man with impeccable fashion sense – eyed Rosie critically. "Hmm. I'd suggest a wrap dress, knee-length, maybe. Right this way."

He ran expert fingers down a rack and deftly selected a burgundy dress with a diamanté adorned V-neck and empire waist for their approval.

Rosie's eyes widened at the sight of it. "God, it's beautiful."

He smiled, sweeping up a pair of peep-toe black heels to accompany it, and offered her the ensemble. "Would you like to try it on? The fitting room is over there."

Rosie accepted, marvelling at the sleek feel of satin through her fingers, and made her way to the corner he'd pointed out. Dawn followed, but Rosie rounded on her at the door.

"You wait here."

"But I want to see!"

"You can see at the ball. I'll just be a minute."

She disappeared behind a heavy curtain, and Dawn vacillated. With a huff, she turned away to browse another rack, and the attendant materialized beside her again.

"Something for you, too?"

"Um… no, thank you – I have a dress already."

"Are you sure?" He extended a silky, floor-length black gown – marbled through with bold strokes of gold – and lifted one sheer, billowing sleeve out to the side to show the silhouette properly. "This would suit you perfectly."

Dawn bit her lip, eyeing it, and tried not to look at the price tag. "Oh, go on, then. Let me try it on, at least."

She ducked into a fitting room with the sleek dress cradled to her breast and managed to slip it on and return to her regular clothes before Rosie emerged from her own cubicle. She was just handing it back to the attendant with a sheepish expression when Rosie reappeared, and Rosie cocked her head as she caught sight of it.

"Well take that one, too," she announced, not bothering to ask

Dawn what she thought of it – it was written all over her face.

The attendant smiled and rang them both up before Dawn could protest, and then packed them delicately into chic boxes for transportation. He handed Rosie the shoebox with her heels, too, and she dipped him a cordial smile as she turned for the exit laden with her parcels.

Immediately outside, Dawn stopped her with a small frown. "You didn't have to buy the other one, Rose."

"I know," Rosie said, "but it's lovely. I'd like to see you in that."

Dawn opened her mouth, closed it again, and gently blushed.

"Least you can do is carry the bloody thing," Rosie continued, handing her the whole lot.

Dawn grumbled good-naturedly as she settled the boxes in her arms, and then they meandered back the way they'd come. They passed a signpost pointing down a lane to one side, and she asked, "What about the museum?"

"Next time," Rosie said genially. "I don't want to rush it. Let's find somewhere to sit, grab a sandwich or something."

"Ooo, yes – I'm starving, actually."

"Thought you might be, seeing as you dragged me out before breakfast this morning."

Dawn smiled and traipsed amiably along beside her until they found what they were looking for. Grabbing a coffee and a bite to eat, they came upon a bench across from a life-size bronze statue of Laurel and Hardy and settled to enjoy the mild morning.

"You're not really going to make me sing karaoke, are you?" Rosie said between bites of her sandwich.

"I'm quite sure I can't *make* you do anything."

"Maybe not, but all you have to bloody do is ask. I find it exceptionally difficult to say no to you, you know."

Dawn smiled. "Now *that* I'm going to file for future reference."

"Don't. Ask. Me."

"I won't," Dawn promised.

Rosie rolled her eyes, not believing her for an instant. She swallowed the last bite of her sandwich and then, frowning at the boxes, said, "We didn't get you any shoes."

"I have shoes, Rose. Besides, the dress is long – I could wear trainers underneath and no one would know."

"You're not wearing trainers!"

"Why not? I think it's a great idea, actually."

"Absolutely not! If I have to wear heels, so do you."

"You could wear trainers, too."

"With a knee-length dress? Don't be ridiculous."

Dawn's eyes flashed mischief. "Even if you wore trainers… I'd think you were attractive."

Rosie scoffed. "Don't get funny. I'm wearing heels, and you'll be wearing heels. C'mon" – she got up with an air of finality – "let's go get you some."

"Sit down, Rose. I *have* a pair of heels."

Rosie hovered over her; eyes narrowed. "Do you really?"

"Yes," Dawn replied. "I actually have a dress, too."

Rosie dropped back onto the bench and thumbed the top of the boxes, feeling suddenly awkward about her assumption. "You… don't have to wear this one."

Dawn covered her hand with her own. "This one is gorgeous, and I'm absolutely going to wear it. Thank you."

A small smile lit Rosie's face, and then she looked up abruptly as a squeal of tires echoed through the quiet morning.

"Ride's here," Dawn chirped, hopping up and bundling their parcels into her arms.

Rosie voiced a hearty groan as she got up to follow her to Liz's idling car at the end of the street.

# CHAPTER TWENTY-FOUR

**B**ack at the Inn, Rosie cradled a cup of strong tea between her trembling fingers and tried to relax after the harrowing return journey. Dawn, meanwhile, had opened the box that guarded her new dress and now held the gown up to inspect it once more.

"Rose, this is really gorgeous… Honestly, thank you."

Rosie smiled. "I'm glad you like it – you'll look lovely in that."

Dawn smiled, too, and hung it carefully in the cupboard. She came to sit beside Rosie, and then her expression turned a little melancholic. "I can't believe tomorrow is the last day. It's gone by far too fast."

"Hasn't it?" Rosie agreed. "Can't believe it's already been a week."

Dawn stole Rosie's teacup and took a sip. Making a face at the lack of sugar, she asked, "Is Mary fetching you?"

"No, she has a meeting, apparently. I said I'd take a taxi home." Rosie glanced at her sideways. "Coming with me? It's a long drive – be bloody boring on my own."

Dawn took a moment to scrutinize her. "I live in the other direction."

"You don't have to."

"Come with you, or live in the other direction?"

Rosie smiled. "Live in the other direction." She rescued her tea back from Dawn's clutches and caught Dawn's gaze with an impassive expression. "Don't go back to your sister's. Come home with me."

"Oh, Rose…" Dawn sighed. "I can't just… besides, what will Mary think?"

"It's more important what *I* think," Rosie huffed. "Mary's too opinionated anyway."

"Takes after you," Dawn quipped.

"I'm rattling around that bloody house," Rosie pointed out. "Just me in there, now."

"Well, I suppose I could come and stay… for a little while, anyway. Just until I get back on my feet, I mean."

Rosie nodded, satisfied. "That's settled then."

Dawn watched her for a long moment, but Rosie merely sipped her tea.

"About those shoes…" Rosie prompted. "Let me see them."

Dawn groaned. "You're not still on about the bloody shoes…" But she got up to retrieve them and shortly held out a pair of black ankle boots for Rosie's inspection. "Satisfied?" she asked. "Heels and everything."

Rosie's lips quirked approvingly. "Very nice – they'll go perfectly with that dress."

"Told you. By the way, are you going to manage in heels with your sore ankle?"

Rosie almost blushed. "It's completely fine, actually. Wasn't that bad of a sprain, after all."

Dawn laughed and got up to make her own cup of tea. She deposited her boots on the corner of the kitchen table, and Rosie wandered over with her empty mug.

"I'll have another," she said.

She put it down and turned to lean her back against the counter beside Dawn. As Dawn added the trappings for a new brew, Rosie watched her hands, intrigued by how graceful they were despite the ordinariness of their task. Her gaze roved upward, taking in Dawn's side profile: the soft wave of her short silver hair, tucked behind one ear, the sweep of her fringe above dark eyes, the fine structure of her cheeks and jaw. A small smile played across her lips, but then Dawn looked in her direction, so she smothered it.

"Something wrong with the way I make tea?" Dawn said, raising an eyebrow.

"No," Rosie replied, and the smile returned. "Not at all."

"What, then?"

"You're just… lovely."

"Oh."

The kettle clicked off with fortuitous timing, and Dawn turned away to busy herself with the hot water so Rosie wouldn't see her blushing. She finished stirring and held out Rosie's cup, and Rosie accepted it affably.

"Thanks," she said, making her way back to the couch.

Dawn waited until the heat in her cheeks faded and then came to sit beside her.

As she settled, Rosie inquired, "Anything fun planned for the last day of our trip tomorrow?"

Dawn swallowed the sip she'd just taken and flashed her an impish expression. "Thought you'd never ask. We're doing the predator experience."

Rosie blanched. "The *what*?"

"There's a place down the road, and they let guests meet the wolves, and—"

"*Meet* the wolves? Nothing about that sounds *fun*, Dawn."

"It's supposed to be very educational."

Rosie snorted. "Oh, excellent – when I'm lying there all torn to pieces, I'll think about how educational the experience was."

Dawn giggled. "They're tame. Basically big dogs – you like dogs, don't you?"

Rosie fixed her with a glare. "*Whippets*! Not bloody wolves!"

Dawn patted her hand patronizingly. "I'm sure you'll survive."

"If I don't, I'm going to kill you."

"I'll take my chances. I think they're lovely – such majestic animals."

Rosie flopped back against the back of the couch. "We couldn't have just gone to a petting zoo – *no*, we have to go run with the bloody *wolves*!"

"I don't think running is a good idea," Dawn commented sagely.

"Oh!" Rosie howled. She ran her hands down her face in exaggerated frustration and then glared. "I'm quite convinced you're trying to do away with me on this trip!"

"Nothing's further from the truth," Dawn countered jovially.

Rosie narrowed her eyes. "Really?"

"I do *like* you, you know, Rose."

"I'm not sure if I like *you*."

Dawn laughed and leaned amiably against her side. "Thought you said I was lovely?"

"It appears I was wrong," Rosie snarked, settling an arm around her shoulders. "You're a bloody fiend. Throwing me to the wolves – honestly!"

"It'll be good practice for when we go to Africa," Dawn teased. "I've heard you can walk with lions there."

Rosie spluttered, but Dawn suddenly turned and smothered her retort with a cheeky kiss. Caught by surprise, Rosie's indignance abruptly abandoned her beneath a hitching in her chest. The kiss turned from timorous to turbulent, and when Dawn finally released her, Rosie sat weakly back with a blush rising on her cheeks. When she'd recovered, she retreated behind a dark frown and said, "You're getting quite forward."

Dawn sipped her tea. "Stopped your whinging, though."

Rosie scoffed before changing the subject. "What are we doing for the rest of today? Hope it's something fun, seeing as it might be my last day on earth."

Dawn snorted but decided she'd baited Rosie enough for the time being. "I thought we could just lounge about here. Watch a bit of telly or something."

"Sounds perfect, actually," Rosie allowed. "This week's taken it out of me."

Dawn's lips twitched. "Getting old, are you?"

Rosie gave a long-suffering huff and wrapped her hand over Dawn's mouth to shush her. "What have I said about that word!"

Dawn mumbled something incoherent against her fingers, and Rosie released her. Eyes sparkling, Dawn shifted upright. "You're so damned easy to bait."

"You don't need to take so much bloody pleasure in it," Rosie grumbled.

"Can't help it. It's fun."

Rosie settled back against the couch cushions with a smile. "It is fun, isn't it?"

"And easy," Dawn repeated. She leaned back against Rosie's chest with a contented sigh, and clarified, "So damn easy, being with you."

Rosie tucked her arms around her, pressed a kiss to her hair, and whispered, "Don't get funny."

# CHAPTER TWENTY-FIVE

As she bustled Rosie out to the coach the following morning, Dawn sang, "Who's a-fraid of the big bad wolf!"

Scowling, Rosie dug in her heels and made every inch of the way as difficult as she possibly could, but Dawn was incorrigible. Before she quite knew how Dawn managed it, they were aboard, and the coach was pulling away with them securely inside. As they trundled down the drive, a bag of crisps materialized from Dawn's pocket, and then the sound of cheerful crunching jarred Rosie's taut nerves.

After a prolonged moment of gritting her teeth, Rosie hissed, "Give us one of those."

Dawn jovially held out the packet, and Rosie snatched it, slid open the window and tossed the whole lot off the bus. Dawn gave a long, slow blink, and then, with a deadpan expression, pulled another packet out of her other pocket. Rosie thumped her head back against the seat with an explosive huff as foil rustled, and Dawn stuffed an exaggerated handful of crisps into her mouth. She crunched them gleefully, pulling ludicrous faces as she chomped on her snack.

"You're such a child!" Rosie cried, trying her best to remain irritable.

But she was no match for the sheer expressiveness of Dawn's face, and soon laughter pealed from her lips. Dawn grinned and offered her a second dip, and Rosie accepted with an air of defeat. She stuffed her mouth just as full as Dawn's, and the rest of the short drive was spent trying to outdo each other's outlandish expressions of enjoyment.

But at last, they arrived, wiped crumbs from their coats, and composed themselves to exit the coach. As Rosie was about to step off the last stair, Dawn leaned down from behind and whispered in her ear. "I do hope wolves aren't partial to the smell of crisps."

Rosie jerked to a halt, clinging to the safety rail on a swift surge of anxiety, but Dawn gave her an unceremonious shove down onto solid ground and grinned as she followed her out. Rosie rounded on her, but their little group – five in total – was already being ushered into an open-sided orientation shed, and Dawn scooted ahead. Rosie settled for cussing under her breath and dragged her feet, trailing in well behind the others. Dawn flashed her a cheeky grin when she finally arrived and patted the spot next to her on a low bench. Mutinous, Rosie sat down as far away as possible atop the little space, but Dawn scooted up close.

"No," Rosie warned, as Dawn opened her mouth. "That's quite enough of your badgering, thank you."

"I was only going to say that you're looking particularly delicious today."

"Sod off."

Dawn winked lasciviously and then turned her attention to the woman giving the introductory talk from the front of the room. Rosie took a breath to settle herself and did her best to absorb every word as Abby – one of the handlers – explained that they currently had three wolves on site, two females and a male from the same litter.

"Sierra, Meeka and Yuma are timber wolves," Abby explained. "But they're hybrids. They have some Czechoslovakian wolf dog bred into them because it's illegal to let pure-bred wolves run free in Britain."

At thirty-one weeks old, they were still technically pups and deferred to their handlers as the leaders of their pack. Abby explained some of their behaviours and outlined the etiquette involved when accompanying the wolves. "*You'll* be walking with *them*, not the other way around. They're pretty agreeable, but there are certain protocols that need to be observed to keep them – and you – comfortable. Jed's going to call them in now so that we can introduce you – you'll become members of their pack for the afternoon."

Rosie's lips tightened, and she reached for Dawn's hand. Dawn squeezed her fingers comfortingly, but Rosie froze as Jed, a strongly built man in his late thirties, unleashed an almighty howl. Within seconds, the three wolves came tearing out from the edge of the trees, bounding up to Jed and then greeting Abby beside him. With mild interest, they turned to scrutinize the pale, assembled faces, and Rosie suddenly found she couldn't breathe. Pups, they'd said. These were bigger than full-grown Alsatians.

"That was a back-to-pack howl," Jed explained in his deep, calm voice. The wolves shifted their attention to him as he spoke, and he informed the group that wolf packs have eight distinct howls. "Their hearing is nine times better than your average dog, too, so they can communicate over pretty big distances."

"The pups are dying to meet you all," Abby smiled. "So, if you'd like to slowly get to your feet and hold out a closed fist, they'll do the rounds."

The group obliged, and as Jed walked into their midst, the wolves took that as the signal to inspect their new friends. Under Jed's gentle instruction, Dawn extended her fist to Meeka, the smaller of the two females, as she came sniffing. Rosie cowered at Dawn's side, out of reach of the wolf's muzzle. Meeka spent a long moment sniffing Dawn's hand, and then gently grazed it with her teeth.

"I think she likes you," Jed grinned, and Dawn's eyes shone.

Meeka stuck her head around Dawn to get to Rosie next, and Rosie stiffened like a board.

"It's all right," Jed said quietly. "She won't hurt you. Meeka here is a lovely soul – just hold out your fist so she can get to know your scent."

Under the intelligent, watchful gaze of the wolf, Rosie raised a trembling hand. Meeka huffed over her white knuckles and then took her whole fist in her jaws. A tiny squeak escaped Rosie, but the wolf gave half a wave of her tail and let go, brushing past her to inspect the next person. The wolves cruised amongst them, taking their measure, identifying their scents, and Rosie didn't move as she endured greetings from Sierra – who was more boisterous than Meeka – and Yuma, the male, and the biggest. He seemed disinterested in Rosie, barely snuffing at her hand before moving on to Dawn, and then swiftly on to the others.

"He knows we're going into the forest," Jed explained with a smile. "Always does the barest job of introducing himself – I reckon he thinks that the quicker he sniffs everyone, the quicker we get in the Landy and go."

"He's not wrong," Abby said. "I think everyone's comfortable enough – let's head out. All right, ladies?"

Dawn nodded, enthused, but Rosie eyed the wolves. They were getting restless, eager for their outing, and it was putting her on edge. She steeled herself; the walk was supposed to be an hour, they'd said – she could get through an hour, couldn't she?

"Right," Jed announced, yipping at the wolves. "Everyone to the Landy!"

The wolves bolted, racing for the open-backed Land Rover Defender outside. Abby opened the tailgate for them, and they bounded effortlessly into the back as if it were the most natural thing in the world. Abby hopped up to sit with them, while the others climbed into the vehicle itself.

"Bit of a squash," said Jed apologetically. "The bigger van is at the shop. Not far, though – just a couple of minutes."

Dawn and Rosie squeezed into the back seat beside two other ladies, with Rosie closest to the window. It was open, thankfully, and Rosie turned her face to the evergreen breeze as they sped along a small track coated with pine needles. They pulled up again before Rosie's claustrophobia became more than a niggle, and she was happy to wait for a beat as the wolves leapt free and dashed past her window.

"C'mon, Rose," Dawn urged, leaning over her to open the door. "They'll leave us behind in a minute!"

"Can't say I'd mind," Rosie sniped, but she got out anyway.

"We're just going to take it nice and easy," Abby was saying as they rounded the front of the car to join the others. "Just a nice stroll through the woods. There'll be plenty of opportunities for you to take pictures, so keep your cameras at the ready if you have them."

"Damn," Dawn whispered to Rosie. "One of these days I really must get a camera and learn how to use it. Remind me, before we go to Africa."

They set off, and the wolves raced ahead, foraging in the woods around their surrogate leaders. The pups rough-and-tumbled as they went, bounding onto fallen logs, nipping, chivvying, and chasing each other through fallen leaves. Dawn and Rosie settled to walk at the back of the group, and a calm quiet fell as no one uttered another word, content simply to marvel at the wonder of walking with wolves.

"See," Dawn murmured, so only Rosie could hear, "this isn't so bad, is it?"

"Well," Rosie said grudgingly, "nothing's eaten me yet."

Dawn's hand brushed against Rosie's, and Rosie clasped it briefly. She was rewarded with a shy smile from Dawn, and, taking a deep breath of the fresh, pine-scented air, she decided that maybe Dawn was right – this wasn't so bad, after all.

But a wolf bounded suddenly at them from a dark thicket, and Rosie yelped and pulled away from Dawn. They froze, three feet apart, swivelling slowly as Meeka circled around behind them.

"All right there, you two?" Jed's voice calmly called. He strode back to join them, an impish smile quirking his broad mouth. "You're straggling – Meeka's worried. She wants you to rejoin the pack."

Dawn grinned, and Rosie released a shaky breath.

"A-are you sure?" Rosie stammered.

Meeka circled behind her again and then came to stand at her side, staring up at her expectantly.

"She knows you're afraid," Jed said to Rosie. "She wants you to keep up so that you're safe."

"That's a whole lot of speculative translation if you ask me," Rosie snapped softly.

"Put your hand down," Jed said. "There, next to her head."

Rosie really couldn't see any other way out of her situation, so, holding her breath, she obliged. Gently, Meeka bumped her muzzle against her palm and then flattened her ears.

"You can stroke her head, now," Jed smiled.

"*What?*" Rosie squeaked.

"Go on," Dawn whispered.

Rosie closed her eyes – at least if the wolf bit her, she wouldn't have to see the blood – and, infinitely slowly, curled her fingers sideways until they were touching the top of Meeka's head. The wolf didn't move, and Rosie risked a peek with one eye. Meeka was watching her with calm patience and, tentatively, Rosie scratched behind an ear. The wolf's head tilted obligingly, and Rosie's touch became firmer as her confidence trickled back.

"You can stroke her back, too, if you want," Jed said, content that the wolf's body language was exactly as it should be. Curiosity besting her, Rosie did so and was surprised at the coarse, almost greasy feel of Meeka's fur. "Wolves have a double coat,"

Jed offered automatically – an explanation he'd obviously given a hundred times. "Long guard hairs on the outside keep them dry, while a thick, soft undercoat keeps them warm."

Rosie gently probed a little deeper through Meeka's fur and was pleased by just how silky her under-fur was. Smiling despite herself, she looked up and met Dawn's warm gaze.

"Want to try?" she murmured, knowing full well that Dawn was dying to.

Dawn looked to Jed for permission. He dipped his head cheerfully. "Go ahead. Approach her from the side, put your hand out, like Rosie did, and wait for her to flatten her ears – that's her way of saying it's okay."

Carefully, Dawn followed his instructions, and Jed – watching Meeka's relaxed stance – nodded that it was okay for Dawn to stroke her.

"Oh my God," Dawn whispered with a grin, "she feels amazing! I'd never have guessed wolf fur was so rough!"

Meeka obligingly tolerated their affection for a little longer, but then, with a quirk of her ears in response to a playful yip from her sister, she pulled free and trotted off. After a few steps, though, she stopped and turned to look inquiringly in their direction.

Rosie smiled. "Yes, we're coming."

Meeka waited until all three of them had started walking again, and then turned and raced off to see what her siblings were up to.

"She'll keep coming back if you fall too far behind," Jed said affably. "Wolf packs are supposed to stick together."

"We'll keep up," Dawn assured him, and he smiled as he strode off.

When they were alone again, Rosie gave a happy sigh.

Dawn grinned. "Enjoying yourself, are you?"

"Absolutely hating it," Rosie said with a smile.

Dawn chortled, and they picked up their pace enough to keep up with the group.

A soft sort of silence accompanied them, lending a mystic air to their trek, and the group spoke little as they followed narrow paths through the deep woods. Damp loam muffled their footfalls, and the quiet breeze sighed around them, bringing the fresh and invigorating scents of the forest. The wolves wove back and forth, following whiffs that caught their interest, and Dawn and Rosie watched, captivated. There was something surreal about being out in nature with three apex predators calmly escorting them, and a strange liveliness coursed through their veins. By the time they reached the cusp of the ridge, their cheeks shone pink, and their eyes sparkled. As they came to a halt with the vista sweeping away beneath them, the wind chased delicious shivers across their skin.

"Dear God," Dawn whispered reverently, staring, "would you just look at that?"

"I'm glad you made me come," Rosie murmured back.

In the distance, forest, field, and fen stretched in every direction to the edges of the world and faded into oblivion behind craggy peaks. Directly below, the grand Lake Windermere dominated, shimmering against a patchwork of green and silver, tiny splashes of spring colour visible upon its banks. The little group stared out, awed, and nearby, a low, soulful howl started. Shortly, it was joined by two more, and then the wolves were singing around them. Jed and Abby threw their heads back and added their own voices, and Dawn and Rosie exchanged glances.

"Sod it," Dawn said.

She upraised a howling of her own and Rosie, caught up in the wonder and the wolfsong, joined in, too. Goosebumps prickled, and a fierce joy was whipped to freedom by the wind. Rosie's body shook with the effort of pouring her heart and soul into the wild cry, and it went on, and on, and on, until at last, the harmony faded to echoes, and she found herself with tears streaming down her face. Dawn caught her eye, and then her hand, and her own cheeks were damp above a trembling lip as she pulled her into an emotional hug. They clung to each other, supporting each other through the bittersweet abatement of a beautiful moment.

Something nudged between them, and then Meeka was there, too, her head pressed into the group hug, ears flat, eyes closed. Rosie's fingers found their way to the wolf's head, tangled there with Dawn's, and Meeka looked up, her amber eyes filled with a strange, wild intelligence.

"God," Rosie whispered, gently tugging at Meeka's ear, "you're absolutely beautiful."

"Aww, thanks," Dawn murmured back.

Rosie chuckled. "I was talking to the wolf, you—"

Dawn opened her eyes and winked. "I know."

But the mild jest had done the trick, and the moment released them. They pulled apart, Meeka bumping each of them with her nose as she turned away, and Dawn linked an arm through Rosie's as they followed the wolf back to reality.

## CHAPTER TWENTY-SIX

As they climbed into the coach an hour and a half later, Rosie gave a happy sigh. "That was incredible!"

"Meeka really seemed to take to you," Dawn smiled. "Too bad they wouldn't let you take her home."

Rosie held up a small toy wolf and stared at it with a sorrowful expression. "Bloody bastards. I guess this'll have to do instead – looks like her, at least." She tilted her head sideways at Dawn, and her lips curved into a warm smile. "Thank you, for making me do that. I think you might have a point about that whole 'facing your fears' malarkey."

"Your wolf walk was much more enjoyable than my tree-top disaster," Dawn said darkly. "So, the theory's a bit give-and-take."

"It's all right – we both enjoyed the wolf walking, and we both despised the tree climbing, so we're two for two."

"I didn't think you minded heights?"

"Heights don't bother me in the slightest – what does, is watching you scared out of your wits. I could do without that, thank you."

"Aww, care, do you?"

"Don't get funny," Rosie snapped automatically. But then she fixed Dawn with a searching gaze. "I do, you know. Care."

Dawn smiled and reached for her hand. "I know."

They travelled back to the inn in companionable silence, each content to lose themselves in the amazing memories they'd made that morning. When the coach pulled up, they strolled out and ambled across the lawns, teasing each other that there were wolves watching them from the treeline. But nothing except small birds stirred across the way, and they made it inside without incident. They traipsed up the stairs, and as soon as their room door had shut behind them, Rosie pulled Dawn into range and stole a hearty kiss from her surprised lips.

"What was that for?" Dawn gasped, her cheeks turning pink as she ducked her gaze from the intensity of Rosie's burning blue eyes.

Pleased that she'd caught her off-guard, Rosie smiled. "You're just... wonderful."

Dawn looked up again. "D'you know, Rose," she joked softly, "if you keep saying things like that, I might fall for you."

Rosie's lips quirked. "Don't you dare!"

Dawn leaned back against her grip and gave an impish shrug. "I can't help it if acerbic is my favourite personality flavour."

Rosie laughed and let her go. "Shall we have some tea?"

"Yes, why not," Dawn said, her gaze flashing to the clock. "We've still got a couple of hours until we need to get ready."

"We've got *ages* before we need to get ready," Rosie corrected, turning to put the kettle on.

"*You* don't," Dawn shot back as she fetched two mugs from the cupboard. "If you start now, you *might* just make it by the skin of your teeth."

"I don't need five hours to put on a dress, Dawn."

Dawn raised a challenging eyebrow. "If you're late, I *will* go down without you."

"*If* I'm late – which I won't be – then fine. You can save us a seat."

"Absolutely not – if you don't get a seat, it'll be your own damned fault."


Five hours passed in a blur. Rosie had tea with Dawn, took a nap, and then, as Dawn vacated the bathroom an hour before the farewell ball was due to start, she ran herself a luxurious bubble bath. Dawn, wet hair wrapped in a towel, folded her arms across the front of her bathrobe and managed a new level of disapproving glare.

"*Honestly*, Rose – a bubble bath? We've got to be downstairs in an hour! You're definitely going to be bloody late. I'm warning you – if we don't get a seat…"

Rosie grinned. "I'll be ready in ten minutes."

"Ten—" Dawn pressed her fingers against her temples. "I swear to God, I'm going to forcibly remove that phrase from your bloody vocabulary!"

Rosie's grin widened as she hustled her out of the bathroom. "Honestly, Dawn, would you sod off so I can bathe? You're going to make me late."

Huffing, Dawn left her to it – but hammered on the door forty minutes later to chivvy her once more. "You'd better not still be in that bloody bath!" she called.

*Splash*. "I'm not, Dawn."

"Bugger it," Dawn snapped, peevish. Rosie's tardiness was the only quirk she couldn't quite handle. "I'm going down! I saw cars arriving through the window already – apparently half the planet's been invited – and I want to be sure we get a chair somewhere."

Rosie blew a swathe of bubbles noisily off her fingers. "All *right*. I'll meet you down there in—"

"If you say ten minutes, I'll come in there and drown you!"

"…ten minutes."

Dawn's hearty groan could probably have been heard in the lobby, and Rosie stifled a giggle.

"Hurry *up*, Rose," Dawn admonished.

Rosie reclined, burying herself in the bubbles, and listened to Dawn's retreating footsteps with amusement. As soon as she heard the outer door shut, she got out and dried herself off – usually, she didn't like to arrive at events on her own, but it was completely worth it to irritate Dawn. She dried off her hair and donned her dress, stockings, and heels. For good measure, she tugged a white shawl out of the closet and settled it around her shoulders, and then, dressed, sat in front of the mirror to put on her face. With a small sigh, she decided that copious amounts of makeup were in order this evening. Luckily, numerous supplies were left out on the dresser, and she smiled as she inspected the selection. Clearly, Dawn had made quite an effort with her own appearance, to judge by the sheer volume of products lined up, and – adamant she wouldn't be outdone – Rosie picked up the concealer and began.

At last, she was ready, and she inspected herself in front of the long mirror behind the bathroom door. She'd done a fine job with her makeup, if she said so herself, and had even managed to blow-wave her blonde hair into something vaguely stylish. The burgundy dress, too, was devilish – the colour suited her perfectly and lent her eyes a sparkle to rival the summer sky. Satisfied, she turned smartly for the door and made her way downstairs.

But in the shadow of the swathes of draping that decorated the entrance to the party, she hesitated and wished she'd just gotten ready and come down with Dawn. Ahead, a sea of glittering people surged, bedecked with expensive fabrics and sparkling gems, and she baulked, inadequate. The taunting discomfort was a feeling that she knew all too well, and her nostrils flared suddenly as she realised what was off.

This was a GALA – not just a farewell dinner.

She backed away a couple of steps. This was her worst nightmare, the utter bane of her life for the last thirty years, and there was nothing on earth that would make her set foot through those doors. God, it felt like Richard would appear at any moment, offer his arm – which she'd have no choice but to take – and steer her in to parade her among his cronies like she was only worth the obscene diamonds at her throat. Absently, her trembling fingers caressed the soft skin of her neck. But they found only a thin gold chain, and she took comfort from its simple feel, clinging to the reminder that there was more to life than shallow glitz and empty glamour. Taking a deep breath, she chided herself for her ridiculous fears – Dawn was in there, waiting for her. This was the farewell ball of their wonderful trip together, something to be celebrated. Why the hell was she hiding in the corner? Squaring her shoulders, she stepped through the doorway. And stumbled to a halt.

For there was Richard, holding out his arm.

"Ah," he smiled. "There she is."

# CHAPTER TWENTY-SEVEN

Time stood frozen for a long, appalling moment, but then the lights and music and crush of the crowd came crashing down. Rosie made to bolt, but it was too late. Richard looped his iron arm through hers, as he had a thousand times before, and – as she had a thousand times before – she found herself too meek to do anything but obey. He piloted her through the fray, pausing here to share a joke, there to greet a haughty associate, and Rosie felt a familiar warmth in her stomach that suggested she might be sick.

"I didn't think you'd come to the gala," he whispered into her ear as they navigated the room, "so I arranged to have it brought to you. Charitable sponsorship, and all that. Funny, you know – drop the chance to meet a couple of celebs and no one ever says no."

Rosie quailed, unnerved by his sheer audacity, and he towed her into the spotlight amidst a swaggering array of preening sports agents. There, he homed in on a strapping young footballer with an expensive suit and a surly face, and presented Rosie as one might a precious gem.

"Ollie! This is my wife, Rosie, whom I was telling you about."

Cool ebony eyes appraised her, judged her wanting. The smile on his face never faltered, but she knew it was insincere – it always was, with these young superstars.

"Can I get you a drink?" Richard continued, slapping the young man on the back. "Cognac, perhaps?"

"Rum and coke, bruv," Ollie corrected in a bored tone.

Richard boomed a laugh. "Of course! We'll be right back."

A tiny slip of resistance stirred in Rosie, and she dug her heels in – but his hand moved to grip beneath her elbow, and he lifted her forward. "C'mon, now, Rose," he growled. "Don't test me this evening, would you?"

He manhandled her around the dance floor towards the bar, and she winced at his steely fingers; she'd have bruises tomorrow if she objected any further. The crush of people pressed in around her, making her feel light-headed, and her conviction crumbled by degrees. Numb, she let him propel her in whichever direction he chose.

But a glint of gold suddenly caught her eye, and she stopped dead. The crowd parted, just for a moment, and the gold took form into bold swashes across velveteen black, draped in elegant lines around a silhouette at the far end of the bar.

Rosie swallowed, staring, and Richard faded into obscurity.

Dawn sat facing the door, her side profile proud and lovely in the modest lighting. The dress Rosie had bought for her clung proudly to her full figure, accentuating it in all the right places, and Rosie found she couldn't tear her eyes away. Dawn's dainty fingers – bejewelled with delicate silver rings – tapped the bar counter, and Rosie was mesmerised for a long moment by their graceful movement. An eternity passed, but then Dawn happened to glance in her direction, and Rosie felt the earth implode beneath her feet. Somehow, she was moving – a mercurial tide, torn free from the vague, insistent impediment at her side – gravitating towards the only thing that mattered. In slow motion, she saw Dawn spring to her feet, watched the play of emotions unfold across her immaculate face – a flicker of surprise, warmth, and then, a darkening of righteous fury. Time inched forward, infinitely closing the distance between them, and then all in a rush it caught up.

Light and sound crashed in, and Rosie caught Dawn by the collar of her dress just as she was about to surge past and confront Richard. She spun her into a kiss so devastating it knocked the breath out of them both, and Dawn dissolved into her fierce embrace. It didn't matter that half the room was watching – it wouldn't have mattered if all the world was. The only thing that mattered to Rosie, right at that moment, was Dawn.

She pulled back to cup Dawn's magnificent visage between her hands and lost herself in the galactic depths of her gaze. Dawn, rocked by the sheer force of Rosie's unexpected affection, held tight to her waist, too stunned to speak.

Rosie hesitated, and then whispered, "I, uh… noticed."

Dawn blushed. She opened her mouth to respond, but Richard suddenly snatched Rosie away by the wrist. She loosed a sharp, startled cry as he hauled her into the reach of his rage, and his bullish bulk dominated her smaller frame.

His voice came low and hoarse, hot against her face. "What in the *hell* do you think you're doing?"

Rosie gaped, too surprised to struggle. For a brief, cosmic moment, she'd forgotten that Richard existed. The reminder crackled ominously through the thunder in his glare.

"You're embarrassing yourself!" he snarled.

The room fell to a deathly silence as he loomed over her, threatening to break her once and for all. His glare lifted to encompass Dawn, too, and a rare malignancy danced in his expression. He took a menacing step towards her, but Rosie suddenly wrenched her wrist free and tucked Dawn firmly behind her.

Finally, she found her voice.

"I'm not embarrassing myself, Richard," she said softly. "You are. Everyone is staring at *you*."

Richard exploded with a roar, shoving Rosie into a cocktail table with a deafening crash, and in the background, there was a flurry of frantic calls for security. He rounded on Dawn, snarling savagely as he caught her by the throat and, with frightening ease, hauled her upward until the tips of her toes barely brushed the floor. Dawn clawed at his hand, choking.

"You'd steal my wife from me?" he thundered, shaking her like a rag doll. Dawn's eyes bulged, reflecting a primal fear. "You filthy little bitch!"

A strangled gasp tore from Dawn's lips, and Rosie ripped herself free of the broken table. Something feral possessed her; something wild, fierce, and deadly. She snatched up a beer tumbler and launched herself at Richard, smashing it viciously against the side of his face. Glass shattered, and he tossed Dawn aside with a yell, throwing up his hands to stem a gush of blood as it cascaded from his cheek. Dawn toppled to her knees, clutching at her throat, and Rosie – fuelled by a lifetime of suppressed anger – took advantage of Richard's distraction to kick him one where it hurt the most.

He crumpled with a tiny whine, bloody hands dropping to cup between his legs instead, but Rosie did not dally to witness her victory. She was already spinning, reaching for Dawn. Shaking with the violence of her emotions, she threw herself down and gathered Dawn into her arms, and Dawn buried her face against her shoulder to stop herself from sobbing. Rosie clutched her protectively against her chest, fixing her fierce gaze on Richard as the security guards finally showed up to haul him away. They cuffed him, and he caught Rosie's glare as they dragged him to his feet.

"Jesus, Rose," he spat. "You're a fucking psycho."

"Burn in hell," she hissed.

He was gone, then – towed unceremoniously out by two burly bouncers – and Liz dropped down beside Rosie. She beckoned urgently to someone else, and then Ed the doctor materialised too.

But Rosie snarled at him, and he held his hands up in supplication.

"Here, now, Rosie," said Liz tentatively, "let's let Ed look Dawn over, make sure she's all right…"

"I'm not moving," Rosie warned softly. "If you try to make me, I'll kill you."

"Rose…" Dawn croaked, pushing against her to lift herself up a little. "Let him… see."

With her lip curled over her teeth, Rosie hesitated a moment, but then grudgingly obliged. She relinquished her grip just enough for Dawn to turn her head.

Dawn faced Ed with a tremulous smile and rasped between halting breaths, "I'm… all right… Doc. Bit shook… is all."

A dark frown encompassed Ed's brow. "You're covered in blood, my dear – nothing all right about that."

Dawn looked down at herself, and Rosie's grip tightened protectively as she, too, craned her neck to see where Dawn was hurt. But after a second, Dawn gently pried open the slick fingers of Rosie's right hand to expose her lacerated palm. Ed's bushy eyebrows almost disappeared into his wispy hairline, and he hurriedly grabbed a fallen serviette for Dawn to press against it.

"Gently, now," he warned. "There's likely bits of glass in there."

Rosie diffused, staring over Dawn's shoulder at the offending appendage as if it belonged to someone else. Dawn took advantage of her lapsed grip to turn in her arms and, very gently, pulled Rosie's hand down to where Ed could easily see. Crimson blossomed through the cloth, dripping slowly down her slender wrist.

"Come on, ladies," Ed said, quiet but firm. "Let's get you out of here. I need to bandage that, Rosie, and I want to look at Dawn's neck in better lighting. Liz, if you would?"

Liz nodded, reaching out to help them to their feet. Dawn disentangled herself from Rosie's limp clutches and took Liz's hand, pulling shakily upright. Ed helped Rosie up, supporting her as her knees briefly betrayed her, and then the four of them shuffled from the room.

"Kitchen has proper lights," Liz suggested as she led the way.

Ed nodded approval, bolstering Rosie as she listed. Dawn slid an arm around her waist from the other side, pressing close.

"C'mon, Rose," Dawn whispered, "let's get you to a chair."

"She's running on adrenalin," Ed said over Rosie's head, "so I'm not surprised she's feeling a little faint. We'll get her fixed up in no time, though."

"Should we go to a hospital?" Dawn asked, a concerned frown creasing her face.

"If you want to," Ed replied, "but I don't think it's necessary. Let's assess in the light, and then I'll advise."

Dawn put her trust in the good doctor, and they settled Rosie onto a bench in the kitchen beneath a fluorescent lightbulb. There, Liz brought Ed a basin and a jug of water, and he peeled the sodden fabric off Rosie's hand. He flushed her palm with care, critically appraising the fine cuts that crisscrossed it. The bleeding had backed off, and he turned her hand this way and that against the light, watching for any suspicious glints. Liz fetched the first aid kit as he did so and passed him a pair of tweezers when he asked for them. He removed two small slivers of glass, cleaned the lacerations thoroughly with soap and water, and then declared her out of the woods.

"Nothing too serious," he assured Dawn. "Your friend has a knack for sustaining only minor injuries, it seems."

The reprieve fell balmy, and then Liz failed to suppress a high-pitched giggle through her nose. When Dawn raised a quizzical eyebrow at her, she squeaked, "*Friend*. Yeh, right. Never seen 'friends' share a kiss like *that*."

Rosie opened one eye from where she had her head lolled back against the wall. "Shut up, Liz."

A relieved smile broke across Dawn's face at Rosie's snark, and Liz laughed.

"Reckon she's fine, Doc," Liz chirped with a grin.

Around a sigh, Rosie muttered, "Oh, go play in traffic." But she stayed still as Ed applied disinfectant and dressed her wounds.

When he was done, he turned his attention to Dawn and gently inspected the angry red marks beneath her jawbone and across her throat. Grimacing, he said, "It's going to bruise quite a bit, love – you'll be a right sight, and tender, for a few days. But there'll be no lasting damage."

"Except for the psychological," Rosie interjected darkly.

"Well, yes," Ed agreed. "There is that. I'm so sorry – no one should have to experience something like this."

"Told you I didn't like Richard," Dawn muttered to Rosie.

"You also told me you were going to run him over with a bus," Rosie replied. "I'm still waiting."

"I haven't had *time*," Dawn said primly. "But I'll make it a bloody priority now."

Gently, Ed interrupted. "All right, ladies – I think you two could do with some rest. I would recommend skipping the rest of the party and turning in early."

"*What?*" Liz burst out. "They can't skip the party – they are the party!"

"Bloody right we are," Rosie growled, cutting Ed off as he opened his mouth to reiterate his advice. She got to her feet, and he gave a genial shrug instead. Sensing no further argument from the mild doctor, Rosie turned to Dawn. "Well? What say you?"

"I'm all for not letting that bastard ruin the last night of an otherwise fabulous trip," Dawn said, "but… are you sure you're feeling up to it, Rose?"

"Honestly, Dawn," Rosie huffed, holding up her bandaged hand. "It's just a bit of blood."

"Which you got all over my lovely new dress!" Dawn shot back.

"Richard's fault," Rosie stated.

"Bastard," Liz chimed in happily. She held open the kitchen door for them, but Dawn paused.

"I'm serious about the blood, Rose. If we're going back to the party, I want to damn well change."

Rosie pouted. "But I *like* this dress on you."

Dawn rolled her eyes, caught her arm through Rosie's uninjured one, and dragged her out in the direction of the lift. The bemused doctor watched them go, shaking his head with a rueful smile. They disappeared around the doorframe on a tide of renewed energy, and decided he'd never met two women so wonderfully audacious in all his life.

# CHAPTER TWENTY-EIGHT

Rosie clicked the door of their room shut behind them and paused to lean her forehead against it with a sigh.

"Okay, dove?" Dawn said from behind her.

Rosie turned around. She contemplated Dawn for a long moment, and then said, "God, look at you…"

A grimace crinkled Dawn's face. "I know, I'm a bloody mess."

"Yes," Rosie agreed with a small smile, "you are."

"You're not much better off," Dawn scoffed, gesturing at Rosie's own bloodstained gown. Her white shawl hadn't fared much better, either – in fact, it was beyond saving.

Rosie's smile turned wry as she inspected herself. "What a waste of a bloody dress. I'm extra miffed about yours, though."

"Suited me, did it?" Dawn teased, giving a little twirl.

Rosie made a show of appraising her and pursed her lips critically. "Well, you were passable, I suppose."

"What! I am a TEN, thank you very much."

Rosie grinned at her indignance. She pouted in mock sympathy and offered, "You're a twenty, darling."

Dawn huffed expansively. "Now you're just being ridiculous."

She turned for the bathroom to wash up and change, but Rosie caught her with her good hand.

"Wait, Dawn."

Dawn's put-upon indignance fizzled at her tone. She stopped and turned to face her. "What is it?"

"I'm… sorry."

"For what?"

Rosie frowned and traced a finger tentatively along one of the red marks on Dawn's neck. "For this. God, I never dreamed he'd hurt you…"

Dawn considered that for a moment, and then raised an eyebrow. "Well, you probably shouldn't have kissed me in front of him, then."

Rosie groaned and hid behind her hands. "In front of the whole bloody room, you mean."

A gentle laugh pealed from Dawn's lips, and she looped her arms around Rosie's waist. "Yes – in front of the *whole bloody room*. So much for discretion."

"You're the one who said it doesn't matter what anyone thinks," said Rosie defensively.

"I know, and I meant it. Still, you… surprised me."

Embarrassed, Rosie dipped her chin, but Dawn leaned to meet her eye and added, "Pleasantly."

Rosie looked up, and her gentle smile returned. "I couldn't help it – you were just… I've never seen you look like that."

"I've looked like that plenty – at literally every party we've ever been to. I always dress up."

"I know," Rosie said slowly. "But tonight… I noticed."

"Hit you like a cricket bat, did it?" Dawn teased.

"A cosmic epiphany, more like," Rosie replied. She took a breath before she went on, groping for the right words. "I'm serious, now – you're just… I thought my heart might explode when I saw you, Dawn. It might, still."

"Oh, Rose…" Dawn whispered, overwhelmed by the sincerity

in Rosie's voice. She gathered her carefully into her arms. "I do love you, you know."

Rosie sighed against her shoulder, content to stand there with her for the rest of their lives if that was an option. "I love you, too. Always have, I think."

Dawn smiled against her hair. "But you've only just noticed?"

"Takes me a while, sometimes," Rosie murmured.

"Makes two of us," Dawn replied, hugging her tighter.

After a moment, Rosie asked, "Are we really going back to the party?"

Dawn pushed back, searching her gaze. "Do you want to?"

Rosie thought about it. "Yes, I think so – if only because the idea terrifies me, and someone once told me that we should do the things that make us afraid."

"Someone wise?" Dawn said with a smirk.

"Oh, incredibly wise – so wise she's a smart-arse."

Dawn snorted. "Come on, then, let's end this holiday properly. I want a drink, and I want to dance, and I want to watch you sing karaoke."

"Karaoke is *not* part of the deal."

"Scared, are you?"

"You're not leveraging your fear theory to swing this one – I'm not scared, I just don't *want* to."

"We'll see," Dawn grinned, extricating herself from Rosie's clutches. "First things first, though – what are we going to wear?"

"You have another dress," Rosie reminded her.

"All right, then – what are *you* going to wear?"

"What I should have worn in the first place, slacks and bloody trainers."

"Not a prayer," Dawn scoffed. "I like you in a dress."

"I don't *have* another dress."

"I do."

"We've established that."

Dawn rolled her eyes. "I *mean*, I have two – when I packed,

I wasn't sure which one I'd want to wear, so I chucked them both in." She scooted to her closet and began rifling, and Rosie loomed like a thundercloud at her shoulder.

"*Why*, then, did you drag me bloody dress shopping in the first place?"

"Mine'll be a little loose on you, Rose," Dawn pointed out with a wry smile. "But for our purposes now, we'll make it work – we've already made our big entrance, after all."

"God, tell me about it."

Dawn pulled out two black dresses and, after a brief inspection, handed her the shorter one. "Here, this one's a bit smaller, I think."

"Thanks," Rosie said, secretly relieved she wouldn't have to show up in casual wear.

"Do you want to shower first?" Dawn asked.

Rosie raised an eyebrow. "Most of my blood is on you, I think."

"Fair point," Dawn allowed. "But listen, now, Rose – if it takes you longer than ten minutes, I'll go without you again."

"Don't you dare!"

"Don't make me," Dawn challenged as she ducked into the bathroom. She was clean and dressed in a matter of minutes, and Rosie, for once in her life, shortly followed suit.

"Wow," Dawn mused when she rematerialised moments after she'd disappeared into the shower, "that's without a doubt the quickest I have ever seen you get ready."

"I'm not bloody going down on my own this time," Rosie said darkly. "Here, do up my zip and help me redo my hair, would you? I'm bloody useless with this bandage on."

Dawn helped her finish up, applying a fresh batch of makeup for her, too, and soon, they were ready. They appraised each other, both in well-cut, if slightly worn, black dresses. Dawn's was long, with tiny white-silk flowers sown down the gossamer sleeves, and Rosie's flowed to just below the knee, tailored and trimmed with delicate silver filigree.

"You look lovely," Dawn smiled.

Rosie held up her bulky, bandaged hand. "I look ridiculous."

"You don't," said Dawn, earnestly. "Are you ready?"

"As I'll ever be."

Rosie hesitated in the doorway once more, listening to the party back in full swing beyond the draping. But this time, Dawn stood solid at her side, one arm looped through hers, and, taking a breath, she lifted her chin to wade into the fray. Smiles and impressed nods greeted them, and raised glasses marked their progress across to the bar. As they reached it, Liz suddenly appeared beside them, and she covered her mouth with her hands to suppress a delighted squeal.

"Blimey!" she squeaked. "And you came back in hers-and-hers dresses! You two are absolute ledge!"

"*Hers-and-hers* dresses?" Rosie growled, glaring.

"Drink, luv?" interrupted a voice at Rosie's shoulder.

All three women swivelled, and the footballer, Ollie, held out a tray of shooters.

He nudged it forward. "Toast, yeh? To your absolute annihilation of that wanker."

Rosie narrowed her eyes but accepted one of the small glasses. "What is it?"

Ollie grinned, offering Dawn and Liz, too. "Tequila."

"Excellent!" Dawn said, snatching one. "C'mon, Rose – loosen you right up."

Rosie gave a derisive sniff. "We've a bit of class around here, you know. Where's the bloody salt and lemon?"

One of Ollie's cronies held out another tray with the requested additions, and Ollie winked.

"At your service, Miss," he said, in his poshest accent. Rosie rolled her eyes as she reached for the trimmings. Dawn and Liz followed suit, and then Ollie raised his shot glass. "Cheers to you mint birds – bigger balls than Richard ever had!"

Dawn choked on hers, snorting it back up through her nose.

"Good God," she gasped as her eyes watered. "I'm too bloody old for this bollocks!"

Rosie sighed and handed her a serviette, and then slugged hers without flinching.

Dawn muttered, "Show off."

Ollie and his boys laughed in good taste, and then he tipped them a jaunty salute. "Enjoy the rest of your evening, yeh? You well deserve it. C'mon, lads, let's bounce."

They sauntered out, trailing a bevy of agents trying to win Ollie's attention, and Rosie scoffed as she turned back to the other two.

"Bloody ridiculous, the lot of them," she said.

Liz shrugged. "Free tequila, though."

"Aren't you supposed to be working?" Rosie snapped.

"What? Oh – yes, I am," Liz said with a grin. She twirled away to get on with whatever it was she was supposed to be doing, and Rosie turned to Dawn.

"*Finally*. God, it's like everyone wants a piece of us, this evening."

"You are rather the talk of the town," Ed commented, joining them.

"Oh!" Rosie huffed. "Not you, too!"

Dawn smiled. "Hello, Ed. Thanks for fixing us up."

Ed raised his bushy eyebrows. "No problem – you two are tough old birds."

"You'll be bleeding too," Rosie warned, "if you use that word again."

The corners of Ed's eyes crinkled. "Pleased to see that you're back to your indomitable self, Miss Bishop. Would you like a drink?"

"Is *everyone* trying to get me drunk this eve—?"

"Yes, please, Ed," Dawn interrupted. She raised a challenging eyebrow at Rosie. "One glass of wine, Rose. You won't get drunk off one glass of wine."

"I *might* get drunk off one glass of wine," Rosie countered. "You don't think I will, but I might."

"It'll be the tequila," Dawn chortled, "not the bloody wine."

"Fine. One glass of wine, then."

Ed ordered for them, and then tipped his hat and left them to it. Rosie brooded into hers, watching him go, and Dawn patted her arm affectionately. "He's all right, Rose."

Rosie sniffed. "He is, I suppose."

"Cheers," Dawn said, raising her glass. "Here's to ending off the trip on a good note."

The carefully cultivated frown on Rosie's face lingered for a moment longer, but then she smiled. "All right. I'll drink to that."

Dawn pouted. "And then we'll dance?"

Rosie laughed at her endearing expression. "Yes, dear. And then we'll dance."

## CHAPTER TWENTY-NINE

Dawn was quite right; one glass of wine did not make Rosie drunk – it was the other three and two more shots of tequila that did it. They danced, and laughed, and danced some more, until Rosie wobbled, and Dawn had to catch her.

"All right there?" Dawn grinned.

Rosie steadied herself, wincing as she bumped her sore hand, and then met Dawn's gaze with flushed cheeks and a twinkle in her eye. "I'm fantastic, actually – a little tipsy, maybe – but fantastic." She pulled Dawn closer with her good hand and added, "It's all your fault, you know. I was doing such an excellent job of being miserable, before."

Dawn laughed, soft against her ear. "Happy, are you?"

"You're going to ruin – bloody ruin – my reputation, Dawn."

A slower song came on – a haunting ballad – and they swayed gently together.

"I'm not sorry," Dawn whispered.

"Neither am I," Rosie agreed with a smile. Dawn pressed closer as the music lilted, and Rosie held her tight. The moment stretched sweet, but at last, Rosie pulled back. "God, this song is putting me to sleep."

"Past your bedtime, is it?" Dawn quipped.

Rosie huffed and cupped a hand against the side of her mouth to shout towards the DJ. "Oi! Put on something more lively, you scallion!" He saw her lips move and lifted one headphone, but then shook his head, unable to hear her over the music.

"I know what'd liven things up," Dawn suggested mischievously.

Rosie narrowed her eyes. "No, Dawn."

Dawn pouted. "C'mon, Rose…"

"Absolutely not. I've not had nearly enough wine."

"Please?"

"Saying please is cheating, damn it!"

Dawn let her lip wobble, and Rosie threw her head back and fisted her good hand.

"Fine!" she snapped. "Just the *one*, mind."

"Just the one," Dawn smirked. She skipped over to the DJ booth and announced, "One karaoke, please!"

The tattooed youngster grinned. "Song?"

"Something easy," Rosie interjected, her tone icy with warning. "Something I know the words to."

"How about 'I Need a Hero'?" Dawn suggested. "I'm dying to hear you sing that – and I know you know the words; you were mouthing them along with the movie."

Rosie released a sigh, and Dawn took that as permission.

"Do you have the version from Shrek Two?" she asked the DJ.

"*Really?*" Rosie said.

Dawn grinned as the DJ nodded and pulled it up in his system.

"Here we are," he said, holding out a mic. "Ready?"

"No, wait!" Dawn exclaimed. She scooted down off the stand and dragged a chair into the middle of the dance floor – effectively capturing the attention of everyone else left at the party – and Rosie snatched the mic with a death grip as others followed Dawn's example. Soon, there was a small, grinning audience, just for her.

Rosie cleared her throat, and then, in a low, sultry voice, purred into the microphone, "Dawn Clermont... I'm going to kill you."

"Sing us a song first!" Dawn shouted, grinning.

At the edge of the room, Liz dimmed the lights so that the minor spotlight on the DJ stand illuminated Rosie distinctly, and the crowd whooped. Rosie's deadly gaze swivelled to spy her. "Also have a death wish, do you?" she asked, voice echoing over the speakers.

"Worth it!" Liz called, scurrying over to grab a perch beside Dawn. Into Dawn's ear, she whispered, "How in the hell did you get her to agree?"

"Dutch Courage," Dawn replied sagely. "And... I said please."

On the small stage, Rosie inhaled deeply and closed her eyes. The music rose – a mellow, haunting piano solo that caused the hubbub to die down – and then, with soft, unexpected resonance, she began to sing.

"Jesus," Liz exclaimed under her breath. "She's got the most fabulous voice!"

"Lovely, isn't it?" Dawn whispered back with a smile.

The audience fell into captivated silence as the first verse slipped like silk from Rosie's lips. She poured her soul softly into the microphone, lilting longing through every lyric, and drew emotion from every person in the room. Her voice tremored to beautiful silence as the piano faded behind the intro, but then the backing track and chorus kicked in with a dynamic burst.

Rosie's eyes flashed open, and she met it with such a surge of power in her voice that the crowd loosed an approving cheer. Mischievous, she adapted the song to a feminised version and was rewarded with a rouging of Dawn's cheeks. Dawn shrank into her seat as Liz elbowed her enthusiastically, and Rosie shot them a wicked smile as she warmed up to the beat. She pushed more and more fervour into her performance until, at last, she stepped right off the stage to corner Dawn as it reached a pivotal point. The song crescendoed, crested, crashed down around them, and then Rosie hauled Dawn to her feet to sing with her. They duetted the last part, attempting to outdo each other in showiness, and the enthusiastic crowd clapped in time, egging them on.

"I'm going to do my death-cat now, Rose!" Dawn yelled between lyrics –

"*No*, Dawn, don't you dare!"

– "Ready?!"

Dawn took up an ungodly yowling at the top of her lungs, and Rosie dissolved into fits of laughter. The crowd echoed it from all quarters, and then the whole room was on their feet, singing, dancing, making utter tits of themselves.

But at last, oh, at last, it came to an end, and as the music ebbed away, Rosie caught hold of Dawn's shoulder to steady herself against the jollity echoing through her bones.

"Good God," she gasped, breathless with amusement. "*Death-cat…?* You're mad!"

"I knew you'd like it," Dawn smirked, pleased with herself for eliciting such genuine laughter from her.

Rosie shook her head, straightened herself up, and said, "Shall we get one more drink? I'm scarily sober after that experience."

"You bloody nailed it, though, Rose," Dawn said approvingly, making for the bar by way of agreement. "Christ, it's been a lifetime since I heard you sing."

"And it'll be another lifetime before you do again."

Dawn gave a conspiratorial wink. "There'll be other parties."

Rosie scoffed. "But not enough wine in the world. I'm bloody exhausted, now."

"Too old, are you?" Dawn asked nonchalantly. She ducked without even looking as Rosie swung at her, and came up grinning. "Another tequila?"

"God no – wine's fine. One more glass, though, Dawn, and then, really, I have to go to bed."

"Bit unsteady on your half-inch heels?"

"Yes," Rosie snapped. "Because apparently, I'm *old*."

They flopped onto two stools at a small cocktail table, and Dawn stretched her own aching feet out in front of her. "I don't know how you still wear shoes like those, honestly," she said, eyeing Rosie's stilettos, which were, in fact, closer to three inches high.

Rosie fixed her with a wry expression. "Lifetime of practice, m'dear."

"Well, they've always suited you," Dawn said. "Still do – your legs look fantastic. I don't know whether to be jealous or... fascinated."

"*Fascinated?*"

Mischievous, Dawn propped her elbow on the tabletop, cupped her chin in her hand, and pointedly fixed her gaze on Rosie's stockings. "I am, a bit."

"Want them all wrapped up with yours, do you?" Rosie said brazenly.

Dawn jerked upright, blushing at the abrupt turnaround, and Rosie's eyes sparkled. "Tit for tat," she smirked.

Dawn groaned. "Forgot how clever wine makes you."

"It's not the wine," Rosie corrected primly, "it's the bloody tequila you keep plying me with." With an air of finality, she tucked her legs firmly beneath her cocktail stool, and Dawn laughed.

A waiter brought them a glass of wine each before they'd even called him over to order it, and Dawn leaned back in her seat to glance at the bar. From behind the counter, Liz waved, and Dawn blew her a grateful kiss. "I'm going to miss that girl," she sighed as she turned back to Rosie.

"She's lovely, isn't she?" Rosie agreed.

"Is that *approval* I hear...?"

"I do approve of some people, you know," Rosie huffed, affronted. Pointedly, she lifted her glass in salute to Liz, and Liz beamed. "Liz is all right."

"She is, indeed." Dawn raised her drink, too. "Well, Rose – here's to a wonderful trip."

"Or, at least, to not falling from a tree, drowning, or being eaten by wolves," Rosie said, clinking her glass against Dawn's.

Dawn smiled around a sip and then sighed. "Can you believe it's all over tomorrow?"

"It's flown by," Rosie agreed. She met Dawn's gaze, contemplative. "I've had fun though, and – to be very honest – I'm quite glad I came."

Dawn smiled. "I'm quite glad you did, too."

"Life's full of surprises, isn't it?" Rosie mused. She drained her glass and then set it down with gentle finality. "Right, you. I'm buggered – my hand is throbbing something fierce, now, and my feet hurt."

Dawn nodded, stifling a yawn, and gently probed at her tender neck. "It's been a day, that's for sure. Let's turn in, shall we?"

"Yes, let's. Show's all over bar the crying, anyway," Rosie said. "It'll be just me, you, and the crickets, in a minute."

"I sort of want it to be just you and me and the crickets," Dawn admitted, making her way towards the door. "I've had about as much adventure as I can handle for a while, I think."

"God – *finally*," Rosie grumbled.

Dawn laughed and chivvied her towards the lift.

# CHAPTER THIRTY

Safely inside their room, Rosie cradled her sore hand against her chest and wilted onto the couch with a groan. She kicked off her heels and gingerly wiggled some feeling back into her toes, and Dawn perched beside her to follow suit.

"Why do women always have to wear bloody heels?" Rosie said darkly, leaning back against the cushions and lifting her legs onto the couch.

"Concept to please the patriarchy," Dawn said sagely. She tossed her ankle boots aside and eyed Rosie's elegant, stocking-clad calves with a cheeky grin. "Can't say I disagree with them, though."

"You're not still going on about my bloody legs."

"Bloody am."

"Well, if you're so obsessed why don't you give me a foot massage, then?"

"Only if you do mine first."

Rosie scoffed. "I've only got one hand, remember."

She straightened her legs over Dawn's lap, and Dawn trailed a playful finger along the silky stocking below her knee. Softly, she brushed along Rosie's shin – and Rosie flinched with a yelp. Dawn snatched her hand away in surprise. "What? What did I do?"

"Nothing," Rosie said, quickly reassuring. "You didn't do anything." She sat upright, gingerly probing at the sore spot on her leg, and yelped again as her fingers found their mark.

Dawn squinted to see. "Jesus, Rose – you're purpling up, there. God, and here – and here… And there, on your arm, too."

Rosie craned her neck to see a mark near her elbow and grimaced. "Must be from crashing into that bloody cocktail table."

Dawn's face crumpled with concern. "We've still got a bit of that anti-bruise stuff Ed gave us for your ankle – c'mon, get changed out of that dress and stockings and I'll grab you a robe, too."

She got up and headed to acquire the aforementioned items, and Rosie levered herself upright on the couch. For a moment, she scowled at her right hand, so trussed up in bandages that she could barely see her fingers, and then, resolute, tried to reach for the zipper on her back with the left one instead. As she did so, she leaned on another rising bruise and hissed through her teeth.

"All right?" Dawn said, returning armed with the bruise remedy and a fluffy bathrobe.

"I'm fine."

"You don't seem fine," Dawn said, looking her over. "You're going to be bloody black and blue, tomorrow."

"Says the woman who looks like Sweeney Todd had a go at her neck."

"You married him," Dawn shot back.

"And I regret it," Rosie said. Scowling, she leaned further forward, still trying unsuccessfully to get a grip on the zipper without leaning on her sore hand. But, at last, she dropped both arms in irritable defeat. "Sod it. Guess I'll sleep in this, then."

Dawn put down the robe and ointment and gestured to her. "Don't be ridiculous. Stand up and come here. Let's get that dress off you."

"You know," Rosie remarked dryly as she got to her feet, "I sort of thought I'd be more enthused to hear you say something like that."

A giggle escaped Dawn. "Shut up, you daft thing – turn around so I can undo it."

Rosie obliged and started pleasantly at the feel of Dawn's fingers against her spine.

"Sorry," Dawn said over her shoulder. "Did I hurt you?"

"No," Rosie breathed. "No – quite the opposite."

Dawn pulled the zipper down as far as it would go, and then Rosie turned to face her again. Dawn's fingers lingered near her shoulder blades, cool against exposed skin. "Quite the opposite?"

Rosie blushed but kept her chin up to meet Dawn's steady gaze. "Yes. I… like the feel of your hands."

Dawn smiled and softly trailed them down to the small of her back. "Like this?"

Rosie bit at her lip and closed her eyes. "Yes… like that."

Dawn leaned in to place a delicate kiss against the side of her neck, eliciting a shiver. Her lips skimmed upward, and then she whispered into Rosie's ear, "Stop distracting me – I'm trying to fix your bruises."

She let go and pulled away, and Rosie's eyes flashed open beneath an irritable scowl. "You're such a bloody tease."

Dawn grinned. "You'll learn to love it – stay still, now."

Carefully, she slid the sleeves fully off Rosie's shoulders, and Rosie found herself still utterly aware of Dawn's fingers as they brushed down her arms. A small frown creased Dawn's brow as she concentrated on being gentle, and then the dress abruptly slipped free and fell to the floor. Suddenly in nothing but her underwear, Rosie froze, but Dawn had the grace not to stare; she reached for the bathrobe, wrapping it firmly around Rosie. She hesitated, then, and said, "Stockings…?"

Rosie exhaled slowly, feeling strangely vulnerable, and nodded.

Dawn caught the look on Rosie's face. She stretched her hands out in front of her, took a deep breath, and announced in a presenter's voice, "I'M GOING TO TOUCH YOU NOW!"

A snort of laughter escaped Rosie, and the mounting tension dissipated. "Get on with it, then."

Dawn slipped her hands inside Rosie's robe, hooking the stockings and sliding them down in one smooth movement until the elastic caught around her knees instead. "Ha!" she crowed, pleased with herself. "Piece of cake."

"Yes, very slick," Rosie sniped, somewhat disappointed despite her fluctuating nerves.

"Sit down so I can get them all the way off."

Grumbling, Rosie dropped back onto the couch and lifted first one leg and then the other for Dawn to roll the stockings down and remove them. Free at last, she hiked the robe up a bit for Dawn to apply the ointment to every rising bruise she could see.

"Not exactly how I'd hoped our last night would go," Rosie sighed.

Dawn cast her an impish glance from where she knelt on the rug. "Had plans, did you?"

"Well, not exactly…"

"Not exactly?"

Rosie raised an eyebrow. "Is that disappointment I hear?"

Dawn hauled herself up with a shrug, and then – as if she didn't care either way – said, "Maybe." She gestured for Rosie to move over and settled beside her on the couch. "Drop that robe off your shoulders a bit, now – I saw a bruise by your collarbone, too."

Rosie did as she was told, and Dawn gently applied more ointment. When she was done, she scooped a last dollop and smeared it onto her own neck, and Rosie rolled her eyes.

"Come here, you nitwit, let me do that – you're missing most of the bloody bruises."

She snatched the tub and cupped it in her bandaged hand, and Dawn tilted her head to the side at her prompting. Feather-light, Rosie spread the balm across her throat and under her jaw, and Dawn watched her with hooded eyes. Rosie completed her task, but her fingers lingered, gently caressing. Perfectly still, Dawn closed her eyes, and Rosie slowly outlined her décolletage with an artist's finesse. She traced the curve where the neckline plunged into a deep vee, eliciting a soft gasp from Dawn, and her own breath caught a little shallower. Fascinated, she watched pleasant surprise flicker across Dawn's expression in time with the arc of her fingertips, and then Dawn suppressed a shudder. Her eyes opened, bright as the night sky, and Rosie found herself irrepressibly drawn in until her lips pressed against Dawn's. Gently, she explored Dawn's mouth, dropping the tub to cup her bandaged hand carefully around the nape of her neck instead. The other laced through Dawn's hair, and Dawn melted against her. Like velvet, Dawn's fingers skimmed the back of her shoulders where the robe had slipped down, and Rosie's heart beat a little faster with each inch they mapped. The kiss deepened, experimental, and Dawn's hands grew bolder, reaching further, gently pushing at the robe to move it down out of the way.

But Rosie pulled free suddenly, catching at the robe with her good hand to prevent it from sliding much further down her front. "Wait, Dawn, the lights… I – um—"

"It's all right – I know what you mean," Dawn whispered, pressing a reassuring kiss to her trembling lips.

She slid to her feet and turned everything off so that only the glow of the pale moon beyond the window lifted the dark. Taking Rosie's hand, Dawn helped her up and pulled her gently back into her arms. She soothed her with soft kisses, manoeuvring her towards the bed until they perched together on the side. There, Rosie's courage built, and she claimed Dawn's mouth again with more confidence. This time, when Dawn slid the robe off her shoulders and down her back, she did not resist. A soft moan escaped her as Dawn trailed electric fingers down her spine and up again, and Dawn hitched a breath in response.

She paused for a heartbeat, murmuring against Rosie's lips, "God, Rose, you're… magnificent."

Softly, Rosie whispered back, "And you're still fully clothed."

A giggle escaped Dawn, and Rosie raised an eyebrow. "Go on," she said. "Turn around so I can get at the zip."

Dawn hesitated. "Are you… sure…?"

"Are you?" Rosie challenged.

Dawn bit at her lip, but then shifted so that her back was to Rosie. "Well, we're halfway there, I suppose…"

Rosie carefully caught the zipper with her good hand and slowly slid it down. "Might as well, then."

Her fingers traced fire against smooth skin, and Dawn gasped. "M-might as well."

Rosie moved closer, pressing butterfly kisses along the top of Dawn's shoulders as she slipped first one, and then the other, sleeve of the dress down. The gown dropped to Dawn's waist, and Rosie nipped with her teeth until Dawn groaned and pressed back against her. Skin met skin suddenly, and Rosie froze with a gasp. Dawn clutched at the bed covers as a shiver sang between them, and a long moment passed before either of them was brave enough to move. Slowly, they drew apart, and then Dawn shifted to face her in the dark.

Shyly, she adjusted her bra strap and cleared her throat. "You know… I've had plenty of sex, Rose. But I've never felt… like this."

"What, turned on and terrified and terribly inadequate all at once?"

Dawn smiled softly. "Yes, that. All of the above."

Rosie's lips curved, too. "I feel like a bloody virgin all over again."

"Well, *technically*—"

"Stop it."

"All right," Dawn said, eyes asparkle in the moonlight. "Technicality aside. We're not virgins, though, are we?"

"Common bloody knowledge that you're far from it."

Dawn smirked. "You've had your share, too."

"Fair," Rosie said. "But not… like this."

"No," Dawn agreed. "Not like this."

Rosie drew her into a hug, and sighed, shivering pleasantly at the lack of boundaries between them. "Why do you make me feel like I'm sixteen again?"

"I could ask you the same thing," Dawn replied. She pressed a kiss beneath Rosie's ear and then drew back to catch her gaze again. "But we're not sixteen, Rose… We're bloody grown women – and I know what I want."

Rosie's response quivered. "And… what *do* you want?"

Gathering her courage, Dawn offered a single word. "You." She pressed her fingers against Rosie's sternum and pushed her down onto the bed, and Rosie sank back, powerless to tear her eyes away from Dawn's bottomless gaze. Dawn hovered above her, quavering upon one last moment of indecision, and then whispered, "Will you… let me?"

Rosie bit at her lip, and slowly drew her down into sweet oblivion.

# CHAPTER THIRTY-ONE

In the half-dark of very early morning, Rosie lay on her side with her bandaged hand tucked awkwardly above her head, watching Dawn sleep. The duvet was tucked up to the bruises on Dawn's throat, almost hiding them, and her eyes were closed in soft repose. She looked so peaceful without her lively face displaying her every emotion, and Rosie smiled as she observed the unusual contrast. Dawn's visage was never usually so relaxed; it was a bright canvas, illustrating her every thought, every feeling, in its full, spectacular magnitude. In fact, even in sleep, her face was often animated, echoing her dreams. This morning, though, it was utterly calm but for the faintest hint of a smile curving one corner of her lips. Rosie's own smile widened as she noticed it, and her heart swelled a little more.

As she watched, Dawn's nose twitched, and then she stirred and reached up a sleepy hand to rub it. When her eyes fluttered open, she caught Rosie's gaze and blushed.

"Rose..." she mumbled, lifting the duvet to hide her face. "Why are you staring?"

Rosie's response was merely a bemused shake of her head,

and Dawn peeked out to catch the end of it.

"What's the matter?" she asked suspiciously.

"Nothing," Rosie quietly replied. "I'm just... admiring you." Dawn's blush deepened, but Rosie caught the top of the duvet and held it down before she could retreat under it again. "Am I not allowed to do that?"

"I think *admiring* is rather a strong word."

"Looking, then."

"Why?"

"I'm sort of... amazed... that you're here."

Dawn gave a slow blink. "As opposed to the other six days I've been here?"

Rosie batted her shoulder and blushed, too. "You know what I mean."

Lowering her gaze, Dawn managed an awkward smile, but the colour did not leave her cheeks. Rosie watched her until she looked up again, and when their eyes met, they contemplated each other for a long moment. Rosie caught her lip between her teeth, searching for something meaningful to say, and at last, Dawn sighed.

"Well, we've firmly crossed the line, Rose. Now what?"

"I was sort of hoping you'd tell *me*."

Picking at the duvet still tucked up to her chin, Dawn wavered for a moment more. Rosie searched her dark gaze, seeing her own insecurities reflected there, but at last, Dawn gathered herself. "Well," she said, braver than she felt, "I liked... exploring... with you."

An explosive exhale escaped Rosie. "Did you really?"

Dawn glanced at her sideways. "To be honest, I thought about legging it this morning, but I fear it's a bit bloody chilly outside."

"Ha, HA. You're bloody lucky *I'm* still here, never mind *you*."

"Too much for you, am I?"

Rosie smiled at Dawn's goading. "You're... something, all right. I never imagined..."

She trailed off, and Dawn softly prompted, "What?"

"I never imagined we'd be here, is all. I can't quite believe it, I think." She caught Dawn's eye. "I have a lot of… emotions, at the moment."

"Good ones, I hope."

Dawn hid behind her jokes, but she was fearful of what Rosie might say next, and Rosie knew it. Rosie tilted her head, and her gaze softened. "Good ones, indeed."

Reassured, Dawn smiled, bright and pretty in the early morning light, and gifted Rosie a kiss. Then, she drew back and said, "You know, we probably should get up, Rose. We have to check out today, after all − and I know you haven't even packed yet."

Rosie blinked sardonically. "Well, you certainly know how to douse the moment. But you're right, I haven't packed." She rolled out of Dawn's embrace and sat up, leaning on her sore hand as she did so.

A pained hiss escaped her, and Dawn asked, "What's wrong?"

Rosie held up the now-crooked bandage with a wry smile. "Forgot about this." She paused to take stock of her physical well-being and then sighed. "God, I hurt all over, actually."

Dawn shimmied upright beside her and gingerly dabbed at her bruised neck. "Me too. That was one hell of a night."

"Had its ups and downs," Rosie agreed, moving stiffly to the edge of the bed. She reached for her robe, discarded on the floor the night before, and groaned heartily as she straightened again. When she had it on, she tipped her head sideways at Dawn with a wicked smile. "The right kind of ups and downs, too, though."

Dawn grinned and threw a pillow at her. "Oh, you've a cheek this morning!"

Smirking, Rosie caught it and cast it aside. She adjusted her robe, and then, with an exaggerated effort, dragged herself to the kitchen.

"Are you making tea?" Dawn called over, watching her with a bemused expression.

"I'm perfectly capable of making tea in the morning," Rosie shot back.

Dawn grinned. "Not *completely* useless, then – and since you're making yourself useful, I'm going to take a shower."

Rosie rolled her eyes. "Hurry up, or your tea will be cold."

Dawn smiled, watching her bustle around the kettle. "I *know* I'm not the one who needs to hurry up. When you're done pottering around the kitchen, get packing, would you?"

Rosie glared daggers, and Dawn gifted her a cheeky wink as she headed for the bathroom.

An hour and a half later, Dawn tossed a suitcase into the hall and snapped at finally-showered, recently-reappeared Rosie. "Are you *ever* going to be on time?"

Rosie made a show of moving slowly and gave a hearty groan. "I got thrown onto a table and had my hand half-cut off last night, Dawn. If you must know, I'm a little stiff this morning."

"I'm surprised," Dawn breezed in quick-fire response, "because I was quite sure you'd loosened up good and proper by the time you went to sleep."

Rosie went bright red, but she raised a defiant glare. "Don't get funny. Are we going, or not?"

"Well, I suppose that depends on whether or not the bloody taxi's still waiting."

With a huff, Rosie stuck her nose in the air and strolled back into the room. Shooting a sly glance at Dawn through the open door, she proceeded to faff, meticulously combing through every cupboard and in every corner for anything they might have 'forgotten'.

"*Really*, Rose?" Dawn said, her exasperation peaking as she stalked back in to chivvy her. "Let's *go*."

Rosie smirked. "Irritating you, am I?"

"More than you know."

"We've still got ten minutes."

Dawn lifted her gaze to the heavens and manhandled her out into the hall. "Bloody cabbie's been here half an hour already!"

"Pay him extra, then."

"God – would you just—" Dawn closed the door behind them and turned to face her with a dangerous glint in her eye. "Do you know, I think I've changed my mind about you, Rose. This isn't going to work, after all."

"Oh?" Rosie raised her eyebrows, accepting the gauntlet thrown. She advanced suddenly, and Dawn backed up until she found herself pinned against the door. An inch away, Rosie looked her up and down, and whispered, "You're a terrible liar, Dawn."

Before Dawn could protest, Rosie caught her up in a kiss that made her wilt against the veneer. When she released her, Dawn listed against the door frame with her hand pressed over her thundering heart. "Christ, Rose, you bloody cheat! Am I *ever* going to win an argument with you again?"

Rosie laughed. "You haven't got a prayer." She caught one suitcase handle carefully with her bandaged hand, shifted her handbag over her shoulder with the other, and sauntered off down the passage. "That's payback, for kicking me out of bed this morning."

"Cow," Dawn grumbled, hefting the other case to follow.

Outside, the day had sprung pretty and mild, and they took deep breaths of the fresh country air as they pulled their suitcases across the drive. The patient cabbie tipped his hat and took them off their hands, and Rosie turned for one last look at the scenery and the Inn.

"Are you ready?" Dawn asked, shouldering against her.

"Yes," Rosie mused. "I'll miss this, though."

Dawn smiled. "Maybe we'll come again."

Rosie caught an arm around her waist and nodded. They surveyed the rolling lawns and vibrant woods for a moment more, and then Rosie said, "Still coming with me, I hope?"

"Well, my bags are already in the car," Dawn said with an expansive sigh, "so I suppose I might as well."

Smiling, Rosie opened the door for her, but a shout stopped them. Liz came bulleting out of the inn, her blaze of red hair streaming out behind her, and before Dawn's face had quite finished registering surprise, the youngster threw herself forward to engulf her in a bear hug.

"That's not appropriate, is it?" Rosie asked of no one in particular.

Grinning, Liz released Dawn and caught hold of Rosie instead, and Rosie yelped as she found herself fondly crushed. "Bruises!" she scolded. Firmly, she extricated herself from Liz's grip.

"Sorry," Liz beamed.

Dawn caught an arm around the girl's shoulders and chortled. "Good Lord, are you happy to see us leave, or…?"

"I'm bloody devastated," Liz said, shaking her head earnestly. "It's going to be far too quiet around here without you two."

"Peaceful, though, I expect," said Rosie.

"Boring, you mean," Dawn corrected.

"Bloody boring," Liz agreed. She rummaged in her coat pocket and produced a small paper box. "Here, Dee, I stole you a brownie from the kitchens."

"You didn't!" Dawn exclaimed.

She accepted the gift reverently, and Liz turned to Rosie. "Something for you, too," she winked, holding out a second box. "Blueberry muffin."

Rosie's carefully sculpted scowl melted. "Oh – thanks, Liz."

"Told you I like this girl," Dawn said. She stifled a sniffle. "We're going to miss you, kid."

"Speak for yourself," Rosie snorted, attempting to keep up her ire.

Liz looked between them, and her eyes glistened. "I'm going to miss you both, too – especially you, Rosie."

Rosie's eyebrows shot up in surprise. "What? Why?"

But Liz only smiled. Clearing emotion from her throat, she straightened her coat, tucked her hair behind her ears, and said, "I think your cabbie's ready to go – safe home, now. Hopefully, I'll see you again one day."

"You will," Dawn promised with a small smile. She pulled Liz into one last hug and then turned to slide into the taxi.

"You look after yourself," Rosie said to Liz as she followed suit.

"I will," Liz grinned. "And you look after Dawn!"

She pushed the door shut, and Dawn leaned over Rosie to buzz down the window and wave. Liz waved back enthusiastically until they turned the corner, and she was lost to sight, and then Dawn flopped back against the seat.

"Bittersweet, goodbyes, aren't they?" she said.

Rosie scoffed. "Not all of them." But then she softened. "That one was a bit, though."

"I like that kid. I hope life's kind to her."

"Life's not kind to anybody," Rosie sighed.

"Maybe it'll make an exception. Good things happen, sometimes."

Dawn leaned against Rosie's side, and Rosie tucked an arm over her shoulders.

"Can't disagree," Rosie said. "You happened, after all."

They fell to companionable silence, each watching the world flash by outside the windows, and the drive stretched from minutes to hours. Rosie dozed, her head tucked against the top of Dawn's, and Dawn was content to be still and let her.

Finally, they left the motorway, and Rosie stirred as the car curved around the off-ramp. She lifted her arms to stretch as best she could in the small space, and a small yelp escaped her as she bumped her sore hand against the roof.

"Are we there yet?" she asked acidly, as they coursed into the outskirts of Wilmslow.

"How should I know?" Dawn replied. "Been bloody ages since I was at your house."

But at last, they slowed, turning into a cul-de-sac that Dawn recognised, and the cabbie pulled up onto a gravelled driveway in front of a 1930s three-storey with a bay front and leaded windows.

"Just as ostentatious as I remember it," Dawn chirped.

"In my defence," Rosie returned, "it was Richard who picked it out."

"Bastard."

They retrieved their bags from the boot, paid the cabbie, and turned for the house, but suddenly the front door swung open. Mary stepped out onto the porch stairs, and Rosie stopped dead with a surprised hiss.

Dawn raised an eyebrow. "You... didn't tell Mary I was coming?"

Rosie vacillated. "Um..."

Dawn chortled and pushed past her, heading straight for Mary.

"Don't you bloody tell her anything!" Rosie hissed. She swung for the back of her coat but missed. "Dawn, I'm warning you!"

"Mary!" Dawn called affectionately, dropping her case, and scooting forward to catch her up in a hug. "It's so lovely to see you!"

"Dawn! God – what a wonderful surprise! Mum never said a bloody word!" Mary scowled accusingly over at Rosie, who strode up to shoulder between the potential allies.

"What are you doing here?" Rosie snapped, pulling Mary into a hug far gentler than her tone. "I thought you had a meeting."

"I did – finished early, though, so I thought I'd come see how your trip was." Mary held her at arm's length and appraised them both, raising an eyebrow at Rosie's bandaged hand, and the bruises on Dawn's neck. "Went well, by the look of things."

"It was... fantastic," Rosie admitted. "Had a great time."

"Probably mostly thanks to Dawn," Mary quipped. Rosie's face paled, guilty, but Mary obliviously continued, "Thank God she was there to keep an eye on you – you're bloody miserable on your own."

"Ahaha – yes, quite," Rosie tittered. She blushed, suddenly, grabbed her suitcase and disappeared into the house before Mary could notice and interrogate her.

Mary, of course, noticed. "Something the matter with Mum?" she asked Dawn.

Dawn gave an easy smile. "She's never been good at admitting she's had a good time, your Mum."

Mary narrowed her eyes and looked towards the empty doorway where Rosie had disappeared. Slowly, she swivelled her gaze back to Dawn's serene expression. "Something's... off. What aren't you telling me?"

Dawn opened her mouth, closed it again, caught off-guard by the frankness of the question. God, Mary was certainly Rosie's child.

"What happened to your neck?" Mary pressed, unwilling to let her suspicions rest until she had some sort of answer.

Dawn smirked, granted a stay of execution. She seized upon the question, satisfied to steer the conversation well away from possible insights on things between her and Rosie at this stage. "Oh, your father did that."

Taken aback, Mary's eyes widened, and Dawn smiled as the power shifted firmly back into her corner again.

"What do you mean?" Mary said, lifting a hesitant hand as if she might touch the bruises. "Dad... did this? God, Dawn – what happened?"

"He was at the farewell party, last night. Had a go at your Mum, and I sort of... got in the way. He had me round the throat, for a bit – until Rose bottled him with a beer glass. That's why her hand's bandaged."

"WHAT!" Mary almost seemed to glitch on the spot. She spun on her heel and stormed into the house, catching Rosie unawares in the kitchen. She cornered her there, hands on her hips, and Rosie shrank back against the fridge.

"Now, Mary," Rosie began, faltering beneath the thunder in

her daughter's gaze, "I can expl—"

"Dawn says you hit Dad with a beer glass!"

Dawn smirked at the obvious relief that flooded Rosie's face. "Oh, that. Yes, well… he bloody deserved it." She warmed up to the much safer topic of Richard, content that she wouldn't have to confess about Dawn just yet. "Your bloody father towed me all around the party showing off to his cronies, and then I told him off – and then he got Dawn by the neck, so I broke a glass in his face."

"God, Mum…" Mary paled, and she dropped onto the closest kitchen stool. "Are you… all right?"

Rosie sighed and came across to pat Mary's hand. "I'm fine, Mary. Dawn's fine, too. We've had a bit of a time with him, is all. He, sort of… stalked me around Cumbria, filled my hotel room with a zillion flowers, and tried to make me agree to go to a gala with him – and then when that failed, he made Greenside host it so I wouldn't have a choice. I didn't know anything about it until I got down to the hall – and then he appeared out of nowhere and grabbed hold of me just like old times, dragged me around as if he owned me – caught me completely off-guard, you know – I mean – he was irrational from the moment I arrived, but then when he saw me kiss Dawn he just—"

Rosie choked off, and Mary's eyebrows all but disappeared into her bangs. "When he saw you… *what?*"

Dawn laughed effortlessly. "When she kissed me – some of the old boys had us on for fifty quid that we wouldn't kiss at the ball. I guess Richard didn't take it too well."

"Y-yes," Rosie agreed weakly, her bravado vanished beneath a strange shade of green. "E-easy money."

"Oh," Mary said. She cleared her throat, and let it go. "Quite the party, then. Right. Yes, well, that probably *would* have made him fly off the handle – he's never liked you, Dawn."

"All's well that ends well," Dawn said breezily. "Shall I pop the kettle on?"

As Mary spared one last odd glance at her mother, Dawn

bustled past them both to search out some teacups, and effectively put an end to the interrogation. As an awkward silence threatened to fall, she commented, "You know, your Mum walked with wolves."

Mary's eyes widened, thoroughly distracted by the unexpected change of topic. "She didn't!"

"I bloody did," Rosie said, latching onto it. "In fact, I've a gift for you." She spun away to rifle through her case perched on the countertop and shortly dug out the small wolf toy she'd bought after their adventure. "Here," she thrust it into Mary's bemused clutches. "This one looks just like my favourite one. Her name was Meeka."

The toy hung limply in Mary's grasp. "You... really walked with wolves?"

"She did," Dawn confirmed, "and next we're going to Africa to walk with lions."

"WHAT?" Rosie and Mary exploded at the same time.

"We bloody are *not*!" Rosie spluttered at Dawn.

Dawn winked at Mary, and the younger woman finally grinned. Thumbing the little wolf's soft ear, she turned her smile on Rosie. "God, would you look at you, Mum... You might be banged up to hell, but I haven't seen you this lively for a long time. Something on this trip has definitely agreed with you."

Rosie caught Dawn's eye for the briefest moment and couldn't help the soft smile spreading over her lips. "You know, I think maybe it has."

Dawn blushed and tried not to let Mary see.

## CHAPTER THIRTY-TWO

After downing her tea, Mary announced, "Right, must dash. Just wanted to see you safe home, but I have to go pick the boys up from footie practice, now. Thanks for the cuppa."

She deposited her empty cup by the sink and then held out her arms to her mother. Rosie sighed, but then smiled and gave her a hug, and Mary returned it warmly before turning to Dawn. She caught her up in a great squeeze, too – and deftly whispered into her ear, "I just want you to know, it's pretty damned obvious – but I think it's wonderful."

Dawn's cheeks turned pink again as she drew back, and Mary winked at her as she grabbed her keys and bag off the kitchen counter.

"I'll see you both tomorrow," Mary stated before Rosie could notice Dawn's expression, "and for God's sake, try not to get into any more trouble before then. Honestly – I'd better not see one more bruise on either of you."

"We're not *children*," Rosie returned crossly.

"Could have fooled me," Mary scoffed.

She turned for the door, and Rosie followed her out, watching until she'd safely pulled away. When the car disappeared around the corner, Rosie traipsed back in, shut the door, and latched it. Heaving a hearty sigh, she turned around to lean back against the veneer for a moment, her hands cupped on the door handle behind her. "Phew," she said. "Thank God she's gone – got away with that by the skin of our bloody teeth, Dawn."

Poised in the kitchen doorway across the hall, Dawn watched her with a slightly perplexed expression, her arms folded across her chest. "She knows, you know."

Rosie scoffed. "She bloody doesn't."

"Trust me, Rose. She knows."

Rosie narrowed her eyes, scrutinizing Dawn's face to see whether she was having her on. But a faint tinge still rouged her cheeks, and Rosie wilted back against the door with a groan. "Oh, God."

"She told me she thinks it's wonderful, though – so there's that."

"What? When the hell did she say that?"

"When she hugged me goodbye."

Rosie abruptly let go of the door handle and raked her fingers through her hair. "Oh! That sneaky little wench! How the buggery hell does she know?!"

A rueful smile crossed Dawn's lips. "I'm sure it's nothing to do with the fact that you told her you kissed me."

Rosie spluttered. "But… you side-stepped that so neatly with the bet thing!"

"I did, indeed – but your utter awkwardness was obviously a dead giveaway."

Rosie pulled her hands down to fist them at her sides, and she stared at Dawn with the expression of a trapped mouse. Dawn pushed away from the door frame and crossed to her, slipping an arm around her waist to lead her safely away from the front door before she could bolt.

As she steered Rosie back towards the kitchen, she said, "It's not such a surprise, I suppose. Mary's your kid, after all – astute as hell."

She deposited Rosie firmly onto a stool and turned to make

more tea, and Rosie leaned her elbows on the counter and buried her head in her hands with a groan. After a long moment of wallowing, she looked up again and caught Dawn's eye. "Did she... did she really say she thought it was wonderful?"

Dawn put a steaming cup of tea down in front of her. "She did."

Rosie slid her fingers around the warmth of the mug and retreated behind a glare. "Are you *sure* she was talking about *that*? Did she explicitly say so?"

Dawn sat on the stool beside her and sipped from her own tea. "Well, not *explicitly*. But I'm pretty damned sure, Rose."

Rosie stared into her mug, mutinous and not wanting to accept it, but at last, gave a resigned sigh. "Well, it is what it is, I suppose. I'll bloody never admit it to her, though."

Dawn hesitated, chewing at the inside of her cheek, and then asked, "Are you... sorry you invited me home?"

"What?" Rosie flung her gaze up. "No, Dawn – don't be ridiculous." A fragile expression had settled onto Dawn's face, and Rosie set her tea aside. Gently, she got up and took Dawn into her arms. "Now you listen to me," she whispered, hugging her tight and stroking her hair, "listen, now, all right? I'm not sorry at all. I want you here – in fact, at the risk of sounding horribly clingy, I want you here forever." She pulled back a little and cupped Dawn's face between her hands to meet her gaze with an earnest expression. "I want to fall asleep beside you every night, Dawn, and I want to wake up beside you every morning, from now until my last breath."

Dawn's lips trembled, trying for a smile. "Wow, Rose... I never took you for such a romantic."

Rosie gave an expansive sigh. "You do bring out the worst in me."

She gathered Dawn up again, encompassing her, and Dawn tucked her head against the inset of her shoulder. Quietly, she murmured, "I want that too."

Rosie shifted to kiss her, soft and sweet and full of promise.

Then, she drew back, pressed her forehead against Dawn's, and whispered, "I do love you, you know."

Dawn finally managed a small grin. "I'm going to ruin – bloody ruin – your reputation, Rose."

Rosie laughed, then, and gave her a playful nudge as she pulled free to drink her tea. "You bloody have, already."

"Well," Dawn sniffed, gathering herself, "I'm not sorry."

"You'll stay, then?" Rosie said, raising a challenging eyebrow.

"Wild horses couldn't drag me away."

Rosie huffed happily over her tea, her eyes twinkling.

Dawn met her gaze with an impish expression. "Forever, is it?"

Rosie blinked, slow and deliberate. "Forever, Dawn. None of this half-arse bollocks. You're in, or you're out."

"What about Mary?"

"You said Mary approved!"

"Well, she takes after you, so who knows whether she'll change her mind?"

Rosie got up and pulled Dawn off her chair so she could lace her arms around her waist. "There's no changing of minds on this one, you daft thing."

"Isn't there?"

Rosie faltered, and her grip weakened. "Is there?"

Dawn smiled, amused by her wavering bravado. "No, dear, there isn't. I've never been so sure of something in my life. I do love you, you know."

"I know," Rosie sighed. Quietly, she added, "I can't believe you came."

"Of course I did, you invited me," Dawn said, lips quirking.

"I mean back into my life," Rosie clarified.

"Bloody good thing I did – honestly, I don't know *how* you coped without me."

Rosie gave a derisive huff and pushed her off. "I was doing just fine on my own, thank you very much – perfectly happy being perfectly miserable."

"Of course," Dawn grinned. "Tell you what, I'll try not to let you get too happy, all right?"

"Fat chance," Rosie scoffed. "Far too bloody late for that."

Dawn laughed and drained her mug. "Come on, are we going to sit around here all day or are we going to unpack?"

Rosie scowled. "I hate unpacking."

Dawn raised an eyebrow. "If I'm to stay *forever*, Rose, we have to do something about the state of this house. First, unpacking, and then, we'll clean. Have you seen the colour of your windows?"

"I *like* dirty windows."

"Well, I don't. I like to see the world a little bit brighter."

"Course you do," Rosie grumbled, "you're a painful bloody optimist."

"Guilty as charged," Dawn grinned. She hitched up her suitcase, raised a challenging eyebrow, and gestured for Rosie to lead the way.

"I *hate* unpacking, Dawn," Rosie reiterated darkly, hefting her own case off the kitchen counter to drag it into the hall.

Dawn's lips twitched in amusement. "It's not so bad, Rose. You never know, whilst we're unpacking, there's a good chance we might get... distracted."

Rosie tripped over her own feet. She stumbled to a halt at the base of the staircase, supporting herself on the bannister. "Distracted?"

Dawn caught hold of her from behind. Leaning up, she huffed into her ear, "Yes, dear... *distracted*." Soft as fire, she nipped at the side of Rosie's neck, and Rosie groaned as her knees buckled. She sank weakly back against Dawn, but Dawn let go and shoved her gaily forward again.

Rosie took a small moment to compose herself, and then valiantly lifted her case to ascend the stairs. "Correction," she said, clearing her throat as she took the first step, "I do believe I love unpacking."

Behind her, Dawn laughed.

# EPILOGUE

*Three Weeks Later*

Dawn laid a gentle hand on Rosie's shoulder and hovered in the half-dark. Tentative, she whispered, "Morning, sleepy head."

Rosie stirred with a groan and squinted sideways at the clock before assuming a murderous expression. "It's five-thirty in the bloody morning, Dawn," she growled, pulling the duvet up to cover her face.

"I know, but… here, I brought you some tea."

Rosie snatched the duvet down again and glared. "It's *Sunday*."

Dawn held the cup out like a peace offering to a vengeful god and put on her best pout behind it. Rosie narrowed her eyes, but then, with an expansive sigh, hauled herself up and flopped back against the headrest. Mutinous, she beat her pillows into submission behind her and then reached for the steaming mug.

"People have been killed for less, you know," she grumbled. "Why in the hell are you awake so early, anyway?"

"It's Sunday," Dawn said, perching on the edge of the bed beside her.

"I've just pointed that out."

"Mary and the kids are coming for lunch, today," Dawn clarified.

Rosie stared at her as if she'd lost her mind. "For *lunch*, Dawn! That's eight hours away!"

"Seven and a half," Dawn corrected mildly.

Rosie forced herself to take a deep, calming breath. "Seven and a half, then – still a bloody lifetime, quite frankly. Why are you up already?"

Dawn dipped her gaze ruefully. "I wanted to get a head start on cooking and things. I just... I want today to be perfect, Rose."

Rosie blinked at her. "It's only a Sunday roast."

"It's not," Dawn said, and Rosie cocked her head.

"Is that a hint of stress I detect?"

Dawn blushed and dipped her chin. "Maybe."

Rosie expression softened, and then put her cup down on the side table and reached for her hand. "It's only Mary and the boys coming."

Dawn squeezed her fingers, attempting to draw comfort from her solidity. "Yes, but... they've only flashed in for a couple of flying visits, so far – this is the first time we all have to sit down together for any amount of time."

"They don't *know* anything, Dawn."

"Mary does," Dawn sighed. She shifted to face Rosie properly. "What if she... doesn't really approve? What if she's just being polite, and actually thinks we're completely mad? I don't know if I can sit through an entire afternoon wondering that, Rose."

"You don't have to wonder," Rosie said. "I can answer that for you – we are completely mad."

With a groan, Dawn threw her head back and squeezed her eyes shut. "I'm serious, Rose!"

"I thought you said it doesn't matter what anyone thinks?"

"This is different – it's your bloody *daughter* we're talking about!"

"And Mary adores you," said Rosie, more gently. "Always has – in fact, when she was little and you were still around a whole lot, she never stopped talking about you."

A half-hearted smile rose on Dawn's lips, faded again. Quietly, she said, "Do you see why it matters to me, Rose?"

The corners of Rosie's lips dipped in response to the tugging in her heart. "All right, then – we'll make it perfect, all right?" She stroked Dawn's back reassuringly, and then jested, "Can I drink my tea first, at least?"

Stifling a small sniffle, Dawn nodded, and Rosie shifted sideways and held out an arm. "Come here, then. Sit with me a minute." Mute, Dawn slipped under the covers and curled up next to her, tucking into her embrace with a halting sigh, and, softly, Rosie thumbed the side of her ribs. "We'll figure it out, Dawn. It's just… new. For everybody. It'll be all right, you'll see."

They sat quietly for a time, Dawn cuddled up with her head pillowed against Rosie's chest as Rosie sipped her tea, and the world began to stir beyond the bedroom windows. Birdsong fluted, gaining strength as the sun pulled into the sky, and at last, Rosie put down her empty cup.

"Are you all right?" she whispered, giving Dawn a squeeze.

"Better now, thank you," Dawn murmured.

Rosie brushed a kiss against her hair and then leaned to press one against her lips, too. Pulling back again, she caught Dawn's eye and stared, and a small, lopsided smile tugged at her mouth.

"What?" Dawn mumbled, after a moment.

Gently, Rosie's smile widened. "I can't believe you're real, sometimes." Dawn blushed, soft pink in the early morning sunlight, and Rosie slowly shook her head. "God, you're beautiful. You make my heart so… full."

"Stop it," Dawn said, pushing half-heartedly at her shoulder. Her blush deepened, and Rosie grinned. She kissed Dawn in earnest, then, and Dawn's worries melted to pleasant warmth as she gave in to Rosie's enthusiasm. But finally, she came up for air and caught Rosie at arm's length. "Stop it," she scolded, unable to suppress a smile. "We've only seven bloody hours, now, and that lunch isn't going to cook itself."

She firmly extricated herself from Rosie's clutches, and Rosie laughed as she let her go. "It *could* cook itself if you'd just let me pick up a ready-made from Tesco."

Dawn rounded on her. "If you mention Tesco ever again for the finer things in life, I'm going to walk out that door and never come back."

Rosie raised an eyebrow, her eyes sparkling. "Well, you could try…"

"Come get me, would you?" Dawn huffed.

Rosie crossed to her and took her in her arms. "I would."

"Really?" Dawn whispered.

"Really," Rosie confirmed.

A few hours later, Dawn stood in the bright kitchen, frantically twirling a wooden spoon through a mixture that refused to bind. "Rose? Rose!"

"*What?*" Rosie responded, from directly behind her shoulder.

Dawn nearly leapt out of her skin, but luckily remembered to release the side of the mixing bowl before spinning to face her. Thoroughly distracted, she raked flour-covered fingers through her hair. "Did you – um – did you set the table, yet?"

Rosie rolled her eyes. "*Yes*, dear – that's the third time you've asked me." She leaned around Dawn to assess the progress of whatever was in the bowl and then glanced up at Dawn's lighter-than-normal locks. "You've flour in your hair, now, by the way."

With a yelp of dismay, Dawn tore her hands down – and accidentally caught the end of the wooden spoon and catapulted the bowl off the counter. Rosie ducked as Dawn lunged frantically for it, but it eluded her and splattered over half the kitchen floor. Dawn wilted against the counter with a groan, staring glumly at the mess.

"Well," she said sadly, "pudding's ruined. That was going to be an apple pie…"

"It'll be all right," Rosie said gently, gathering her up. "I'll pop out and get a ready-made one from Tes– … Waitrose."

Dawn's lip wobbled. "Thanks, dove."

Rosie drew her into a hug, and then Dawn straightened and squared her shoulders.

"It'll be all right," Dawn repeated Rosie's words with a sharp nod, more to reassure herself than anything else.

Rosie spared a smile for her bravado and gifted her a kiss. Tasting apples on her tongue, she drew back with a teasing laugh. "*Were* there any apples left for the bloody pie?"

Dawn did her best to look affronted. "A chef has to *taste* things, Rose, m—"

Rosie caught her mouth up again, cutting off her protests, and the kiss turned long and languorous. Dawn relaxed at last, her anxiety replaced by that warm ache that she could never quite describe. Rosie felt the tension leave Dawn's shoulders and pulled back, just a little, with a mischievous glint in her eye. "I do *like* you with flour in your hair, by the way," she said.

"Oh really," Dawn murmured, running her floury hands down Rosie's back.

"Mmm," Rosie purred. "It's very sexy."

Dawn giggled. "I'm not sure sexy is the word."

"I am." Rosie dipped for another kiss, and Dawn gasped against the sweep of her tongue. Suddenly, she found herself backed against the kitchen counter with Rosie's mouth pressed to the side of her neck, and, with a groan, she threw her head back as Rosie nipped at soft skin. Dawn's knees almost failed her as Rosie huffed into her ear, and she clung to the back of Rosie's shirt to keep herself standing as a whimper escaped her.

"St-stop it, now, Rose!" she said, hoarse. "The roast – the lunch won't be ready!"

Rosie supported her upright, grinning, and then Dawn pushed her off with a scowl.

"Honestly," she grumbled, "how can you possibly have *such* an effect on me?"

"I've no idea – but I absolutely intend to keep taking advantage of it."

"Well, not now, damn you," Dawn snapped, retreating behind a business-like brusqueness. "Go and get the apple pie while I clean up this mess – Mary and the boys will be here any minute."

"All right," Rosie smirked, "as long as you promise not to dissolve into a floury mess again the second I leave the room."

"I'm *not* a mess."

"Says the woman nearly brought to her knees by a mixing bowl."

"Just… go!" Dawn cried, flicking a tea towel at her. "Clearly, I've far more chance of keeping myself in control if you're not here."

Rosie laughed and gaily spun to grab her car keys out of the bowl on the kitchen table. As she ducked out, she grinned, "For the love of God, Dawn – keep it together."

A short time later, Dawn fidgeted in the hall, wringing the life out of a tea towel as Rosie opened the front door. The kids tumbled in, Tommy sporting a new stud in one ear – which Rosie was thoroughly berating Mary about as she traipsed up the steps behind.

"Honestly, Mum," Mary was saying crossly, "he likes it – and it's not as if he can't bloody take it out again."

Nate spied Dawn first. He threw himself down the hall towards her and caught an enthusiastic hug around her middle – nearly knocking the breath out of her. "Hi, Nandy!" he chirped.

Pleasantly surprised, Dawn grinned and hugged him back. "Well, hello, Nate!" she said. "You're looking extra-specially handsome today."

"Mum said we should dress nice," he informed her with a nonchalant shrug. "Sunday Lunch is well important."

Dawn groaned inwardly as he scarpered off towards the games room but rekindled her smile for Tommy as he shyly approached.

"Hello, Nandy," he said, sticking out his palm.

"Hello, Tommy," Dawn replied, accepting his handshake with all due seriousness. She winked, then, and added, "I like your ear stud."

He stared up at her for a long moment, and then ducked in for a hug, too. Dawn returned it affectionately, and he whispered, "Thanks – you're much nicer than Grandma Rosie."

She laughed, and he fled to catch up with Nate so they could tussle over who got what PlayStation controller. Rosie approached in his wake; eyes narrowed suspiciously. "What did that little mite say?"

"Nothing," Dawn said with an amused smile. "What does 'Nandy' mean?"

"No idea." Rosie shrugged and turned to glare back down the hall. "Ask Mary, she appears to know absolutely bloody *everything*."

"Hardly," Mary scoffed, doffing her coat and gloves. She spied Dawn, and a brilliant smile lit her face. "Still here, are you?" she joked, gathering her into a hug. "Thought you'd be sick of Mum, by now."

Dawn blushed despite herself but managed to keep her tone jovial. "Well, it's only been a little while – let's see what next week brings." She cleared her throat and changed the subject. "Do tell, why are the boys calling me 'Nandy'?"

Mary's grin widened. "They've a tendency to mumble – they're saying 'Nan Dee' not Nandy."

A momentary silence fell, buoyed by surprise, but then Rosie crowed and clapped her hands together in delight. "*Nan*? Oh! Oh, Dawn – HA! – they've lumped you firmly into the granny category!"

Dawn blushed, pleased – but not about to let Rosie know that. "Shut up, Rose."

Mary grinned and caught an arm around each of them to tow them towards the kitchen. "Something smells amazing around here – is dinner ready? I'm bloody starving."

Later, as they sat at the table around the remnants of a fantastic meal, Mary nodded to the boys that they could return to world domination or whatever it was they were doing on the PlayStation. They scampered, and Mary lifted her wine glass to command her mother's attention and allow them to escape.

"God," she said with a hearty sigh. "Cheers, Dawn, that was fantastic – you've absolutely outdone yourself!"

"I helped!" Rosie snapped.

"You bought a bloody apple pie from Waitrose," Dawn corrected primly.

"After you threw the first one all over the floor!"

"Now, now," Mary grinned, "let's not ruin the moment." She took a deep draught of her wine and then reached for the bottle to top it up. "Anyone else?"

Both Dawn and Rosie held their glasses out, and Mary topped those off, too. She leaned back in her chair and sipped from her wine again, rolling it around her tongue to appreciate the flavours. Pensive, and in no rush whatsoever, her calm gaze roved from Rosie to Dawn and back again, and then dropped down to her empty plate.

Nonchalant, she toyed with the corner of the placemat beneath it. "So… Mum…"

Dawn sank back into her chair, and, opposite, Rosie's fist tightened around her glass. She narrowed her eyes at her daughter's far-too-offhanded tone. "What?"

Mary cleared her throat, more for effect than actual need, and looked up with a devilish expression in her bright blue eyes. "Are you and Dawn…?"

She trailed off, and Rosie's lips thinned. "Well? Are me and Dawn… *what*."

"You know…"

Rosie thumped her glass down with a huff. "I don't know *what* you think you're implying, but—"

Mary laughed, cutting short her indignation. "I'm not *implying* anything, Mum – it's perfectly bloody obvious." Dawn and Rosie exchanged alarmed glances, and Mary's amusement distilled to soft warmth. "Oh, relax – I think it's lovely, and been a long time coming. I'm only pointing out that you don't have to try to keep it a secret – because you're pretty shit at it, to be honest."

Dawn blushed, and Rosie spluttered, but then she glanced at Dawn and shook her head in wry surrender. "Well…" she said ruefully, "it is what it is, I suppose."

"It is what it is," Dawn agreed.

Mary grinned and raised her glass. "Here's to you," she said, "to *both* of you." She sipped and then caught Rosie's eye with a pleasant sigh. "It's so damned good to see you happy, Mum."

Habitual, Rosie opened her mouth to argue, but then an irrepressible smile shone through, instead. She was – happy, that is – and it was well beyond the realms of possibility for her to deny it any longer. Dawn smiled back at her – a tentative, pretty smile – and Rosie's heart gave a little flutter. Shyly, she reached for Dawn's hand across the table, and then Mary cupped her own over both of theirs with a gentle squeeze. Blushing, Rosie glanced sideways at her, and then back across at Dawn, and the moment settled into something soft and bright.

Rosie didn't quite know how the hell it had happened, but suddenly her life was damn near perfect.